BROKEN PRINCE

AN ACCIDENTAL PREGNANCY ROMANCE

LILIAN MONROE

PREVIOUSLY TITLED KNOCKED UP BY THE BROKEN PRINCE

WANT THREE BOOKS DELIVERED STRAIGHT TO YOUR INBOX?
HOW ABOUT THREE ROCK STAR ROMANCES THAT WERE *WAY* TOO
HOT TO SELL?

GET THE COMPLETE *ROCK HARD* SERIES:
WWW.LILIANMONROE.COM/ROCKHARD

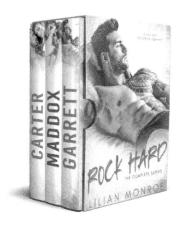

~

1

IVY

THERE'S a special place in hell for people who are jealous of their sisters. My spot has been reserved since I was just a little girl. I'm pretty sure Lucifer himself has a party planned for my arrival, complete with a thousand emerald balloons and a banner that says, 'WELCOME HOME, IVY.'

Whenever I'm near my sister Margot, I bleed green. Envy curls in the pit of my stomach and sends roots into my heart, squeezing my insides until I can hardly breathe.

It's happening right now, as Margot twirls in front of the mirror in yet another perfect, figure-hugging gown—which, by the way, she got for free. Yes, my sister is so beautiful that all she has to do is post pictures of herself online, and brands send her boxes and boxes of free things.

"Which one do you like better?" Margot asks, tilting her head. "I think the blue one might be more appropriate for a royal event, but this pink one would make a statement. Prince Luca seems like the kind of guy who would appreciate a statement." She bites the inside of her cheek. "My stylist asked me to make a decision tonight so that she can put together my shoes and accessories before the event."

Her long, false nails slide down her abdomen as she sucks in her flatter-than-flat stomach. My older sister is tall and willowy, with waist-length blonde hair and blue, come-hither eyes. All she has to do is bat her eyelashes at a man and he falls to his knees in front of her.

Why would Prince Luca be any different? I honestly don't think it matters which dress she chooses. She could show up in flannel pajamas if she wanted to. People would call it *fashion, darling* and put her on the 'Farcliff's Best Dressed' list.

Margot's eyes move to my reflection in the mirror, and her eyebrows jump up in question.

I shrug. "Yeah, either one is nice."

Margot's shoulders fall, and a pang passes through my chest. I know she needs my support right now, and I'm not giving it to her. She's meeting one of the Princes of Argyle tomorrow. The entire royal family of Argyle—the King and Queen, and two of the three Princes—have been invited to our Kingdom of Farcliff following the coronation of Prince Luca's older brother, King Theo.

The Kingdoms of Argyle and Farcliff haven't always had the best relations, but with King Theo in Argyle, and King Charlie here in Farcliff, there are high hopes of reconciliation. The formal dinner tomorrow night is an opening ceremony, of sorts, which will kick off the Argyle family's month-long visit in Farcliff.

My sister—being one of the most famous celebrities in Farcliff—is invited to the ball. Me?

Not so much.

I guess the slightly shorter, slightly chubbier, black-haired version of Margot isn't exactly in high demand.

Did I mention I'm most likely spending eternity in a fiery abyss?

I don't even know *why* I'm so jealous. That dinner sounds

like my idea of death by a thousand boring conversations. I'd rather pluck my leg hairs out one by one than spend time with the guests at tomorrow's event.

Still, I envy her.

Margot's management team has arranged to hook her up with Prince Luca, as he's apparently the hottest thing since sliced bread. They think it'll be good for her 'image' to have her dating a high-profile celebrity like the Prince. The Prince's management team agrees, wanting to bring Argyle and Farcliff closer together. It's a match made in royal Instagram heaven.

For a month, at least. All bets are off once Prince Luca leaves Farcliff again.

I swing my legs off the bed and stand up, throwing my jet-black hair into a messy bun. "Go with whatever dress you think is best, Margie. You know I'm no good at these things."

Margot throws me a look when I say her name. Her *real* name. She changed it to Margot when she started acting, because her agent told her 'Marguerite' isn't fame material. At least our mother died before *that* happened.

"I just want to make sure the Prince likes me." Her eyes return to her reflection in the mirror.

Taking a deep breath, I put my hands on my sister's shoulders. She swings her gaze back to me, and I force an encouraging smile. "He's going to love you. Everyone does. Literally everyone—even me."

Margot cracks a grin and shakes her head. With a sigh, she makes a decision. "I'm going to go with the blue one."

As the personal assistant to Farcliff's hottest star, my life revolves around my sister. It always has. Ever since she landed her first commercial when she was four years old, my sister's life has always taken priority.

Even when Mama's illness got worse and the end was near, my father would still take Margot to her auditions and modeling jobs before going to see his own wife in the hospital. That's what happens when there's an opportunity to lift a family out of poverty—everyone latches on for dear life.

Including me.

Margot is the gravy train that we all need to survive. And because my sister is such a damn saint, she doesn't hold it against us. She shares her wealth and success with my father and me without rancor or the need for anything in return.

So, every day, I swallow my jealousy and get up at the crack of dawn to make sure my sister's days go according to plan.

This morning, in particular, is hectic. I have to make sure the hair and makeup artists are here on time. I need to confirm the limo service and call her stylist to make sure she's finalized the outfit.

I need to make sure Margot eats enough so that she doesn't faint on her way to Farcliff Castle, but not so much that she'll look bloated in her pretty blue dress.

Most importantly, I need to make sure my sister is happy, confident, glowing, and ready to meet the Prince of her dreams.

Margot still has her silk eye mask on when I gently shake her awake. She lets out a cute little sigh—because even in her sleep, she's graceful and perfect—and pushes the pink silk off her eyes and onto her forehead. Her golden hair is still curled from yesterday, splayed out in soft waves on her pillow.

I couldn't look that good when I wake up if I tried.

"Hey, Ivy," she smiles. "Is it time to get up already?"

"Rise and shine, future Princess."

Margot beams at me, and pads to her ensuite bathroom. I hear a yelp, followed by a series of clattering bangs, and I let out a sigh.

My sister's single, solitary flaw is that she can't go anywhere without knocking something over. 'Clumsy' doesn't even come close to describing it. She's a bull, and the world is a china shop.

A really pretty, really feminine, blonde-haired bull, but still.

An accident waiting to happen.

She's lucky she has an entire team of people around her who hide that particular flaw from the public. The Margot LeBlanc that the masses see is graceful, kind, and pretty much perfect.

Knocking on the bathroom door, I wait for her response.

"It's fine," she calls out. "Just the shampoo bottles."

"Okay. Let me know if you need anything."

I make her bed while she showers, and check my phone when it dings. The hairstylist is on her way. Makeup will be late.

Today is all about managing Margot. Her agent, Hunter, arrives at our seven-bedroom mansion at eleven o'clock, prepping Margot with a thousand and one facts about Prince Luca.

"Remember, Margot, don't mention Queen Cara."

"His ex. Right. Got it." Margot nods. "No mention of the Queen of Argyle."

"I mean it, Margot. They were sweethearts their entire lives. When Queen Cara married Luca's older brother, it was a massive controversy in Argyle. Prince Luca was still in Singapore at the time."

"For his operation?"

Hunter nods. "That's something you can focus on—his

recovery from the spinal fracture and how miraculous it is that he can walk again. But not Queen Cara. Not even her name. When she married his brother, Prince Luca went off the rails. Talking about her is a sure way to get the Prince to dislike you."

"I *get* it," Margot repeats. Her voice has a slight edge to it —the most aggression you'll ever hear from my angelic older sister.

Hunter pulls his phone out of his pocket and stares at it as he continues: "Keep the conversation light. He likes sports— he's a big basketball fan. Just be yourself."

"Is she supposed to be herself, or is she supposed to talk about basketball?" I ask, arching an eyebrow.

Hunter ignores me.

I slink to the kitchen, tired of hearing about Prince Luca. It's all they've talked about for months. If I hear the words 'bad boy meets good girl' or 'relationship of the century' one more time, I think I might explode.

Heading for the pantry, I pull out some flour, sugar, yeast, and a few other bits and pieces. My favorite mixing bowl lives in the corner cupboard by the sink, and as soon as I feel the weight of it, my shoulders start to relax.

I love baking. I always have. Mama and I used to spend hours in the kitchen together, putting together lavish desserts from scraps of food that she scrounged from who-knows-where. She taught me everything I know about baking, and every time I make something, I think of her.

As Mama's illness progressed and her tremors became more severe, she stopped being able to bake. She'd sit in the kitchen as I did the work. Mama would coach me through the complex recipes, and then we'd eat the treats together.

It was special. It still is. Baking is the one thing that I'm really, really good at.

6

Right now, I need to think about something other than my beautiful sister, her impending royal relationship, and my own inadequacy.

Cinnamon buns might do the trick.

Slipping on my bright blue apron, I get to work. The sounds of the hairstylists and agents and managers fades into the background, and I inhale the scent of fresh dough. It's the scent of memories, home, and comfort. As soon as my fingers sink into the soft dough, a smile drifts over my lips.

This is where I'm happiest. If I could give up the seven-bedroom mansion and all the money and comfort that Margot provides for me, I would. I'd open a small bakery in Farcliff and I'd sell everything that my mother and I used to bake together.

The *clack-clack-clack* of stilettos on our Italian marble floors informs me my sister is coming to find me. I cover the dough to prove it, and then wipe my floury hands on my apron.

Margot comes around the corner in all her glory. In six-inch heels, she looks even more breathtaking than she usually does. Her makeup is flawless, of course, and her hair is swept to the side in elegant curls. The blue dress was a good choice—it makes her perfect figure look like she's walking around with real-life Photoshop on her body. She smiles at me, but pauses at the kitchen's entrance.

"I don't want to get flour on my dress, but I wanted to say thank you for all your help today. I couldn't have done it without you. I know it's been a tough couple of months, but once this relationship goes public, it should provide a lot more opportunities for us. We'll be real stars, Ivy."

We.

My heart squeezes.

Why am I such an ass?

Here I am, cursing my sister's name, and she's including me in all her plans. Everything she's done to be in the public eye, to make all this money—it's been for my father and me.

We stand on the opposite side of the kitchen. The distance between us is vast.

I force a smile. "I'll have cinnamon buns ready and waiting for you when you come back."

"Can't wait," she says, as if she'll actually eat one. I don't think she's eaten a simple carb in ten or twelve years.

She turns to leave, and then pauses. "Oh, would you mind grabbing my dry cleaning? Marcella didn't have time to do it today with everything going on." Without waiting for an answer, my sister blows me a kiss and disappears down the hallway with her entourage in tow.

I grimace, wincing when the door slams. "Sure, no problem!" I call out into the silence. I listen to the big, empty house, not quite sure what I'm expecting to hear.

Then, with a sigh, I take my apron off and do my sister's bidding.

2

LUCA

QUEEN CARA of Argyle looks radiant as she walks up the wide steps leading up to the Farcliff Castle doors. Her rich, purple gown cinches her at the waist, and my eyes stay glued to the spot on her lower back where my hand used to rest.

Key words: *used to.*

Past tense. As in, not anymore. Never again.

I sit in the back seat of my limousine with a sick feeling in my stomach. My brother, King Theo, smiles at the flashing cameras and lifts his arm up towards them. His wife's tiara sparkles with every photo as she stands beside him. Hot coals glow in my chest, burning me from the inside out.

My lips pinch and my gut churns. My brother, Beckett, watches me from across the limousine.

"You okay?"

I sigh. "Yeah. I'll be fine."

He gives me a tight-lipped smile. "It's good to see you again, Luca." He slides over beside me and pats my knee. "Argyle wasn't the same without you."

"It's been a long five years, that's for sure. It's good to see you too."

I smile at Beckett, and the tension between my eyes seems to ease. Besides Cara, Beckett was my best friend growing up. He's actually my half-brother—our mother had him with my father's brother, which caused about as much controversy as you can imagine—but he's as much my brother as Theo is.

"Try not to let them get to you."

"Who?"

Beckett rolls his eyes. I know who he's talking about—our brother, Theo, and his beautiful, graceful wife, Cara.

Also known as the love of my life, the shatterer of my heart, the bane of my existence, and, unfortunately, my new sister-in-law.

Beckett lets out a sigh and exits the limousine. His lopsided smile greets the flashing cameras, and I take a deep breath. I'm next.

Reaching into my pocket, I pop two painkillers into my mouth. Whenever I get stressed, my body screams with burning pain. Nerve pain. Right now, as I stare up at Theo and Cara, it's bad.

When I walk out, I don't look at the cameras. I ignore the clamoring of reporters and the death glares my eldest brother gives me. I just walk straight toward the castle without acknowledging the crowds.

What do I care about the people of Farcliff? Why should I give a fuck about the journalists and news reporters who have done nothing but tear me to shreds? They'll look for any glance, any facial expression, any word to show how heart-broken I am over Cara's wedding to my brother.

Not that it'd be hard to find something.

Theo's eyes burn holes into my back. I pause on the top step, and I can sense his approach without even turning to see him.

"Behave yourself," he hisses in my ear. "This visit in Farcliff is important."

"For you, you mean."

"For all of us. For all of Argyle. This is your first public appearance since Singapore, in case you've forgotten. It's your chance to show yourself to the world." His trimmed beard has a few white hairs growing in it. He looks old—a fact that brings me more pleasure than it should. He lowers his head toward me as cameras continue to flash. "Just don't make a scene. Your date will be here any minute."

"Wonderful." I roll my eyes. "I'm so glad you were able to arrange a suitable match for me, Your Majesty. Or are you going to take her into your bed as soon as I turn my back, too?"

Beckett distracts the photographers by stepping forward with a dazzling smile. He glances at me for just a moment, giving me a pointed stare.

His eyes say, *Don't do it. Calm down. Get through the night.*

Theo is staring at me, too—and his eyes are blazing. His anger only serves to feed mine. It pours into me like liquid heat, sending sharp daggers through my chest.

Who the fuck is he to be mad at me? I didn't swoop into his life and steal his bride away. *He* did that to *me*. And now, I'm supposed to forget it ever happened?

Fuck. That.

I'll make a scene if I want to.

Cara appears beside him, hooking her arm into Theo's. She smiles at me with soft eyes. The aggression inside me evaporates, replaced with a dull thud in my empty chest.

"Everything okay with you two?"

I incline my head. "Of course, Your Majesty."

"Luca, I wish you wouldn't call me that." Her plump, red

11

lower lip juts out, and I remember sucking that lip between my own not too long ago.

I arch an eyebrow. "Why not? You earned the title."

She earned it by sleeping with my brother while I was getting my spinal cord stitched back together and learning to walk again. She earned it after assuring me that she'd wait for me.

Theo clears his throat. "Here comes your date. Behave."

I turn to the bottom of the wide steps to see a blonde woman with an entourage bigger than ours. Her dress looks painted onto her perfect body, and I can't deny how beautiful she is. Her tits are plump and perky, and every step she takes as she climbs the stairs makes her look more seductive than the last. She walks in like she belongs here, flashing a dazzling smile at me, angling her face toward the cameras.

I feel nothing.

I'm empty, except for the low, simmering rage that always bubbles when Theo's near.

"Your Majesties," the woman says as she curtsies for my brother and his wife. The blonde beauty turns to me, and a slight pink tinge colors her cheeks. She bows her head. "Nice to finally meet you, Prince Luca."

I bring her hand to my lips, staring into her bright, blue eyes. Cameras flash as reporters shout for us to face them. I ignore them, but the woman smiles for the photographers.

I could fuck her for the month I'm here, I guess, if she's not too boring to listen to.

Glancing at Cara, I see her staring at the two of us. Her eyebrows draw together slightly, and she lets her eyes drift down the woman's body.

For the briefest of moments, all my anger melts away and is replaced with bright, zinging interest. I tilt my head, studying her.

Is the Queen jealous?

I quirk an eyebrow as an idea starts floating through my head. Maybe this blonde would be more useful than I anticipated. Taking my date's hand, I hook it into the crook of my arm and motion toward the castle. "Shall we?"

"Please." She smiles at me again, a little more coquettishly. In her heels, she's almost as tall as I am. She smells floral and a little too sweet. My date angles her head one more for the benefit of the cameras, and I resist the urge to roll my eyes.

Cara clears her throat, stealing another glance at us before turning away.

I grin.

Cameras flash.

Shocking as it is to say it, this might actually be fun, in a cruel, twisted kind of way.

We turn toward the big double doors that lead into the castle, and my date stumbles over the last step. Before she goes flying face-first into the ground, I catch her.

Snap-snap-snap. Cameras are trained on us.

My date smiles at me, a blush tinting her cheeks. "Thanks."

"Of course." I put my hand on her back, resisting the urge to steal a glance at Cara.

As soon as we enter the castle, someone hands me a glass of champagne. I down it in one gulp and belch in my fist. The woman—what was her name?—stares at me and then immediately rearranges her features into a smile.

"I was told you were a character." She bats her eyelashes and pushes her chest out toward me.

I guess 'not too boring to listen to' was too much to ask. I could still fuck her, I guess. Cara would hate that.

"I was told you were a good fuck," I answer. I grab another

glass of champagne on our way toward the Great Hall, ignoring whatever it is that comes out of her mouth next.

Farcliff Castle is different from the one at home. This castle just as grand, but it feels colder. There's more stone and steel in it. In the Great Hall, long tables are set up with thick, white tablecloths on them. I let the usher lead me to my assigned seat, at a table with Beckett and my date. Prince Damon and Princess Dahlia of Farcliff are seated next to us, and a few other Lords and Ladies take their seats further down the table.

The King of Farcliff, Charlie, and his Queen, Elle, take their seats at the head table. My brother, Theo, thankfully, is sitting at the opposite end of that table with Queen Cara. I won't have to stare at them all dinner, which I'm sure was done on purpose.

The more distance between us, the better.

Beckett stares at me from across the table, glancing at my date. He cocks his eyebrow as if to say, *You okay?*

I avert my eyes.

I don't know how I feel. On the one hand, I'm seeing my family for the first time in years. I'm happy to see them, but another part of me resents the fact that they never came to visit me. I want to go back to Argyle, but I'm nervous about what to expect.

Beckett stares at me and then his face twists, and he sneezes.

"Allergies?" I ask, spreading my serviette over my thighs.

Beckett grunts in acknowledgement. My brother is allergic to dust, cats, dogs, horses, pollen, peanut butter— pretty much everything except water. He sneezes again, and I hide a grin.

I used to tickle his nose with dandelions when we were kids and run away when he'd get mad. He'd chase me, sneezing the whole time. We were kids. Our childhood was happy.

Now, that happiness seems to have slipped through my fingers.

"Can't take you anywhere," I say with a grin. Beckett sighs, frustrated. Is it wrong that I kind of like seeing people like this? Uncomfortable, in pain, and hurting?

I wasn't always like this. Before the accident, I was a happy person. I liked to laugh.

Snapping your spine and become a paraplegic has a way of changing your outlook on life, though. My family shipped me off to Singapore to get fixed up, and now that I've made a miraculous recovery, they're welcoming me back with open arms.

I'm not broken anymore, so I'm worthy of their attention.

My date shifts in her seat. She reaches into her tiny clutch purse and pulls out a pill packet, handing it to Beckett. "Here," she says with a smile. "I have allergies all the time. These antihistamines are prescription."

Beckett's eyebrows arch, and he accepts the pill with a grateful nod. "Thanks. You're an actress, right? You were in the last *James Bond* movie."

Her face breaks into a smile. "Yeah, I'm Margot LeBlanc. I loved playing a Bond girl. Something about being a villain was really fun and freeing." Her laugh is musical, and she flicks her hair over her shoulder.

Margot. Right. I silently thank my brother for asking.

"Beckett," my brother says, extending a hand. When Margot reaches over to take it, she knocks over my glass of champagne with her arm. I catch it as it sloshes over my plate, and a waiter whisks it away within seconds.

Margot looks embarrassed and apologizes. She glances at Beckett, and they stare at each other for a little bit too long. Beckett's eyes shine, and he smiles at my date like an idiot.

I'm not going to pretend like I'm into this chick, but that doesn't mean that I'm going to let Beckett swoop in on her. Apart from Cara, Margot is the hottest chick in the room. I reach my arm over the back of her chair, leaning into Margot as I glance at my brother. His smile fades, and Margot clears her throat, smiling at me.

I sip my champagne as an awkward silence settles between us.

Princess Dahlia makes a soft noise, smiling politely at us. "So, Prince Luca, please tell us about your recovery over the past few years. You must have worked very hard."

"Never thought I'd have to learn to walk twice," I say, taking another slug of champagne.

Prince Damon nods, and starts telling us about his own brush with death. His was self-inflicted, though. I remember the news reports from a few years ago. It was right before he met Princess Dahlia.

By the time we're onto the second course, I'm half-cut and dying for a piss. I excuse myself from the table, stumbling through the castle hallways, leaning against expensive paintings on the walls for support. I stumble down the hallway, poking my head into lavish rooms.

Are there no bathrooms in this fucking castle?

I pinch my lip together and finally just choose another door at random. Whatever it is, I'm taking a piss in it.

Turns out, it's a formal living room with a balcony. I head over to the balcony, unzip my pants and water one of the plants. Groaning in relief, I zip myself back up and reach into my pocket for a joint.

I can't go back in there without taking the edge off. It's too soon to take another painkiller, and the booze isn't doing anything to distract me from the pain that's starting to pulse down my spine. Weed will help.

Beckett and Margot are making eyes at each other across the dinner table, I'm zoned out most of the time, and I can *still* hear Cara's laugh from across the Great Hall. I light up my joint and take a puff, leaning against the exterior wall as I stare off the balcony.

Farcliff isn't bad, I guess. It's colder than Argyle, but that's because it's much farther north. There are more trees here than in our Caribbean climate, and the air does taste cool and fresh. It's late May, and the whole country is exploding with blooms and the excitement of late spring.

It makes me feel even more bitter than I already do.

Farcliff is like Margot—she's nice, and pretty, and sweet— but all I want to do is fuck her and leave her broken in my wake. This trip to Farcliff is supposed to be the start of a homecoming for me, but all I want to do is ruin my brother's life.

Hopefully, if all goes well, Cara will hate every minute of it. Maybe then she'll get a tiny taste of the torture she's put me through.

As I watch the smoke swirl around my head, a smile curls my lips. My PR team wants me to date Margot? That's exactly what I'll do—but I'm not promising it'll end with a happily-ever-after.

3

IVY

CINNAMON BUNS WERE INVENTED to make bad days better.

My special recipe? I add little bits of apple before cooking them up, so it's like the perfect combination of apple pie and cinnamon bun.

As soon as I pull them out of the oven, I rip one open and stuff the steaming dough into my mouth.

Big mistake.

As soon as the piping-hot bun hits my mouth, I burn the roof of it so badly I lose a layer of skin. I exhale as I chew, cursing myself as I jump around the kitchen.

Typical.

I'm never patient, never smart, never forward-thinking. I always make the same mistakes over and over again. Swallowing my bite, I look at the rest of the cinnamon bun and double down. My mouth is already burned, why not eat the rest of it?

Leaning against the kitchen counter, I mash the dough between my teeth, too angry to taste anything. I'm not even sure why I'm mad. Because I'm too impatient to wait five minutes before eating these? Because my sister is off meeting the prince of her dreams and I'm here on my own? Because as hard as I try, I can't bring myself to dislike my sister even a little bit?

My phone dings on the counter beside me. It's my news app flashing on the screen. The only finger that isn't sticky with cinnamon bun is my pinky finger, so I use that to press the screen. Leaning on the cabinets, I read the headline that appears on my phone:

BAD-BOY PRINCE LEAVES WITH FARCLIFF SWEETHEART:
SPARKS FLY

Heat rips through my chest like a flaming arrow. I scroll through the news story with my pinky finger, pausing on a photo of Prince Luca and my sister with their heads close, laughing at something only they can hear.

Even in a paparazzi photo, the two of them look like they were crafted for the sole purpose of making the rest of us feel inadequate. My sister glows in her blue dress, her hair and makeup somehow still flawless, even after a full evening of eating.

The Prince—well, he's the definition of perfect. Darkish hair, dark eyes, a roguish smile. His jaw is strong and square, and his body dwarfs my sister's in every photo. He has a hand on her lower back, and I can see the hint of a tattoo poking out from his perfectly tailored suit.

I stare at the photos, zooming in on them and leaning forward until my nose is practically against my phone's screen.

The Prince is a little older than my sister. I think I read that he was in his mid-thirties. He almost has a silver fox look about him, and the way he's staring at my sister makes my gut clench.

They're both so damn good-looking. Turning around in disgust, I lean my back against the cabinets and stare up at the ceiling.

I look down at my sticky, cinnamon-bun covered hands and then run my tongue over the raw skin on the roof of my mouth. Is it any wonder that I don't have any royalty knocking down my door? I spend my evenings in the kitchen, baking for no one except myself. I wear ripped jeans and a white t-shirt every single day. I don't talk to men, except if they happen to be driving a taxi or working behind a cash register.

The front door opens, dragging me out of my pity party.

"Ivy!" Hunter calls from the hallway.

"In here." I head to the sink to wash my hands.

His footsteps grow nearer, and he pops his head around the corner just as I untie my apron and hang it on its hook on the wall.

"You have to leave."

"Excuse me?" I arch an eyebrow. "Did you forget that I live here?"

Hunter runs a hand through his dirty blond hair. His eyes are thin slits on his face, and he jerks his chin toward the door. "The Prince and Margot are on their way. They need the house to themselves."

My heart thumps. "Why?"

Margot's agent rolls his eyes. "Come on, Ivy. I know you're a virgin, but you should understand what we've been working toward for the past six months."

My cheeks burn. Liquid fire runs down my throat as I try to swallow. How did he know I was a virgin? Hunter's eyes run down my body as he leans against the doorway, arching an eyebrow. A slimy feeling follows his gaze as it passes over me.

I turn away from him, if only to hide my embarrassment. "Where am I supposed to go?"

"I don't care. You can come to my place if you want."

I whip my head around to stare at him, only to see a disgusting smirk on his face.

I arch an eyebrow. "I'd rather eat sand."

Hunter shrugs, staring at his nails. "Your loss. I could show you what you've been missing."

"Barf. Please leave."

He stares at me pointedly, and I sigh, wiping my damp hands on my jeans.

"Fine. I'm going. They can have this whole entire mansion to use as their fuck-palace in peace. Anything for my dear old sister."

"Good." Hunter pushes himself off the doorjamb and gives me his back. He pauses, looking over his shoulder to grin at me. "Offer still stands if you want to come to my place."

"I just threw up a little in my mouth."

Hunter scoffs and walks back down the hall. His shoes echo on the marble floors, and I wait until I hear the door slam before I move from the kitchen. My shoulders sink, and I make my way to my bedroom to pack a small bag.

Taking my cell phone, I dial my best friend's number.

"Hey, Miss Ivy," Georgina says as she answers. "I see your sister is moving up in the world."

"Don't remind me. Her agent is basically a pimp. It's disgusting. I have to leave my own house so they can have sex."

"Ew. Doesn't your house have, like, a million bedrooms? Why do they need the whole place? Is your sister a screamer?"

"Please don't." I shake my head. I try to fight the grin off my face.

"Don't what?"

"Don't be gross. I have enough of that in my day-to-day life."

Georgie giggles. "Sorry. You want to meet me at the diner? Giselle and I are just finishing up our shift, and Marcus made some extra pie for us. He's testing out a new recipe."

"Be there in twenty."

"I'll have the milkshakes ready and waiting."

I hang up the phone and let out a relieved breath. I've known Georgie and Giselle since I was in kindergarten. The twins have been by my side since we were six years old, through Margot getting famous, through my mother passing away, through my father leaving us to travel the world with his new lover—through everything.

They're my rock, and the only people that can make me feel better about being kicked out of my own house so that my sister can have a dirty, royal sex-fest.

To be honest, all the siblings have been a bit of a surrogate family for me. There are seven of them—five boys plus the twins—and they treat me as their eighth family member.

I hear the sound of a car engine coming up our long drive, so I hurry out through the back door. My Vespa scooter is parked at the side of the house, and I steal a peek around the corner of the house. My leather jacket creaks as I inch closer to the corner, poking just a fraction of my head around so I can see.

My sister is giggling and slinging her arms around the Prince as they stumble up the pathway to the front door. He's taller than I expected, and even from a distance, in the darkness, I can see that he's devastatingly handsome. My chest squeezes when I see him sweep his hand around my sister's lower back, locking his lips with hers.

With my head poking around the corner, I can see her melting in his arms. She lets out a moan, and the Prince tangles his fingers in her hair. My eyes widen and a dagger of heat passes through my stomach.

I wonder if anyone will ever touch me like that? I can almost feel the need rolling off them in waves.

Hunter is correct. I'm a virgin. I've kissed a couple of guys —usually drunkenly, after they resigned themselves to the fact that they were never going to score with my sister—but I've never had a man touch me like the Prince is touching my sister.

My fingers curl around the edge of the building and I stare at the two of them, watching how the Prince's hand sinks into my sister's skin, how she melts into him and presses her body against his.

There's a tightening around my eyes as I squint at them, my hands gripping onto the corner of the mansion. My lips part as my ribs squeeze me breathless. The Prince lets out a low groan, pulling my sister's body into his.

Lucifer cackles and pats the seat he reserved for me in hell.

I know it's weird. I'm watching my sister make out with someone...and I think I'm kind of turned on? Or am I just jealous?

I bite my lower lip, wanting to tear my eyes away. I don't, though, and it's a mistake.

A *big* mistake.

Because while my head is poking around the corner of the house, the Prince's eyes flick up and meet mine. The second his gaze lands on my eyes, embarrassment engulfs me in a bath of fire. My stomach bottoms out, and a gasp stays stuck somewhere in my throat.

If a normal guy saw someone watching as he made out with a girl, he would probably stop what he was doing. A normal guy might call out and ask who it was that's creeping around the side of the building.

Not Prince Luca.

No, the Prince tightens his hold on my sister, and *keeps kissing her as he watches me.*

For an interminable and extremely uncomfortable moment, we stare at each other. His eyes are dark and enchanting, and they keep me rooted in place. I can't look away, or move, or even breathe. Heat blooms in my stomach, between my thighs, all the way down to my toes. He pulls my sister's head back, kissing her neck and lifting his eyes to me again.

My heart hammers against my chest so hard I think it might break through my ribs.

I'm going to pass out.

Tearing myself away from his gaze, I lean my back against the side of the house. My chest heaves as I suck in the cool night air. I close my eyes and try to regain control over my racing heart.

My body is a mess. I'm sweaty and shaking. I'm embarrassed...

...and I like it?

I hear the Prince's low, deliciously growly voice say something that I can't make out, and then the front door opens and closes.

I let out a breath, staring up at the starry night sky. The roof of my mouth is still raw and tender, and I run my tongue over the rough skin. Then I shake my head, get on my scooter, and I drive to the diner.

The whip of the air around my body shakes the last of the heat from my veins. I drive fast—faster than I normally would—wanting to put as much distance between myself and the Prince as possible.

Georgie was telling the truth. She has two milkshakes ready and waiting in our favorite booth in the Grimdale Diner. Her family inherited the diner from their parents, and the seven of them run it together. The booths are still cracked, green vinyl, the jukebox in the corner hasn't worked in years, and the faded pictures on the wall are from old Farcliff and classic Hollywood.

Georgie and Giselle grin at me from one side of the booth. Georgie's midnight blue hair is tied in two braids that hang on either side of her face, and Giselle's bright orange hair is pulled up in a high ponytail. Georgie pushes my milkshake toward me—vanilla, always—and takes a sip of her strawberry-flavored one.

"I should have asked Irving to put vodka in your shake," Georgie grins. Their eldest brother runs the diner, and he's like a big brother to me, too.

Giselle nods her head at me. "You look like you need a bit of alcohol."

"Maybe if I wanted to vomit." The vinyl seat creaks as I slide in, leaning my head against the back and letting out a heavy sigh.

"That bad?"

"Worse."

Georgie flicks a blue braid over her shoulder and grins. She takes another sip of milkshake and waits for me to continue.

"I saw Prince Luca making out with my sister." I grimace.

The twins' eyes sparkle. They nod in unison.

"Go on," Giselle says.

"He *saw* me looking at them..." A blush creeps over my cheeks as I relive the embarrassment all over again. "...and then he kept kissing her while he stared at me."

"Wow, very weird," Georgie says. She exchanges a grin with her twin, and they both nod again. "I love it."

"It was awful." I shake my head, pinching the bridge of my nose.

My best friends laugh, and the embarrassment of the evening fades ever so slightly. I take a sip of my milkshake as Irving drops a big piece of pie on the table.

"Strawberry and rhubarb. I tweaked the crust recipe slightly for extra flakiness. Let me know if you can taste the secret ingredient."

I sniff the pie, and my face breaks into a wide smile. "Ginger."

Irving shakes his head, smiling. "You're too good, Ivy. Didn't even have to taste it."

"Smells amazing." I force a smile, but my thoughts drift back to the Prince. I can still feel the tendrils of heat that tease the edges of my womb, faint reminders of the heat of his gaze...

...while he *Kissed. My. Sister.*

What the hell is wrong with me?

4

LUCA

WHEN MARGOT and I stumble inside, I run my hands over her fit, near-perfect body. She kisses me, and then pulls away. Her cheeks are flushed, and her eyes look a little hazy from drinking. Or did she take something else? Maybe she's a lightweight.

"You want to come upstairs?" she drawls.

Unease twinges in the pit of my stomach. She's far from sober.

Margot arches a fine eyebrow and holds out her manicured hand. I nod, letting her lead me upstairs. Her house is nice, with a wide staircase leading up to the second floor. The place stinks of new money. The rugs are thick, the art is modern, and the decor is sterile.

I hate it.

But I let this pretty, young woman take me by the hand and lead me to her bedroom. Her king-sized, four-poster bed is made, which I like. Nothing bothers me more than someone who's messy.

Margot fumbles with my buttons and I stand there, not moving. I know I would hate myself if I fucked her right now.

She'd wake up and she might regret it, or she might not—but I know I would. When she finally gets my shirt unbuttoned, she pushes it off my shoulders and lets out a giggle.

"Your body is royally *hot*." The actress looks up at me through her eyelashes, giving me her best sexy pout. Her hand drifts down to the outside of my pants.

I glance down at my crotch.

No movement.

I clear my throat. "I have to pee. Bathroom?"

Margot nods to a door beside us, and I gently extricate myself from her hold. I wink at her and give her a soft kiss on the lips before disappearing into her ensuite.

Once inside I let out a sigh. What the hell is wrong with me? Usually, I'd be ready to go. I'd have her splayed out on top of the bed and I'd be plowing her from here to Argyle. Leaning against the sink, I close my eyes and try to gather myself.

It's because of Cara. I know it is. Being close to her at the event tonight threw me off. I just can't get used to seeing her with my brother, even though it's been over a year since they were married. I can't see my life without her by my side. I can't imagine her spending it with someone else.

The day I found out they were engaged was the same day I took my first step after an experimental operation and lots of physiotherapy. It was the best and worst day of my life. I'd thought of Cara constantly after the accident that made me paraplegic, and the thought of coming back to her was what got me through the low, low months that followed.

Then, I became a miracle, and my life became a nightmare. All in the same day.

We were attached at the hip from the time we were toddlers until the time I jumped off a cliff into water that was a little too shallow. When I broke my back, everything changed. I thought I'd be with her forever, and I still can't get used to the fact that it won't happen.

She couldn't wait for me. She couldn't even visit me.

When I was sent off to Singapore for my seventh operation, she kissed me on the lips and told me she loved me. Then, four years later—one year ago—she married my fucking brother and became my Queen.

Is that what she calls love?

I turn the faucet on and let it run, watching the water for a few moments. Then, I open the medicine cabinet and have a look. I glance over my shoulder, listening for any noise on the other side of the door.

I hear nothing.

Margot's got Prozac, Celexa, Zoloft—all three bottles old and expired—a bunch of antihistamines, some bullshit fat-burning supplements, and some Advil. Nothing too interesting. Nothing too fun. Sort of like Margot. I close the medicine cabinet and splash a bit of water on my face. Patting it dry, I rack my brain for a way to get out of this situation.

I need to stay with Margot, if only to make Cara jealous. I don't give a shit about the fact that my PR team wants us together for the month, but I did love the daggers that Cara was shooting at me.

So, I can't insult Margot by leaving—but I also can't fuck her. Not when she's drunk and falling over herself. The way she was slurring her words did nothing to make me want to fuck her. My cock seems to have forgotten how to function properly.

Bracing myself, I open the door, only to see Margot passed out across the bed, snoring softly. My shoulders relax as I let out a sigh of relief, and I slip out through the bedroom door.

Padding silently through the house, I start opening doors at random.

What can I say? I like snooping.

I think you can tell a lot about a person by the way they keep their house. I open a bedroom that's obviously a guest room. Two bathrooms, a home gym, another guest room.

Then, at the opposite end of the house from Margot's room, I finally find a room that seems to be inhabited. It smells fantastic. Like fresh laundry with a sweet, feminine undertone. Maybe a bit like cinnamon? I inhale the scent deep into my lungs, and my cock stirs.

Down, boy.

I walk to the vanity, where pictures are stuck to the mirror. Staring at them, I see a young Margot with a dark-haired girl —her sister? The dark-haired girl has a dimpled smile and eyes that sparkle, even in a picture. In another shot, she has her arms slung around a pair of twins. All three of them are laughing at something.

It feels wrong to be looking at these intimate pictures, but I can't look away. On the vanity is an old, carved box. I flip it open and find old, stained cards. Pulling one out, my eyebrows arch.

Recipes—hundreds of them. They're organized alphabetically and split into meal categories, and the Type A side of me nods in approval. I close the box again and lay on the bed, stretching out across the pillows.

Is it weird for me to be here?

Kind of.

Do I care?

Not even a little bit.

I reach into my pocket and pull out the hard cigarette case where I keep my joints. I light one up as I stare around the room. It's tidy, but it feels like home. My thoughts flick to the girl that was peeking around the corner of the house. Is this her room?

She was staring at me making out with her sister. Maybe she's just as much of a creep as I am. I ash my joint into the glass of water on the bedside table, folding my other arm behind my head. I watch smoke swirl up and dissipate before it hits the ceiling, taking in all the trinkets and pictures that dot the room.

This room doesn't feel as sterile as all the others. It feels lived in.

It feels *real*.

As weird as it sounds, I like being in here. It's like a home I never knew I was missing.

After a time, I get up off her bed and head back to Margot's room. She's still passed out on her bed, so I close the door and head downstairs.

There are very few personal touches around the house. Everything is perfectly displayed, perfectly arranged, perfectly designed. In the living room, there's a huge painting of Margot on the wall, naked, with her arms and legs strategically placed to hide all the fun bits. I arch an eyebrow, tilting my head.

She's definitely hot. Maybe when she's sober, I'll fuck her.

Maybe her sister would want to join.

It's not until I'm in the kitchen that I get that feeling again —the feeling that someone actually lives here. It smells incredible in here. There's a bright yellow stand mixer in the corner and beside it, a tray of fresh-baked cinnamon buns.

My stomach rumbles, and suddenly I feel hungry. No, not hungry. I feel like my stomach is an empty pit, and even if I filled it with all the food in the world, I could still eat more.

I descend on the buns like a pack of hungry seagulls who just spotted a toddler with a corndog. The first cinnamon bun, I inhale in about three seconds flat. The second takes me a few seconds longer, but definitely less than a minute.

I groan in pleasure, stuffing my face with soft, sweet dough, cinnamon, and—apples! I laugh as I rip another cinnamon bun open. There are pieces of apple in here! I ate the first ones too fast, but this one, I really taste. It tastes like doughy magic.

I eat another.

And then another.

And then another.

They're. So. Fucking. Good.

Better than sex. Not that I've had sex tonight, but this food triggers something in the pleasure center of my brain. A rush of dopamine floods through me and I laugh, my mouth full.

I don't even hear the door open, or footsteps, or anything before a voice makes me jump.

"What the fuck?"

I turn around and I see *her*. The girl from the photos. Dark, almost black hair—it's messy, and she has a big red mark across her forehead. She arches her eyebrows, staring at me.

"I said, *what the fuck*? What are you doing?"

I chew, looking her up and down. She's wearing jeans— faded and ripped on the thighs—and a plain white t-shirt. A leather jacket is slung over her arm, and she's carrying a tiny backpack. In the other hand, she has a helmet, and the mark on her forehead makes sense.

I swallow. "I'm eating a cinnamon bun."

Her cheeks flush as her eyes flick to the empty plate behind me. Her lips—blood red, with the bottom lip slightly fuller than the top one and an exaggerated cupid's bow—are perfect. I want to taste them, too. Her eyes flash with anger, and my cock twitches.

"Did you eat them all?" Flinging her bag, jacket, and helmet on the kitchen island, she stomps over to me. The girl stares at the plate and then back at me. I catch that smell again—fresh and sweet and feminine. Desire twinges in the pit of my stomach.

I grin. "They were delicious."

Her plump red lips fall open and she shakes her head. "All of them? I was looking forward to one of those in the morning."

"So? Just buy more."

"I *made* them, you knucklehead." The girl stares at me, eyes blazing, and all I want to do is bend her over the kitchen counter and drive my cock into her. I want to make those cheeks even redder as she screams my name. I want to grab fistfuls of her ebony hair and twist it as she comes all over my cock.

I take a step toward her, suddenly keenly aware that I'm still not wearing a shirt. She seems to realize that at the same time, her eyes drifting over my chest.

I lift a finger up, brushing it over her soft, round cheek. She stares up at me, unmoving, as if she's frozen on the spot —just as she did outside when she watched me with Margot. The tension grows between us. Her lips call out to me, begging to be kissed. Her body is soft, and supple, and exactly what I need right now.

But it's her eyes that make me want her. One is blue, and the other one is a pale green color, and they're both full of pain and hardship and complicated history.

"Your eyes are different colors," I say in a gravelly voice.

She snaps out of her stupor and jerks away from me. "Keenly spotted, Sherlock. Got any other revelations for me?"

Reaching behind me, the girl grabs the plate that used to have cinnamon buns on it. Her arm brushes against my side, and the blush on her cheeks deepens. She keeps her gaze averted, taking the plate to the dishwasher without sparing me a glance.

I grin. "Are you embarrassed that I'm not wearing a shirt? You can look, if you want. You can even touch. I won't bite... unless you want me to."

Finally, she lifts her eyes up to me. "First of all, *ew*. Second of all, I'm not in the habit of having my sister's sloppy seconds, but thanks."

"That's disappointing."

Her blush extends up to her hairline, up to the fading red mark on her forehead.

"What's your name?" I inch closer to her.

She closes the dishwasher, throwing me a disgusted glance. "Ivy."

"Ivy," I repeat, tasting her name on my tongue. "Maybe I should call you Poison, because you're killing me standing there like that."

That dumb line makes her stare at me, and a surprised laugh falls through her lips. She shakes her head as I take another step toward her.

I need her. I need to feel her skin under my palms. I need to taste her, kiss her, make her mine. I need those two-toned eyes to drink me in, and I need to hear her moan in my ear.

Ivy's jaw juts out and her eyebrow arches. "Do those stupid lines actually work?"

"You tell me." I erase the distance between us, sweeping my arm around her back. My other hand runs up her delicate neck, cupping her cheek. I run my thumb over her red lips, dragging it across her full lower lip. Her breath teases the edge of my finger, and my cock throbs between my legs.

Ivy's fingers splay over my bare chest. Her breath hitches. I can see the pulse thumping in her neck as her eyes widen.

Angling my head, I lean toward her. In a moment, I'll taste those perfect lips between mine. I'll curl my fingers into her dark hair and taste her silken, white skin.

I'll kiss the only woman that I've actually wanted to kiss in almost a year...

...but at the last moment, she turns her head and pushes me back harder than I would have expected her to be able to.

Too hard.

I drank and smoked too much tonight—or maybe I ate too quickly. I took one too many painkillers. Maybe I'm still learning how to walk on these unsteady baby Bambi legs of mine, and I'm destined to fall over all the time from now on.

Whatever the reason is, I can't hold my balance and I stumble backward. Arms flailing, legs unsteady, I take another step back, but it's not enough. I twist, hoping to grab onto something, but the edge of the marble countertop is closer than I anticipated.

So close, in fact, that I don't even have time to react until I hit the edge of my head against it, and crumple to the floor.

5

IVY

PRINCE, down.

Blood, everywhere.

Ivy, panicking.

"Fuck. Shit. Fucking shit." I scramble forward, reaching for a semi-clean tea towel as the Prince groans at my feet.

He's making noise, so at least that means he's not dead.

Farcliff Almighty, I almost killed the visiting Prince of Argyle because he tried to kiss me. I can't even imagine how I'd explain that one. Who in their right mind would believe me? Not even Georgie and Giselle would think I was telling the truth.

"Can you sit up?" I step over the Prince, bending over to help him lean against the cabinets. He slumps a bit, so I kneel down and straddle him to offer more support.

I don't even have time to think about the fact that I'm straddling royalty right now, or that his very hard erection was pressed up against my stomach just moments ago. Or, indeed, the fact that I'm pretty sure we were a few milliseconds away from kissing.

Kissing.

Me, the virgin, with him, the Prince of Argyle who happens to be in some weird arranged relationship with my sister.

Right now, all I can think about is the blood pouring out of the gash on his head. I press the tea towel against it to try to stem the flow of blood.

The Prince's hands drift up my thighs and come to rest on my ass. I try to ignore the electric spark in my stomach responding to his touch, or the fact that my panties are soaked—and did I mention I'm straddling him?

Did I mention I've never straddled a man, *ever*?

"This isn't so bad, you know," he says, his voice slightly muffled. "I'd gladly suffer an injury if it meant I could bury my face in your tits." I look down to see his nose shoved between my breasts as I try to keep pressure on his wound.

"You're disgusting."

"I'm only human."

I round my back to put a bit of distance between his face and my boobs, even though deep down, I don't really mind his face being shoved up against my chest.

At the very least, if his face is occupied, he can't look up and see how red my cheeks have gone. I can feel the burn of embarrassment all the way up to my hairline.

Swinging my leg over to put some distance between our crotches, I take his hand and place it on the tea towel on his head.

"Keep the pressure on."

"Yes, ma'am. I like a woman who orders me around." His lips quirk up in a grin.

I roll my eyes. "Give it a rest. I'm trying to avoid you bleeding out on my kitchen floor."

Pulling a drawer open, I find a clean tea towel and swap it out for the blood-soaked one. Then, I take another clean tea towel and wet it. I start mopping up the blood on the Prince's face.

I can feel his eyes on me, but I focus on the task at hand. I mop up the blood on his cheeks, noting how strong his jawline is. He has a bit of stubble—more than I'd expect from royalty, to be honest. It gives him a rugged, kind of roguish look.

I wipe the blood from his smooth, wide brow, and try to get it out of his hair. It's dark, thick, and a bit coarse. There are half a dozen grey hairs poking through on his temple. I feel his hair with the tips of my fingers as I try to wipe a bit of blood out of it, and I start to wonder what it would feel like to twist my fingers into it.

The Prince's lips are full and almost feminine, and he parts them ever so slightly when I wipe the blood off them. His tongue slides out to lick his lower lip, and a jolt of heat passes straight through my stomach.

Once or twice, I glance at his eyes. They're dark, stormy, and utterly sinful. The way he looks at me makes me want to squeeze my thighs together. It makes me want to know what it feels like to have his lips on mine, his hands around my waist, his...

I shake my head. A few hours ago, I was watching him kiss my sister. Now, I'm fantasizing about him being my first?

Get a grip, Ivy.

When I start mopping up his chest, my heart is racing. I take care to not let my skin touch his, but even through the tea towel, I can feel the heat of his body. His chest is hard, muscular, and impossibly broad. I wonder what it would feel like to lay my head there, in the crook between his shoulder and his chest?

I clear my throat.

"I never would have taken you for the nurturing type

41

when you walked in here, guns blazing," the Prince says to break the silence. I flick my eyes up to his.

Big mistake.

My panties are pretty much ruined at this point.

"No?" I manage to say, focusing on the blood that has dripped down to his navel.

"No, you stormed in here like a tough biker chick, all leather and attitude, but you're actually really gentle." The Prince's hand drifts up to my hip, and I don't want to tell him to move it. I like the feeling of his hands on my body. I like the heat of it, and the coiled power that I can sense in every part of him.

Taking care not to look at his eyes, I shrug. "I drive a Vespa, so I'm not exactly a bad-ass biker chick. More like dinky little scooter girl."

Prince Luca chuckles, and the noise makes my stomach clench. I swallow hard, standing up to wring out the tea towel. His eyes are still on me. I can feel them, and it takes everything inside me not to stare back. I've pretty much been wearing a permanent blush ever since I walked into the kitchen.

The Prince groans as he stands up. I focus on the tea towel, throwing out the bloody ones and moving to wipe down the counter. The kitchen looks like a crime scene.

I stop when I see Prince Luca's hand extended toward me.

"I'm Luca, by the way. I never introduced myself."

"I know who you are," I say, dragging my eyes up to his. I slide my palm into his hand, and my whole body turns electric. Heat licks the inside of my stomach as my hand feels like it's burning against his. My mouth goes dry and I struggle to swallow. I'm blinking too much.

Kiss. Straddle. Erection. Panties. Lips. Eyes. Hands.

What were we talking about?

"What's going on here?" We both turn to see Hunter in the doorway. His face is dark, flicking from me, to the shirtless Prince, to the bloodbath on the kitchen floor.

My instinct is to shrink back, but not Prince Luca. Instead, he puffs his chest out and takes a step forward, as if he owns the ground he walks on. Even in my own house, he feels more at home than I do.

"Who are you?" Luca asks, stepping sideways to shield me from Hunter.

My heart flutters the tiniest bit.

Okay, fine—it flutters a lot.

I step forward, putting a hand on the Prince's bicep—a very firm bicep, by the way—and I glance at the Prince with a slight nod.

"This is Hunter, Margot's agent. He's..." I glance at the wiry man in the doorway. "What *are* you doing here, Hunter?"

"I just came to check in. Do you need to go to the hospital? That's a lot of blood."

Luca waves a hand. "I'll get one of the doctors at the castle to look at it. I'd better go." He turns toward me, his gaze making me burn up. "It was nice to meet you, Poison."

"You're not actually going to call me that, are you?"

His grin is intoxicating. How is it possible for one man to be this handsome?

...and why does he have to be promised to my sister?

Prince Luca leans down and brushes his lips against my cheek. His breath tickles my neck and he moves his mouth closer to my ear. My pulse jumps, and sparks fly between my thighs.

"I'll see you again, Poison Ivy."

Before I can respond, he throws a knee-weakening grin. Holding a tea towel against his head, and still sans shirt, the Prince strides out of the kitchen as if nothing at all is amiss.

Hunter stares after him, and then at me. His eyes narrow. "I'm watching you, Ivy. You'd better not mess this up for Margot, or else you'll have hell to pay."

"I was *helping* him." I gesture to the blood on the floor, on the cabinets, on the countertop. "I'm not messing anything up."

"Why wasn't he wearing a shirt?"

"I don't know, maybe because you pimped out my sister and made her hook up with him? Why are you asking me this? Can you leave? You don't even live here, pervert."

Hunter rolls his eyes and walks away. When I hear the door close, I jog over and lock it, even though Margot's agent has a key. I tiptoe upstairs and make sure my sister is still okay. She's on her bed, sideways, still wearing her dress and heels.

My heart thumps. Maybe they didn't have sex after all?

Why does that make me so happy?

I sigh, taking Margot's sparkly stilettos off. I throw a blanket over her, and then I head back downstairs and clean the kitchen. As I mop up the last of the Prince's blood, I blink back tears.

He was probably just upset that his first choice passed out before he could have sex with her, and then I walked in. I was the second choice, as usual. The fool who enjoyed the attention.

I won't cry tonight. I *won't.*

I'm sick of crying over everything that my sister is given, and everything that I'll never have. I don't know why the Prince was interested in me tonight. Maybe that's just what he does. He hooks up with girls, and then flirts with their sisters.

I scrub the kitchen of any evidence of his presence—as

much for my own sake as anyone else's. By the time I'm done, my back is sore, my hands are raw, and all I want to do is collapse into bed.

But when I get into my room, my hands ball into fists. Anger flares in my chest, burning me as I try to breathe.

He was *here.*

It smells like him. I can sense him here, like a whisper in the wind. The bed is messed up. There's ash on my bedside table.

I repeat: *ash on my bedside table.*

What the actual fuck?

My ears burn, and it feels like my head is going to explode. Was he just toying with me that whole time? He snuck into my bedroom, and he thought he'd pretend to be into me? He flirted with me and trespassed into my space just because he thinks he can?

I rip the blankets off my bed and ball them up, tossing them to the floor. Opening the window, I fling the water out of the glass, sending his ash away with it. I wipe my bedside table, but it's still not enough.

I can't sleep here. Not until I clean it of his presence.

He's too dangerous. Too addictive. Too damn sexy for his own good—or mine.

Tonight, I'll sleep in a guest bedroom. Tomorrow, I'll purge my room of him, and then I'll stay the hell away from Prince Luca.

6

LUCA

THE ROYAL DOCTOR stitches me up, and then I jerk off in the bathroom while I think of Ivy. When I come, the wound on my head throbs like hell. I probably shouldn't have done that, but I haven't been that turned on in months.

Feeling Ivy's tight, lithe body on top of mine was almost too much. If she'd have stayed on top of me for much longer, grinding her hips against me without even realizing she was doing it, I might have exploded right there. Her tits smelled like magic. She fitted on top of me like we were made for each other.

How the hell am I supposed to date her sister?

I collapse into bed and dream of the dark-haired beauty with the dimpled smile and two-toned eyes.

WHEN I LIVED IN SINGAPORE, I forgot what it was like to be on a Royal Tour. Every day is full of events from morning until night. On account of my fall, and the fact that I'm still required to do two hours of physical therapy for my back every day, I'm able to skip most of the next day's itinerary, save for the evening meal.

Unfortunately, my brother makes it abundantly clear that I'm expected to attend dinner, at least. It's an intimate meal with only the Farcliff royal family, our family, and a few dignitaries. My date will be here, too.

I pop a couple painkillers in my mouth and wash them down with a gulp of wine. Roughing my hand through my hair, I glance around my room and find my black tie. Slipping it around my neck, I don't have time to tie it when a knock sounds on the door.

When I open it, I'm surprised to see Princess Dahlia standing outside my bedroom door. She smiles at me, flicking her baby blue hair over her shoulder.

"Your Highness," she says. "I hope I'm not interrupting."

"Not at all." I step aside and motion for her to come into my chambers. The Farcliff royal family have been kind enough to provide each of us with our own bedroom, living room, and bathroom. I motion to one of the sofas in the ornate living room, and Princess Dahlia steps over to it. Her gait is soft and almost fairy-like, just like the rest of her.

"I wanted to speak to you before tonight's event," she starts, smoothing her hands over her navy dress. Tilting her head, she stares at me with sharp eyes.

"Okay," I respond, a little bit apprehensive.

"My husband and I were talking about our upcoming tour through Farcliff. You may or may not be aware, but Damon has become a bit of a spokesperson for mental health."

I incline my head.

Dahlia smiles at me. "We were hoping you'd join us."

"Me? I'm not exactly a model for a healthy mind," I snort, shaking my head. My knee bounces up and down and I scratch the back of my neck. It'll be a few more minutes

48

before the pills I took take effect, and an itching sensation is crawling up my spine.

The need.

The addiction.

Her Highness doesn't seem to notice. She tucks a strand of pale blue hair behind her ear and smiles wider. "Of course you're a model for mental health! You survived a debilitating spinal cord injury, and not only lived, but learned to walk again. You're an inspiration, Your Highness."

"You're too kind," I say, resisting the urge to fidget. I clamp my hands together and pray that the pills will take effect soon. Maybe I should have taken an extra one tonight—I know that Cara will be at dinner. I'll be on edge until it's over.

Princess Dahlia smiles. "The tour begins shortly after you're due to leave in a month's time. Damon and I were hoping that you'd stay on for a few weeks, a month or two, tops. We have events and workshops planned to promote mental health resources in the Kingdom."

Dahlia stands up, and I do the same. She extends her hand toward me and I lean down to kiss her fingertips.

"I hope you'll consider it," she smiles. "I understand you've only just reunited with your family, but sometimes distance is a good thing."

Her eyes are sharp, and I know exactly what she's talking about.

Cara.

Is it that obvious how much it cuts me up? Is it so painfully clear to the whole world that she tore my heart out of my chest, smiling politely as she did it?

Of course it is. I've never been good at hiding how I feel.

I give Princess Dahlia a tight-lipped smile and incline my head. "I'll think about it."

"We'd be honored to have you."

49

She leaves, and I'm left alone again.

My thoughts bounce around my head, and I have a hard time keeping up with them. I head to my pill bottle and take two more before finding my joint case and taking out a spliff. Sitting by the window, I light up and take a puff.

I need to take the edge off.

It's more than an edge. My entire body is made up of jagged edges. I crave numbness, if only to forget that I'll have to spend yet another evening in the presence of the woman who broke my heart.

Closing my eyes, I let my thoughts drift to last night.

To Ivy.

The scent of her skin. The feeling of her body on top of mine. The look in her eye when her gaze passed over my bare chest.

Maybe staying in Farcliff wouldn't be so bad. Maybe Dahlia's right, and a bit of distance from my own family would do me good. I can always go back to Argyle after the mental health tour and deal with my issues with Cara then.

The fidgeting in my body is slowing down. My thoughts aren't so fragmented, and my movements start to feel smoother. The tightness in my face eases, and finally, *finally*, I can take a full breath.

As I exhale another puff of smoke through the window, I see a limousine pull up. My date exits the car, extending a hand toward a waiting valet.

She's not the one I'm looking at, though.

Behind her, Ivy steps out. I grin when I see what she's wearing—jeans and a white t-shirt. To her credit, her pants aren't ripped. They're black jeans, at least. She doesn't follow her sister up the steps. Instead, she heads off with one of the valets toward the servants' entrance.

Yes, maybe staying in Farcliff isn't such a bad idea, after all.

I finish tying my tie and gulp the rest of my wine down. It sloshes in my stomach as I race through the door. My steps are loose, and I feel almost unsteady. I float down the hallways toward the servants' areas, avoiding any of the formal reception rooms.

I'm drawn to Poison like a moth to a flame. Isn't that the theme of my entire life? I crave any type of poison, whether it be a pill, or a potion, or a painful heartbreak. I let it swirl in my veins until I feel numb and alive at the same time.

Ivy isn't any different. Her eyes enchant me, and her body puts me under a spell that I never want to be rid of. She has a certain brand of poison that's irresistible to me, and I intend to drink her up until I've had my fill.

7

IVY

THIS MORNING, Margot decided that she needed a babysitter for tonight's event—so, here I am. She's been on edge lately. I've heard whispers of anxiety disorder, but Margot zips her lips if I ever try to bring it up. Deep down, though, I know she needs me.

There's something worrying her, I just don't know what. Maybe the fame and celebrity are finally getting to her. Maybe this relationship with Prince Luca is putting her over the edge.

And as much as I'm jealous of her, I love my sister with all my heart. With Mama gone, and Dad run off to enjoy 'retirement' in the Caribbean, we only have each other.

If she needs a babysitter at the castle, I'll come along.

I follow the red-waistcoat-wearing valet through narrow corridors until I get to the underbelly of the castle.

I can feel the weight of the building on top of my head. I've never been in a building this big, or this ornate, or this important. I inhale the scent of stone and steel, and let the valet lead me to a big room adjoining the kitchens. It looks like the staff's dining room.

"You can wait here," he says with a bow, his eyebrow arching as his eyes pass over my body.

Maybe I should have worn something fancier, but black jeans usually see me through any event. It's not like I go anywhere formal.

I follow my nose over to the kitchens, where a hundred delicious smells make me groan in pleasure. I lean against a wall beside the entrance, watching the hive of activity before me.

A smile tugs at my lips as I watch the chefs work.

This is my happy place. This is where I feel alive—in a kitchen, surrounded by smells and sounds and noises of food being created.

A sous-chef chops an onion while looking over his shoulder and shouting something at another chef. How he's not cutting his fingers off is beyond me. The kitchen is buzzing. My eyes drift over to a door on the side wall. Through it, I can see ovens and mixers, and I already know that's where I want to be.

I slide along the wall, still unnoticed, and peek through the window. I watch one of the pastry chefs pipe delicate roses onto a towering cake before wiping sweat off his brow. My breath catches in my throat, and I lean against the glass to watch.

"Thought I might find you here."

I jump at the sound of Prince Luca's voice. He's wearing that same smirk he had on yesterday. My stomach clenches, and butterflies explode through my abdomen. Their wings tickle the edges of my stomach as a blush spreads up my neck.

"Your Highness," I say. "What are you doing here?"

"Looking for you." The Prince's voice drops, and his hand drifts to my lower back. Fire teases my insides, licking my thighs with delicious heat as his touch spreads warmth through my body.

A crash followed by a shriek makes us both turn our heads toward the dessert room. One of the pastry chefs is holding his head while another runs over. I can sense the panic rolling through the door in waves.

Pushing the swinging door open, I step through.

I don't know why. I have no right to be there. I'm sure they would have kicked me out immediately if not for Prince Luca's presence. The pastry chef's faces turn from shock, to outrage, to polite resignation as they both bow at the Prince.

At our feet, the three-tiered cake—and all its delicately piped roses—lays smashed on the floor. Buttercream icing is smeared from one end of the room to the other.

The young pastry chef holding the piping bag looks at the older man and shakes his head. "I'm so sorry, George, I don't know what happened."

"*Mon dieu,*" the older man says, slipping his chef's hat off and raking his fingers through his hair. "That was our *pièce de résistance.* We have only small bites to serve now." The old man's face crumples, and he shakes his head. "My first time serving dessert somewhere other than Westhill Palace, and I won't have anything to show for it."

His eyes dart up to Prince Luca, and the old man's cheeks turn bright red. I can feel the shame and embarrassment radiating from him.

Putting my hands on Prince Luca's shoulders, I spin him around. "Nice to see you. Bye!" I say to his back as I push him out the door. It swings back toward him and smacks the Prince on the bum. He stumbles forward, whipping around to stare at me through the door's window. His eyes are wide with shock, but I don't have time to worry about that right now.

The young pastry chef's jaw is on the floor, and the old man is looking at me with an arched eyebrow. I don't have time to explain my weird relationship to Prince Luca to them, though, because there's a dessert disaster at my feet. If there's one thing I know how to do properly, it's how to fix a baking mishap.

"Okay," I start. "We can't serve this. What else have we got?"

"We?" the young chef asks, crossing his arms.

George, the old one, must see something in me though, because he nods his head and turns to the stainless steel tables behind him.

"*Tree* raspberry cheesecakes which were meant for tomorrow—Queen Elle's favorites—and two small chocolate cakes which were to be the miniature versions of this one. We have small bites of homemade chocolates and some macarons." I can tell by his accent that he's French, but I don't have time to think about anything other than the desserts in front of me.

The old man takes an apron off a hook on the wall and tosses it at my chest. I catch it, slipping it over my head.

George points to the young pastry chef. "Ben, clean up this mess." He gestures to the floor.

My eyes drift up to the doorway, where Prince Luca is looking at me with a curious grin on his face. He inclines his head and walks away.

I shake my head to clear the thoughts away. I can't think of him right now, or the way he makes my body ignite. Tightening the apron strings, I put my hands on my hips.

"We don't have enough for one big dessert, so how about we do individual ones?"

George quirks an eyebrow.

I nod to the cheesecakes. "Individual raspberry cheesecakes and chocolate cake bites inside a tempered chocolate dome, served with warm raspberry sauce. The sauce will tie the two desserts together. Do you have good quality chocolate?"

"Of course," George smiles.

"Good. Let's get tempering. We can make a praline topping for the cheesecake squares and garnish the whole with the macarons. The whole thing on the individual plates, served to each guest."

The old man puts his hands on my shoulders and stares into my eyes. "Genius, *mademoiselle*. What's your name?"

"Ivy," I answer.

"Well, Ivy, you're a hero."

"Don't know if I'd go that far, but I may have saved the dessert for tonight."

The next hour is a flurry of activity. The three of us work like crazy to create chocolate domes, placing small bites of desserts inside them. I make a raspberry sauce under George's watchful gaze, who grunts in approval as he tastes it. Right as a butler comes to tell us that the guests are ready for dessert, I find some gold leaf in one of the cupboards. With a bit of dazzle on top of the chocolate domes, and a delicate decanter of raspberry sauce, the dessert looks decadent, refined, and—if I do say so myself —perfect.

The waiters whisk the plates away, and I lean back against the countertop, letting out a heavy sigh. I grab a piece of broken chocolate dome—one of the extras—and pop it into my mouth. It snaps delicately between my teeth and then melts on my tongue. I groan, nodding.

"That's good." I try to smile, but I'm exhausted.

George comes to stand in front of me and extends his hand. "Thank you, Miss Ivy."

I smile. "My pleasure. I've never worked in a commercial kitchen before. That was incredible."

The old chef stares at me, crossing his arms. He taps his lips with his fingertip, tilting his head to the side. "I'll be here for the next month, before we head back to Westhill Palace with Prince Gabriel. Would you like to come train with me until then? You're talented, and I could use your energy and creativity in here."

My eyes widen, and I stare around the dessert room. This is my *dream*. It's more than my dream! I'd wanted to own my own small bakery, maybe somewhere in Grimdale. I had modest ideas.

But to bake for royalty? To learn from one of the world's top pastry chefs?

Unreal.

My face breaks into a smile. "Yes! Yes, I'd like that very much."

George nods. "Good. Now get to work, we have a lot of cleaning to do." His eyes flash and a hint of a smile flits across his lips. I glance at Ben, the other apprentice, who grins at me.

"You have no idea what you've gotten yourself into," he laughs.

I smile in response, because I don't want to say the thought that passes through my mind—that even if working here is hell, it can't possibly be worse than being my sister's personal assistant.

This is my chance to do something for myself. To do something I love. I won't be watching my sister blossom, constantly feeling like I'm less than her.

Maybe, working here, I'll finally feel like who I am is *enough*.

8

LUCA

DINNER GOES by in a haze of alcohol and tedious conversation. Margot sits beside me, and even the jealous glances that Cara sends my way do nothing to entertain me.

Only when dessert arrives do I feel any sort of joy sparking in my spirit. The veil of numbness that I've worn all evening shivers slightly, and I see Ivy's touch in the dish that's served.

A few comments are made on the dessert, but no one seems to appreciate the genius on the plate. I saw the cake smash against the ground. I saw the disaster in the kitchen.

To then have it turned into something delicate, delicious, and refined... That takes a master's touch.

Ivy's touch.

When I taste her creation, I feel like I'm tasting *her*. I moan into my plate, imagining her red lips.

I need her.

Or, maybe, I just need a distraction from the woman who decided to marry my brother instead of me.

Being at this table is suffocating. I feel like I'm about to explode, and all I can do is sit here and endure it. My gaze drifts to Cara, even though I know it'll hurt to look at her.

Her beauty. Her smile. Her perfect fucking body that no longer belongs to me.

Maybe it never did.

"...and we're so glad to see Luca recovered so well," Cara smiles, swinging her eyes to me. They hit me like a sledgehammer to the gut, her smile a knife that twists in my back.

Dahlia clears her throat. "We were hoping that Prince Luca would stay in Farcliff for a while longer. He's an inspiration to us all."

All eyes turn to me. Margot slides her hand over my thigh, and I resist the urge to leave the room.

Cara's eyes are the dial that cranks up the agony in my spine. Every time she looks at me, my nervous system screams, and pain shatters through my body. Deep, throbbing pain starts to well up in my marrow, and I need to swallow another pill or three.

I stare at the raspberry sauce on my plate, dragging a spoon through the thick, sweet liquid.

"He's a miracle," Cara responds, her words peppering my chest with poisoned knives.

Miracle.

It would have been a miracle for her to wait for me. For her to stay true to her word. She wouldn't have run off with my brother. She'd have been by my side until I was better.

But no.

She chose the brother that was whole. The one who could walk. The one who could make her a Queen.

I shift in my seat, and my body screams.

The pills have already worn off.

It's Cara's fault. If she'd stop looking at me with her big, brown, magnetic eyes, my body wouldn't be a bubbling cauldron of suffering. If she'd stop slapping me with that honeyed voice, I'd be able to breathe properly.

"So, are you staying?" Theo asks, arching an eyebrow.

The vindictive part of me wants to say no. The cruel part of me wants to tell him I'll be right beside him until Cara comes back to me.

To my surprise, though, those aren't the words that come out of my mouth. "Yes," I say, bringing my spoon up to my lips to taste sweet, tangy raspberry sauce. "I'm staying."

WHEN DINNER FINISHES, I can finally slip away. I feel Margot's eyes on my back, and Cara's gaze in my soul. I don't look back.

Letting my feet carry me down to the kitchens, I ignore the castle staff as they bow to me. I make my way to the pastry room, only to be disappointed when Ivy isn't there.

Stalking through the hallways, I know I can't go back to the formal living room where the two royal families are sitting around, dousing each other in empty compliments.

One good thing about being sent off to Singapore for five years? There were no royal events that seem to have the sole purpose of boring me to death.

Instead of rejoining the dinner party, I head outside and light up a joint. I shake a painkiller from the pill bottle in my breast pocket and swallow it down before taking a puff.

Exhaling, I loosen my tie.

My body immediately relaxes, and the shots of pain that have plagued me all evening start to subside. Heading through the topiary garden, I make my way to the pool at the back of the estate.

The doctor was very clear last night—I can't get the wound on my head wet. But my body is screaming for some water.

When I was in Singapore, being in the water was a big part of my physiotherapy. I've always been a swimmer, but having a spinal cord injury only made me love the water more. It's what got me moving again. It's what built up the muscles in my atrophied legs enough so that I could walk.

So, when I reach the edge of the pool, I strip down to my underwear and slide into the cool water. My joint is still hanging on the edge of my lips, and I blow out some smoke around it.

The cold water hugs my body tight, and I ease deeper into the water. Staring up at the starry sky, I let myself drift to the middle of the pool. One by one, my muscles relax. The burning pain in my nervous system eases as the cold water laps my body.

"You know you're supposed to wait an hour to go swimming after you eat, right?"

I lift my head to see Ivy at the edge of the pool, grinning. She crouches down, running her fingers in the water before shivering at the coldness.

"It's beautiful in here, you should come in."

"Didn't bring my swimsuit to the formal dinner that my sister dragged me to, but thanks." She stands up, crossing her arms over her chest. My eyes drop to her breasts and then slide back up to her face.

Ivy glances at me, arching an eyebrow. "I didn't appreciate the ash on my bedside table, by the way. Or the soiled sheets."

"I didn't soil them," I grin. "I wouldn't do that without you."

It's too easy to make her blush, and far too much fun for me to stop.

"You're disgusting."

"I think you like it."

"Of course you do." She shakes her head.

"When are you going to make me some more cinnamon buns?"

"When hell freezes over."

I chuckle, standing up in the pool. I suck on my joint and nod to Ivy. "Do they let you wander around the castle grounds on your own? Doesn't seem very secure."

"I'm an employee now," she grins, dangling a lanyard in her hand and lifting a bag. "George offered to train me. Just went to the storeroom to pick up my uniform." She nods her thumb at a building tucked behind some trees.

I quirk an eyebrow. Ivy'll be at the castle?

Looks like I *will* be staying in Farcliff. Definitely.

I wade across the pool toward her, resting my forearms on the edge. She takes a step back, as if she's scared of being too close to me.

"Looks like you and I will be seeing more of each other, then." I arch an eyebrow, offering her the joint.

She shakes her head. "I don't know about that, Your Highness. I'll be in the kitchens most of the time."

"I've got a sweet tooth."

Even in the darkness, I can see Ivy blush again. Her eyes drift over my arms, my shoulders, and then over to the edge of the pool.

"Where's my sister?"

"Who cares?"

"Well, you, for one. Aren't you supposed to be dating her?"

I wave a hand. "There aren't any cameras here."

Ivy's brows draw together, and she sits down in one of the pool chairs. She crosses her ankles, staring at me curiously.

"What?"

Ivy's lips quirk into a smile. She shrugs, tucking a strand

of black hair behind her ear. "I've been around a lot of famous people, and I'm just trying to figure you out."

"What conclusion have you come to, Poison? Psychoanalyze me, please. It turns me on."

"You're angry, and maybe a little lonely. You're smart, which means this life bores you."

"That's like reading a horoscope. It could be true for anyone. Try again."

Ivy's eyes flash. She leans forward. "You think that your problems are special, and that the whole universe revolves around you. You expect me to fall to my knees in front of you, just because you're you."

I grin. "No one said anything about being on your knees in front of me, but if you're offering..."

Instead of answering, Ivy just snorts. She pushes herself off her chair and shakes her head. "If you weren't so revolting, you might actually be kind of interesting. As it stands though..." She grimaces. "No, thank you."

Lifting myself out of the water, I watch Ivy's lips drop open as she looks at my body. My feet leave wet, dripping footsteps as I stalk toward her, stopping just a foot away from her. She hasn't moved.

"Poison," I tsk, reaching over to touch her cheek. "Don't kid yourself. You want me just as much as I want you."

9
IVY

JERKING my face away from the Prince, I stumble backward. I stammer something unintelligible and practically run away from him.

How does he manage to make me feel like a blundering fool every time he's around? Even when *he's* the one falling over and getting injured?

My pulse thunders through my veins. My head feels like it's full of cotton candy, and I can't string a thought together. Gripping my new uniform to my chest, I shuffle to the castle and make my way back to the kitchens. George is waiting with some paperwork.

"Sign here," he says, pushing a pen toward me. "You start tomorrow."

Pushing thoughts of the Prince aside, I sign my name with a trembling hand. George smiles at me, his bushy grey eyebrows relaxing as he extends a hand toward me.

"Welcome to the family."

When I make it back to the limousine to wait for Margot, my pulse is still thumping through my veins. I stare up at the twinkling castle lights and let out a sigh. My heart bounces against my ribcage, and my thoughts drift back to the Prince.

When he pulled himself out of the pool, my panties were just as drenched as he was. Is there anything sexier than a muscular, shredded Adonis of a man, dripping in water, staring at you like he's going to eat you?

Maybe it's just because I've never had a man look at me like that. Maybe he's just toying with me.

Maybe I'll end up getting hurt.

Squeezing my eyes shut, I try to ignore the dread curling around my heart.

This is what Giselle calls self-sabotage of the highest degree. Even the *idea* of being with a man freaks me out. No wonder I'm still a virgin. The Prince barely grazed my cheeks with his fingers, and I literally spun on my heels and ran away from him.

Even if he was interested in me, I've definitely sent a clear message about how I feel.

Scoffing at myself, I shake my head. The Prince isn't interested in me. He's toying with me.

I just need to focus on taking care of my sister, and on working on improving myself. Working for George at the castle could bring me one step closer to opening my own bakery. It could be the training I need to strike out on my own.

When Margot slides into the back seat of the limo, her face is drawn and her movements are jittery. She glances at me and then looks away, raking her fingers through her hair over and over again. Her knee bounces up and down as we set off toward home.

I clear my throat. "How was dinner?"

"Fine." She bites her nail, staring out the window.

"Are you okay, Margot?" I reach over to touch her leg, but

my sister flinches away from me. Her eyes are wide, and her skin looks clammy. I frown.

Margot nods her head half a dozen times. "I'm fine. Dinner was fine. The Prince disappeared. I don't think he's into me."

I worry my bottom lip between my teeth, averting my gaze.

Maybe it isn't a game for the Prince? Maybe he *is* interested in me, and not my sister?

Margot's face crumples, and she sucks in a labored breath. I scoot closer to her, trying to put my arm around my sister, but she shrugs me away.

I need to tell her about my apprenticeship at the castle, but I can tell she's not in the mood to hear anything. Maybe her ego is bruised by the Prince ditching her.

Mine would be, too.

Still, I take a deep breath. "Margie, I don't know if I'll be able to be your assistant for the next couple of weeks."

"Do you have to call me that?" Her head whips toward me. Her eyes are tight, and her mouth twists into a cruel snarl.

I shrink away from her. "Sorry. I meant Margot."

My sister huffs, staring out the window. As soon as we make it to the mansion—*her* mansion, I remind myself— Margot speeds to the front door and disappears up the steps to her bedroom.

I nod to the limo driver and trudge behind her. My shoulders feel tense, and I head to the kitchen. I sink down onto one of the island bar stools, staring at my hands.

Maybe I can do both the apprenticeship and the work for my sister. I think she needs me. She's not stable on her own. I can go to the castle in the mornings, and work on her schedule in the afternoons. She rarely gets out of bed before eleven o'clock, anyway.

I map out my schedule in my head, thinking of a script that I can use to tell my sister about it. A part of me thinks she should be happy for me and let me do this apprenticeship, but a bigger part of me knows that she needs me.

She's always needed me, and I've always been there for her. I can't stop now.

So, when Margot reappears in the kitchen doorway, I know exactly what I'm going to say.

But the Margot that stares back at me is completely different from the one who snapped at me in the car. She's calm, with slower, less jerky movements. She's lost the edge to her voice and she isn't fidgeting as much.

Margot slides into a bar stool next to mine and nudges me with her shoulder.

"What were you telling me before?"

She doesn't apologize for snapping at me, which I've come to accept. When you're famous, people treat you like your farts smell like roses, so it's hard to accept that you might be wrong. She stopped apologizing for her behavior a long, long time ago.

I give her a tight smile. "I was offered an apprenticeship at the castle under the pastry chef there."

Margot's face barely moves. She nods.

I take a deep breath. "But I was thinking about it, and I think I can do it while still being your PA. I'll go to the castle in the mornings and come back here to do the afternoon work. It's only for a month, anyway, so I shouldn't burn myself out."

My sister wraps her arms around me. Her limbs feel heavy. "Thanks, Ivy," she mumbles into my chest. "You know I need you, right? I couldn't do this without you."

My chest squeezes, and I kiss the top of my sister's head. "I know, Margie. Come on, let's get you to bed."

When I help my sister into her bed, her head lolls onto the pillow and her arms flop out to her sides. Margot's already passed out.

When I head over to my own room, I let out a heavy sigh. My sister's mood swings are getting worse. I think it's the stress of this relationship with the Prince, or maybe the pressure of being famous.

She reminds me of Mama.

Our mother had Huntington's disease. She had a gene mutation that affected her brain. It started with tremors and uncontrollable movements, and as it progressed, it started affecting her moods. She was more irritable and became a different person. It was difficult to see her change, to see her be mean where she'd been gentle before.

Really, really difficult.

I shake the thought away. Margot doesn't have Huntington's. We got tested just a couple of months ago. The results were negative. She told me so.

As I slip into my own bed, I vow to stay by my sister's side.

Margot has done everything for me. She worked from the time she was a toddler to make sure that our family had food on the table. She's given me a job, and a place to sleep, and as many bags of flour and mixing bowls as I could ever want.

She tortures herself, starves herself, and puts herself in the public eye so that my father and I can have a good life.

In return, she only asks for my support.

As I snuggle into my pillows, I think of the Prince. A part of me wishes I hadn't washed my sheets after he was in my room. Maybe a faint smell would still cling to the sheets where he lay. Closing my eyes, I imagine the lines of his chest, his abs, his shoulders, everything so defined as water dripped down them tonight.

I think of the bulge I saw between his legs, and excitement teases up my spine.

Letting out a sigh, I know I can never have him.

He's promised to my sister, and the last thing I want to do is betray her.

WHEN I WAKE UP, the sun is streaming through the windows and someone is knocking on the door. Groaning, I drag myself off my pillows. My head is still throbbing where my stitches are, and my body screams with pain.

Just like it does every morning, and every afternoon, and every night unless I dull it with drugs.

Before I answer the door, I open my bedside table and catch the pill bottle that rolls to the front. Swallowing a couple of painkillers, I slip my feet into slippers with the Farcliff crest embroidered on them and drag myself to the door.

Beckett stares back at me, lifting a cup of coffee toward me, and a small silver platter with a cinnamon bun on it.

"These were sitting on this trolley," he explains, nodding to the breakfast trolley by my chamber doors.

I accept them with a grunt.

"You look like hell." He looks me up and down and then steps past me into my room.

"Thanks." I try not to wince as I turn to face him. It'll be a few more minutes before my pain dulls, and every movement is agony. Every step feels like I'm walking on a bed of hot coals. The soles of my feet burn. I lower myself down onto a sofa and take a sip of coffee, grimacing at its bitterness.

"I didn't think you'd sleep here tonight."

I arch an eyebrow. "No?"

"Thought you'd have an after-party at your new girl-friend's house." His eyes flash, and a wicked tingle flashes through my heart. He has a thing for Margot. I can tell.

If I were interested in her, it might be a problem. Since I'm not, though, it's merely entertaining.

"After-parties aren't my thing."

Beckett snorts, and I turn to the cinnamon bun. When I tear it open, I see little pieces of apple in it. My lips curl into a smile as I think of Ivy's special touch.

Seems like hell has frozen over, because she's baking for me already. She must be downstairs, working with the pastry chef.

"Where did you disappear to last night?" Beckett asks, eyeing me from across the room.

"Why? You keeping tabs on me?" I stare at my brother as I chew the sweet dough.

Damn, Ivy's good. This cinnamon bun is unreal.

My brother doesn't answer the question. "So, where were you?" There's an edge to my little brother's voice, and the mean part of me likes the fact that he's jealous.

"Went for a dip in the pool."

"In the middle of a dinner party?" Beckett's brows draw together, and I wonder if there's anything else going on. Is this simple jealousy?

I haven't seen my brother in over two years. None of my family came to visit me while I was getting treatment. They video-called me, and sent me messages and emails, but no one made the trip to come see me. Beckett included.

If I'm completely honest, I might have pushed them away. Maybe I told them one too many times that I didn't want them to see me like I was, broken and immobile, and they finally listened.

Now, there's an undercurrent of animosity between us all, and I don't exactly know why.

Beckett nods to my head, where the stark white bandage leaves a streak against my dark hair. "You never told me what happened to your head."

"I fell over and hit my head in Margot's kitchen."

Beckett arches an eyebrow. "I won't ask what you were doing in the kitchen."

"Eating cinnamon buns, actually," I grin, raising the pastry up. I don't mention Margot's sister—it's too much fun to see Beckett squirm.

My brother glances to the wall behind me, and I can see him gathering the courage to say something. I wait patiently until he starts, munching on my breakfast. It feels like Ivy made it especially for me.

Beckett finally swings his eyes over to me. "Theo wants me to take you and your girlfriend out on Farcliff Lake today. Something about a yacht and a photo opportunity."

"Maybe Theo should worry less about our public image, and more about actually ruling Argyle. Why are we here, anyway? We should be home, taking care of our people."

Beckett shrugs. "We need to improve trade relations with Farcliff. Dante is in Argyle running things while he's here."

Our other brother, Dante, decided not to make the trip to Farcliff. I don't blame him. He's always shied away from the public eye.

"It's a farce," I grunt.

"You should worry less about Argyle's image, and more about your own."

"What's that supposed to mean?"

"Never mind. Be ready in two hours." Beckett opens his mouth as if to say something, then shakes his head and stands up. He throws one more glance my way and leaves without another word.

I finish my breakfast, mulling over the conversation. The way Beckett looks at me feels like he's suspicious of me for some reason.

My family should be doting on me. They should be showering me with love and affection, and congratulating me on my recovery.

Instead, I feel like a stranger.

An intruder.

A reject.

Downing the rest of my coffee, I lick the sticky cinnamon off my fingers and stand up. The burning feeling in my extremities has faded, and the familiar, soothing numbness is starting to take hold. I stretch my neck from side to side, closing my eyes to clear my head.

When I open my eyes back up again, my vision seems sharper. I pull some clothes on, making sure to slip my hard case containing my weed into my back pocket, and a few backup painkillers into my breast pocket. I pat them with my hand, letting out a breath.

Knowing that I have the drugs in my pocket calms me down. It's not that I want to take them right now, it's just that I need to know they're on hand.

When I walk out of my room, my steps feel light. A soft smile drifts over my lips as the drugs take hold of my body. My spine feels good as new. The tingling and burning in my extremities is gone, and the ache in my marrow fades to nothing.

For the next hour or so, I'll be pain free. I'll be normal. Healthy. Whole.

I let my feet take me down a wide staircase and around to a servant's hallway. I already know where I'm going. It's as if an invisible tether is dragging me down to the kitchens, pulling me toward Ivy. My Poison.

Well, one of them, at least.

When I get downstairs, Ivy is pushing the exterior door open, carrying a bag of garbage. Two big, floury handprints mark her ass.

I grin, following her outside.

"How was your first day?"

Ivy flings the trash bag into a dumpster before turning to face me. She has another mark of flour across her forehead. Strands of black hair try their best to escape the bun on top of her head, framing her in a fuzzy black halo.

"George is a slave driver," she huffs.

"Will he notice if you're gone for a few minutes?"

Ivy's eyebrow arches.

I nod down the path. "I need your help with something."

Ivy glances at the closed door leading back to the kitchens. Her eyes flash, and a grin tugs at the corner of her lips.

She shrugs. "Why not? Lead the way, Your Highness."

11

IVY

I WIPE my hands on my apron and glance one last time at the kitchen door. Prince Luca grins at me.

"Scared of big bad George?"

"I'm scared of big bad *you*."

He laughs, extending his hand toward me. I slip my palm against his, and a zing of heat flows up my arm. Tingles fly through my body, making my face flush as he curls his fingers around my hand.

"You shouldn't be scared of me," he says softly, glancing over at me.

My heart jumps.

I'm not scared of the Prince. Not even a little bit. Not even when Hunter told me to stay away from him, or when the newspapers say he's been volatile and angry since he had his spinal injury.

Not even when he's dragging me away from my brand-new job at the castle to take me to Farcliff-knows-where.

The only thing I feel when I'm around Prince Luca is excitement. It's a deep, pulsing excitement that starts in the pit of my stomach. It sends waves through my whole body, until I can't keep the smile off my face.

The Prince squeezes my hand.

"I like you, Poison."

"Thank you."

"That's it? Just 'thanks?'"

I shrug, fighting to keep the grin off my face. "If I told you I liked you now, it would seem false. It's like when you compliment someone and then they respond by saying they like your shoes, or something. It's not usually true."

The Prince chuckles, and the sound sends flutters through my chest.

"Plus," I continue, "the jury's still out on you. I wouldn't want to lie by saying I actually like you."

I love making him laugh. When Prince Luca smiles, he looks like a different person. He loses the harsh lines on his face. His eyes soften. He looks so much more *human*.

Every photo that I've seen of the Prince, he's scowling. Every news story talks about his accident, and his miraculous recovery. None of them talk about his smile, or his laugh, or the magnetic energy that seems to draw me to him.

Not that I've obsessively Googled him for the past two days, or anything.

My heart rattles against my ribs with every step we take. As we wind our way through the Farcliff Castle grounds, the wind rustles through the trees and carries the Prince's scent toward me. I inhale, feeling almost drunk as I walk beside him.

Drunk on him.

On his presence. On his aura. On the irresistible pull that draws me closer to him.

The path veers to the right and starts to climb. The Prince lets out a soft sigh, shaking his head.

"After my accident, they told me I'd never walk again. The thought of spending the rest of my life in a wheelchair nearly killed me. It all comes down to the mind."

The path narrows, and the Prince lets me walk ahead of him. I can feel his body behind mine, sending pulses of heat coursing through my veins.

Gulping, I try to take a full breath. No one has ever had this effect on me before.

"How did you learn to walk again?" I force myself to ask.

"Sheer determination, luck, and lots of physical therapy."

The Prince's hand drifts to my waist, and he nods to a small pathway which intersects the one we're on. My skin tingles where he touches it through my shirt. My breaths are shallow, but not because of the climb. It's because of Prince Luca.

I step onto the small pathway, holding a tree branch out of the way for the Prince to step under. His chest brushes mine as he walks across, his eyes meeting mine. There's a fire burning inside him, and in the silence of the woods, I can hear it crackling.

When his hand reaches up to brush a strand of hair off my cheek, I close my eyes and lean into his touch. Everything he does makes my heart skip a beat. My stomach clenches, and I force myself to glance at the narrow forest pathway.

"Where are we going?"

Prince Luca grins. "Well, ever since I learned to walk again, I've made a point to do it every day. I've been exploring the royal grounds, and I found this spot just last week. Being in nature, on these paths that would have been unavailable to me. Being here makes me feel alive."

He turns down the path, jerking his head for me to follow him. A lump forms in my throat as I stare at the Prince's broad back.

I've judged him harshly. I've thought of him as nothing but a player, a bad boy, a sleaze. But what if there's more to him than meets the eye?

Being told you're paralyzed for life—that must do something to a person.

My eyes drift down to his narrow waist, and over his bum.

"You staring at my ass?" he asks without turning around.

My eyes widen. "No," I lie.

The Prince chuckles, the sound sending more shivers teasing through my core.

"If you were walking in front of me, I'd be staring at your ass," the Prince says, glancing over his shoulder. His lips tug into a grin, and the heat of his gaze makes my cheeks burn.

What am I doing here? I should be in the kitchens with George, learning how to make pastries. Instead, I'm being dragged off into the woods by a Prince.

I shake my head to push the thought away. The woods open up and we arrive at a small clearing overlooking Farcliff Lake. The forest stops on a cliff's edge, and a gentle wind washes over my face. The far shoreline is lined with trees, and the waters of the lake look clear, blue, and cold.

Prince Luca smiles. "It's places like this that make me feel like myself again. Small enclaves where my feet carry me, away from people and their problems. All we did was walk for ten minutes and look where we are."

His eyes move to me, and I see a softness in his eyes I haven't seen before. Then, a flash crosses his face.

"Should we jump?"

"W-What?" I stutter, glancing at the cliff. My stomach surges, and I take a step back. "No."

Isn't that how he injured himself in the first place? He went cliff jumping with his brother, Prince Beckett, and

Queen Cara, and jumped in a spot where the water was too shallow.

Does he have a death wish?

Prince Luca laughs at the expression on my face.

He cups my cheek. "The only thing that makes me feel more alive than walking is an unbelievable surge of adrenaline."

Prince Luca grins at me, drops his hand, then takes off sprinting and launches himself off the cliff.

I scream, the sound echoing across the lake as Prince Luca flies through the air. He flips, landing feet-first in the water with a tiny splash that would make Olympic diving judges proud. I stumble to the edge, gasping.

My heart races and I scream again. "Luca!"

The surface of the lake stays dark and utterly prince-less. The wind rustles through the trees, and a songbird calls out behind me. My breaths are short and quick as I scan the water.

Nothing.

"Shit. Shit. Ahh..." I fist my hand into my hair and then tighten my bun, my eyes scanning around me. I left my phone in my bag at the castle. Going to get help and coming back would take at least twenty minutes. There aren't any boats on the water over here, and not a single soul in sight.

I crawl to the edge, a rock tumbling over the cliff. It lands in the water with a splash, and I feel like I'm going to throw up.

The seconds tick by, one by one.

Thump, thump, thump.

All I can hear is the beating of my own heart as panic starts to lace my blood.

He's dead. Drowned. Broken his back again. He'll bob up to the surface, face down, and I... What will I do?

My mind spirals deeper and deeper into black panic.

Then, with a crash, Prince Luca breaks the surface. He flicks his head back and a shower of droplets dot the water. His smile is blinding as he glances up at me. His arms spread wide, and his laugh echoes up toward me.

"Come on!" he calls out. "It's great in here."

"No fucking way!" I scream.

The Prince laughs, beckoning me with his hand. "Come on, Poison. Live a little!"

Staring down at him, something shifts inside me. Maybe it's his smile, or it's the fact that my whole body feels like it's on fire when he's around.

Maybe it's the fact that he lost his ability to walk after a devastating injury, and I just watched him jump off a cliff without hesitation. He stared in the face of his deepest fears, laughing as he punched through them.

Whatever it is, it compels me to stand up. It almost feels like I'm watching myself from above as I take four steps back from the cliff, sucking in a breath to steel my nerves.

Then, I run toward the edge of the cliff.

For the few, short seconds that I fly through the air, I can't think. My mind is completely clear. It's clear of the jealousy that has plagued me since I was a kid. It's clear of fear, and worry, and resentment. It's clear of desire.

Only when my feet break the surface of the water and the cold shocks my senses, do I yelp. I close my lips at the last moment, sinking into the freezing, inky water of Farcliff Lake.

The cold takes my breath away. I sink down, down, down, opening my eyes underwater to see blackness all around me. With one powerful kick, I propel myself upward. I kick my way to the surface, coming up with a gasp.

Prince Luca is there, and he wraps me in his arms. I lean into his warmth, panting. We swim toward the edge of the water, pulling ourselves up onto a flat rock that's been warmed by the early summer sun.

The Prince peels his shirt off over his head, revealing a chiseled body and bronzed skin. His physiotherapy must have included hours in the gym during his recovery, and a treacherous part of my brain wonders what it would feel like to run my tongue up between his abdominal muscles, licking the water droplets clean off his skin.

I lay beside him, letting out a sigh and shaking my head.

"Did you enjoy that?" He grins.

"I think so."

The Prince props himself up on his elbow, angling his body toward mine. I blame the cold water, because I find myself shifting my body closer to his warmth. His hand drifts up my soaking-wet shirt to my face, sliding across my jaw.

His touch is soft, yet possessive.

My heart goes *boom, boom, boom* against my ribs.

"Thank you for jumping with me," the Prince says, his eyes soft as they drop to my lips.

"I didn't think I would do it."

He grins. His thumb brushes my lower lip, and a delicious shiver tumbles down my spine. It circles in my stomach and teases between my thighs.

I want him. I don't even know what that means, really, except that I know I want the Prince to kiss me and touch me like I belong to him.

A drop of water falls from his hair onto my cheek, and the Prince wipes it off. The touch makes me shiver, and a sigh slips through my lips.

I reach up to hook my hand around the Prince's neck, and without even knowing what I'm doing, I pull him down toward me.

The Prince brushes his lips over mine gently, so gently.

His breath washes over my skin as my nipples pucker under my wet clothing. Pulsing waves of heat course through my body, and I forget that I was cold a few seconds ago.

Angling my lips up toward his, he pulls away and chuckles. His lips trace my jaw, sending waves of fire coursing through me. Finally, the Prince's hand slides back to the nape of my neck, and he stares into my eyes.

"Where did you come from, Poison?"

I can't answer. He's stolen the words right from my mouth. I gulp, and the Prince's eyes flick to my lips. Then, without another word, he finally, *finally* kisses me. The instant his mouth touches mine, liquid heat pours through my veins. I part my lips and accept his kiss, curling my fingers into his wet hair.

A moan slips through my lips and the Prince swallows it down as if it gives him sustenance. He shifts his body over mine, and the weight of him makes my whole body thrum.

Deepening the kiss, the Prince swipes his tongue across my lips and claims them as his own. Fire burns inside me. My cold, wet clothing clings to my body, making me feel like I'm burning even hotter.

The Prince's hand drifts down to my shirt, and he palms my breast. His thumb runs over my pebbled nipple, feeling it through my drenched clothing. I gasp, nipping at his lips as I try to have more of him.

I need more. I need *him*.

My body screams for him—his touch, his kiss, his everything.

I thought I'd been kissed before. I thought that those sloppy, drunken embraces in dingy nightclubs counted as kisses.

I was wrong.

Nothing could have prepared me for the electric heat that

the Prince delivers to me. Every time his finger brush over an exposed sliver of skin, sparks erupt and goosebumps follow. I arch my back, hooking both arms around his neck as he moans into my mouth.

He tastes like honey and danger. Like adrenaline and sweet sin wrapped into one. I rough my hands through his hair, gasping when he drops his head to my breast. Pulling my shirt down, he takes my hardened nipple between his teeth.

The cold air coming off the lake mixes with the Prince's hot breath, and my head spins. Sparks tease my thighs, and my legs part of their own volition.

I've never wanted anything as badly as I want Prince Luca. My hands trace the outline of his muscular shoulders, his wet skin all the way down to his defined waist.

He brushes his hand over my breast again, bringing his lips up to kiss me once more.

"You taste even better than I expected, Poison," the Prince whispers.

I shiver, not knowing how to respond. My head is a mess. All I can think about is the molten lava coursing through my veins, the undeniable heat that's sparking between my thighs, and the deep, pulsing desire that's starting to overwhelm me.

I've never felt like this. I've never been with anyone—let alone someone like Prince Luca.

I've never felt ready to give myself to anyone...

...until now.

12

LUCA

Ivy's skin tastes like magic and cinnamon and sweet, forbidden fruit all swirled into one. I claim her lips again. I can't get enough of them. That lush bottom lip that she's been teasing me with is finally between my own.

My cock is hard as a rock, pressed up against her leg as she grinds her hips toward me.

Then, as soon as it started, it's over.

The sound of someone calling out above us makes Ivy freeze, and she scrambles away from me. She pulls her shirt up over her exposed breast, glancing up to see the source of the voice.

I lay back on the rock, panting. My heart races in my chest, doing its best to break free from its cage. Turning my head to glance at Ivy, I see her smoothing her hands over her head.

"I should get back," she says. Her cheeks flush when she meets my eye, and then she touches her shirt. It's still dripping wet from our dip in Farcliff Lake, her nipples calling out to me through the sopping fabric.

Ivy shakes her head. "How am I going to explain this?"

"You could tell the truth."

She gives me a sideways glance and shakes her head. "I'm sure that would go over well. I already got a stern talking to from my sister's agent about you. I'm not supposed to go anywhere near you."

I arch an eyebrow. "Is that right?" I grin. "Yet, here you are."

Ivy doesn't answer. Instead, she just lets out a dry chuckle and shakes her head. She glances up at the sun, as if she's trying to determine what time it is.

"I probably do have to go, though. I'm supposed to go to some stupid yacht party with my sister, because apparently she's incapable of doing things on her own." Ivy gulps, shaking her head. "That's not what I meant."

"Sounds like it *is* what you meant," I say, standing up with her. "I'm going to that stupid yacht party, too, so at least you have that to look forward to."

Ivy's cheeks burn brighter, and she shakes her head. "I can't. If anyone knew about this"—she moves her finger between her and me—"I'd be dead. I shouldn't have kissed you."

I fight a smile. "No?"

My hand goes to her hip, and I pull Ivy close. She lands against my chest, her hands splaying against my wet shirt. Closing her eyes for a moment, she inhales deeply and shakes her head.

"I shouldn't be here."

"But you are."

I brush my lips against Ivy's, tasting them one last time before we head back. The walk back to the castle is slightly shorter from the bottom of the cliff, and before we clear the trees, I hang back.

"I'll give you a five-minute head start. You know—for your reputation."

Ivy laughs, nodding. "That's very kind of you. It still doesn't explain why I'm soaked."

"Say you tripped and landed in the pool."

"On my way to the dumpsters?"

I shrug. "You got any better ideas?"

Ivy's eyes flash. "We have to pretend this never happened, or else I'll be in big trouble. I mean it, Your Highness."

"I don't think I'd be able to pretend it never happened even if I tried."

Ivy lets out a breath, staring at me for a long moment. She sucks that lip between her teeth and worries at it, and another wave of desire threatens to overwhelm me. Then, she sets off toward the castle. The floury handprints on her ass have been washed off, but it doesn't stop me staring as she walks away.

It's only when I get back to my chambers that I realize that I haven't had to take a painkiller all morning. Even after jumping into the water and crashing into its icy depths at top speed, I haven't needed to dull anything.

I pop a painkiller into my mouth out of habit more than anything, knowing that the reason I haven't needed any was because I was with Ivy.

WHEN BECKETT and I make it to the pier for the yacht party, I can already see some paparazzi sneaking around the marina. I don't know why they bother hiding. It's obvious they were called here on purpose. This is a photo op. It's all arranged.

Our bodyguards whisk Beckett and me toward the massive yacht. When we get near the boat, I hear excited shouts behind me.

A limousine pulls up, and Margot emerges. Her hair is gleaming in the sun, and her thin sundress leaves nothing to the imagination. She's wearing oversized sunglasses, but she still manages to smile and wave at the cameras. I resist the urge to roll my eyes.

Does she actually enjoy this? The cameras, the attention, the lack of privacy?

Beckett lets out a sigh behind me. "Damn..."

I glance at my brother, and he clamps his mouth shut, turning his eyes away from my supposed girlfriend. I look back at her as she struts down the pier.

The way the paparazzi clamor for her makes me want to retch. When I see her wave for the cameras, I understand why Ivy was so hesitant to be seen with me. She knows that anything she does could be blown completely out of proportion.

I know that already. That's the reality I've been living, too. I'm the prodigal son who learned to walk again, returning to spread my message of hope to the masses. I'm the miracle boy, healed from his cliff dive. The man who would never walk again, walking.

If I act like anything less than a hero, I get torn apart by the media.

But I'm used to it. Ivy's not. She still lives her life in the semi-unknown. She's adjacent to fame, but she's doesn't feel the direct heat of the spotlight.

A small part of me wants to respect that. I want to shield Ivy from it all, and let her keep that pure, innocent spirit that she has. Would she have jumped off that cliff if she was worried about cameramen hiding in the bushes?

Maybe not.

Behind Margot, Ivy emerges from the limo. No one snaps a photo of her. No one even seems to notice her.

But I do.

Ripped jeans. White t-shirt. Baseball cap. Sexy, angry scowl. She looks exactly how I feel.

My heart thumps, and all the blood rushes between my legs. The two sisters walk up toward us. Margot hands her purse to her sister before slipping her hand in mine. She reaches her head up to kiss my cheek, and I glance over her shoulder at Ivy.

The dark-haired girl glowers. Her eyes shoot flames at me, and I grin.

Is she jealous that I'm holding Margot's hand, or is she just scared that I'll say something about our kiss?

"You look great," I say to Margot, leading her up the gangway to the yacht's exterior deck. I can hear the paparazzi shuffling behind us, rushing to get into boats that will follow us out onto Farcliff Lake. Beckett hovers, saying an awkward hello to my date.

Ivy follows. I can feel her movements behind me without even having to turn around. There's an invisible connection between us, and it takes all my self-control to play the part of a doting boyfriend for a woman I care nothing about.

A few more celebrities and socialites have been invited, and they're all waiting for us on board. Staff buzz around to everyone, refilling cocktails and passing around appetizers that no one eats.

How my brother Theo thinks this will elevate Argyle's reputation, I have no idea. But it does allow me to spend the afternoon in close proximity to Ivy, so I'm not complaining.

Ivy slinks behind us, forgotten by everyone except me. I can sense her presence everywhere. When I inhale the scent of seaweed and boat fuel, I can just detect the faint notes of cinnamon and sweetness hovering underneath. Glancing over my shoulder, I see her slip inside the interior of the luxury yacht.

Margot drags me to the bow of the boat, where large sunbeds have been set up. Beckett plants himself on one of them, slipping his dark sunglasses over his eyes. He's never too far away from Margot. Margot shimmies out of her sundress, revealing a barely-there black bikini.

Beckett lets out a soft groan.

Margot glances at me, adjusting the tiny bikini over her ample breasts. She smiles coyly, and then lays down on one of the sunbeds. I follow her, taking my shirt off and glancing at the upper decks of the yacht.

It feels almost wrong to be here with Margot. I know I'm supposed to. I'm the broken Prince who's fixed again. I'm Humpty Dumpty, all patched up and better again, and Margot is the belle that's supposed to be by my side.

An itching sensation starts to grow in my body, starting between my shoulder blades and spreading out through my body. I pat my pockets, feeling for the small pill case that I took on board. When I pop a painkiller in my mouth, Margot glances at me. I can't see her eyes through her sunglasses, but something about her look makes me pause.

She gulps, and then turns her head to face forward again.

Resisting the urge to scream, I lean back on the large sunbed beside Margot. I've done everything I was supposed to. I left Argyle to get fixed. I didn't complain when my brother stole the woman I loved. I agreed to come to Farcliff when all I wanted to do was go back to Argyle for the first time in five years.

I agreed to be seen with Margot, for the good of the Kingdom.

But now?

Now, all I want to do is break all the rules. I can almost

feel Ivy's gaze through the tinted windows—or am I imagining it?

Margot moves closer to me on the sunbed. A speedboat passes us, full of photographers. Margot leans into me. She arches her back and puts her hand on my chest, angling her face so that the cameras get a good picture. I'm sure her ass will be on full display.

"You're really playing this up, aren't you? You and me?" I look down at the actress, putting my arm around her.

She shrugs. "Isn't that why we're here?"

I have to hand it to her, the woman is a professional. Margot leans into me as another speedboat passes by. She angles her body just so, and I can already tell the photos will be all over the internet.

She knows what she's doing.

A part of me respects her for it—Margot doesn't want anything from me. She's not asking to be my girlfriend. She knows exactly what to do to get the media excited, and she does it. After the first night, when we kissed and I left her in her room, she hasn't tried to kiss me in private again.

It's a job to her.

Another part of me hates it. Here is this beautiful, presumably smart woman, parading herself in a skimpy bikini for the sake of a few photos.

With a sigh, I shift away from her and stand up. Margot glances up at me, eyebrows arched. She nods to the cameras, as if to ask where the hell I'm going when there's work to do. I don't have the energy to say anything to her.

This whole experience is exhausting. The yacht, the celebrities, the photographers—it's all bullshit. It's all fake. It's some concocted PR publicity stunt with the sole purpose of making my brother, the King, look good to the people of Farcliff.

Never mind the fact that I don't want to be in the public eye. Never mind the fact that I have to spend time with Cara every day, pretending to be polite. Never mind the fact that Margot's preening and posing disgusts me.

I'm craving something real. Something genuine.

Some*one* genuine.

So, I let my feet take me to the yacht's inner decks.

The yacht's main salon has a bar on the bow side, with rich teak wood polished to perfection. Uniformed bartenders wait behind the bar, their bowties straight and smiles painted on. I glance over to the long couches and tables, but I don't find what I'm looking for.

Poison.

It's an apt nickname. It feels like she's injected something into my veins. It makes me feel numb and alive, and it makes me want more, more, more. Her scent swirls around me all the time, and when I close my eyes, I imagine what it would be like to taste her.

Really taste her.

If she's poison, then I'm a willing victim.

13

MARGOT

I TRY NOT to let the disappointment sink in too deep when Prince Luca gets up to leave. He doesn't say a word to me as he walks away, and sourness coats the back of my throat.

Is my ego so bloated that I can't handle a single guy who isn't interested in me?

Shaking my head, I let out a sigh. Our relationship isn't even real. It's as fake as my nails, and the only reason I'm playing along is because it's my job, and I'm a professional. With the exposure that my relationship with the Prince will bring, I know the phone calls will start rolling in for the next big role of my career. I'll be turning thirty in less than a year, and for a man, it might not matter. For a woman in the spotlight?

My crow's feet are the subject of much discussion.

Anxious thoughts needle at me, and I do my best to blink them away. I think of the white, sealed envelope that I've hidden at the back of my closet.

I told Ivy that the results were negative, but the truth is that I'm too chicken to open it up.

Sighing, I lean back in the sun bed as the itching starts at the base of my spine. I know this feeling. Swirling thoughts. Tingling sensation. Churning stomach.

The first panic attack I ever had was three years ago, when I was twenty-seven years old. I was in Hollywood, starting the first day on set for the biggest role of my career. Right before I stepped in front of the cameras, I forgot all my lines from one second to the next. My vision started to tunnel. I couldn't breathe, and my chest ached like I've never experienced before.

Have you ever heard of a film and TV actress who was scared of being filmed?

Yeah, me neither.

Now, I go to therapy every week and I take a cocktail of anti-anxiety medication. It helps, mostly.

But ever since that white envelope arrived in the mail, things have gone downhill. My medication isn't as effective. My therapist knows I'm holding back.

Every time I knock something over, or fall, or feel my hand trembling, I take it as a sign.

I have what Mama had.

You might think it's just the anxiety talking. Of course, if you have an anxiety disorder, having a fifty percent chance of developing a degenerative brain disease does nothing to help. But what if I told you that mood changes and things like anxiety and depression are a *symptom* of Huntington's, too? It's a feedback loop that just gets louder, and louder, and louder.

So loud, in fact, that I can't enjoy the first rays of sunshine of the year, or the fact that I'm on a luxury yacht with literal royalty.

I haven't even told Ivy about the anxiety, or the sealed white envelope—why would I? She's always been the good one. The healthy one. The perfect one. She wouldn't understand what it's like to be under the kind of pressure I'm under.

Plus, whenever she's disappointed with me, the way her eyes pierce through me is worse than any panic attack I've ever had.

Being famous feels like being locked in a tower, staring at the world below me. It's luxurious, and well-stocked, and I can have anything I need, but I can never go down to the ground. I can't walk among the people of Farcliff without being mobbed, I can't go to the grocery store or go for a haircut without pictures of it ending up online.

I know, I know. I sound like an entitled, ungrateful brat. I'm thankful for everything that I have, and I'm happy that I can provide for Ivy and my father. It's just sometimes, I wish I was a normal person with a normal life.

I wish I didn't have to take medication to feel normal. I wish I didn't have to refuse Ivy every time she offered me a treat she baked for me, just for the sake of staying skinny.

Instead, I'm locked up in a high tower, torturing myself.

"Deep in thought?" Prince Beckett asks from the sun lounger next to mine.

I force a smile. "Something like that."

The itching at the base of my spine gets stronger, and my fingers start to fidget. I adjust and re-adjust my bikini, trying to ignore the thoughts that are starting to circle in my mind.

"Thanks for those antihistamines," the young Prince says with a shy smile.

I frown, and then remember. "Oh, at the welcome dinner! Of course." I nod. "My allergies are bad year-round. I know how painful it can be when you can't stop sneezing."

The Prince sits up and moves to the chair next to mine. He waves his hand toward a waiter, who brings over a couple of drinks. I accept one with a smile. Alcohol isn't my favorite substance, but it'll do for now.

The drink sloshes as my hand trembles, and I bite down on my bottom lip to stop my mind from spiraling out of control.

"So, what's causing you so much grief?" he asks, taking the tiny umbrella out of his drink and sliding it behind his ear.

I smile, surprised that a Prince would do something so...*normal*.

Shrugging, I take a sip of the cocktail. "Just work stuff."

And the fact that my life is slowly spiraling out of control, and all I can do is watch.

"Is it about my brother not giving you the time of day?"

I glance at Prince Beckett's face, trying to see any sign of mockery. Was it that obvious that I was offended? Am I that pathetic?

He looks earnest, though, so I smile. "He's not my type anyway."

Prince Beckett's eyebrows jump up. "No?"

I shake my head.

"So, what *is* your type?" The Prince pushes his sunglasses up onto his head, and I can see a sparkle in his dark eyes. His eyebrow arches. "Perhaps a guy who's six foot four with abs of steel, a roguish smile, and chocolate-brown eyes?"

He gestures to his body, and I laugh.

"I like ones who wear drink umbrellas in their hair."

"That's oddly specific." He grins, taking a sip of his drink. "Do you always tell people exactly what they want to hear?"

"Part of the job." I wink.

"Isn't your job to be yourself? As far as I can tell, everyone loves you."

I let out a sigh. "My job is to give the public a part of me, every single day."

"Sounds like my job, too."

I smile at the Prince, and a quiver passes through my chest. Clearing my throat, I turn away from him. I take a sip of my drink, wishing it were stronger. When I put it down on the small side table beside my lounge chair, tension eases between my eyes. Now, I don't have to worry about trembling and spilling it.

I'm a mess. I don't deserve Prince Luca's attention—or Prince Beckett's, for that matter.

So, when the Prince turns to me and smiles, I keep my head facing forward. I close my eyes and lay back on the lounge chair, pretending to enjoy the rays of sunshine that warm my skin. I pretend that I can't sense his movements, and I can't smell the faint scent of his cologne.

I close myself off from him, just as I've closed myself off from every man who ever made advances at me.

It's the reason that I agree to enter into these ridiculous publicity stunts like dating Prince Luca. It's the reason I don't mind being dragged through the tabloids every time I breathe.

If they knew the truth about me, it would be much, much worse.

14

LUCA

WALKING up the steps to the second floor of the yacht, I do a lap of the luxurious cabins and living rooms, but I still can't find Ivy. This floor has a dining room at the front end of the boat, complete with another bar, and then a hallway leading back to the bedroom cabins.

The yacht is huge, and well-equipped, and frustratingly easy to hide in.

It's not until I get to the top deck that I see Ivy, tucked under a small awning. She's crouched down with her nose tucked into a book, her hat and sunglasses covering most of her face. Unlike her sister, she hasn't stripped down. The small parts of her skin that are exposed are already starting to turn pink in the sun.

How this girl and the bronzed, blonde model below could be related, I have no idea.

"Hiding from me, are you?" I sink down onto the floor beside her, stretching my legs out.

"Isn't that exactly what I told you I'd do?" Ivy swings her eyes over to me. "Tell me something, Your Highness—are you allergic to shirts?" Her eyes sweep down my body, her cheeks turning pink before she turns back to her book.

I grin. "You didn't seem to mind before."

"I was focused on trying to stop the blood gushing out of your head."

"That explains the kitchen," I grin. "What about the other times?"

Ivy's lips twitch. "The other times, I was wondering what it would be like to lick melted chocolate off your abs." She turns her head to look at me. "Is that what you want to hear?"

"That can be arranged. Do you prefer milk or dark?"

Ivy's cheeks turn red, and she shakes her head. "You're not supposed to be talking to me."

"Says who?"

"Says me—and my sister, and my sister's entourage."

"Well, the only person I care about out of that lineup is you, and I don't believe that you don't want to talk to me."

I lean my back against the railing behind us, glancing up at the blue sky. Ivy sucks her lower lip between her teeth, and I grin. I've only known her a day, and I already know that that small movement is a sign that she's off-balance.

"What are you reading?"

She closes the book, and I catch a glimpse of the title— something about baking. Maybe some homework the royal pastry chef gave her.

"Is there a reason you're here?" Ivy demands. "Shouldn't you be making out with my sister right about now?" She angles her body away from me, staring out at the lake. The tree-lined shore shrinks away from us, and the only sound is the wind whipping around us, the cry of a few seagulls, and the yacht's motor. Faint music trickles up toward us from the decks below.

"Maybe I should, but I don't want to," I answer.

Ivy gulps, and I watch the movement of her throat. Her lips drop open, and all I want to do is taste them again.

"I wanted to see you," I say.

Ivy scoffs. "Right."

"Is that so hard to believe?"

"What's your angle, here? One sister isn't enough, so you want to make headlines by bagging two of them? Newsflash: the media doesn't care about me, so you're not going to gain anything by trying to get with me."

"Are you saying I'm going to bag you?"

"Please. I'm saying that whatever your motivations are, they're pointless. I'm not a prize to be won, so you can fuck off."

"That's quite the one-eighty from this morning," I grin. I know she's mad, but a part of me loves hearing foul words coming out of her pretty mouth.

"I saw the way you were looking at my sister. I know I'll always be second-best."

I let out a frustrated sigh. "Your sister is a *job*, Ivy."

She just sighs, shaking her head. "I knew it was a bad idea to follow you through the forest today. I don't..." Ivy releases a breath. "I'm not cut out for this type of romance, or affair, or whatever you want to call it. You shouldn't be here."

"Look me in the eye and say it like you mean it."

Her hands grip her book, and she turns to face me. She bites down on her lower lip, raising her eyes to mine. I can see the pulse in her neck thumping, and I long to run my tongue all the way up her delicate neck.

"Why are you here?" she whispers.

I lean into her, dropping my lips close to her ear. "Because I want to be."

A faint shiver passes through Ivy's body. I keep my head close to hers, closing my eyes for just a second. What is it about this girl that drives me wild?

Ivy snaps her head away from mine and clears her throat. "Shouldn't you be canoodling with my sister, or something? I saw a couple boats full of photographers salivating at the thought of seeing the two of you together."

I arch an eyebrow. "Are you jealous, Poison?"

"Stop calling me that."

"You didn't answer the question."

Ivy's eyes flash. "Am I jealous of my supermodel-turned-actress sister, around whom the entire universe orbits? Hmm, let me think about that for a second." She shakes her head and drops her voice. "I wish I could say no, but that would be a lie. I've been jealous of her since before I learned the meaning of the word."

In that simple sentence, that single moment of vulnerability, I feel closer to Ivy than I've felt to most other people. I, too, know what it's like to feel crushing jealousy for a sibling. Wasn't I the one who stewed in a vat of green envy when I heard that Theo was marrying Cara? Aren't I the one who crawled back to my family, feeling alienated and oddly ashamed, and jealous of their healthy, able bodies?

The hurt in her face makes my chest sting, because I understand it. To her core, I know how Ivy feels right now. Envy is a dirty, insidious poison that seeps into your veins and eats you from the inside out. It makes you question everything and everyone, and leaves you a husk of the person you once were.

I put my hand on her thigh. "You shouldn't be jealous, Ivy."

Ivy glances at me. I watch her swallow, my eyes following

every movement she makes. Her lips part, and her tongue slides out to swipe across it. A shiver passes through me.

"Do you enjoy toying with me? Making me feel bad?"

"I enjoy toying with you, but not to make you feel bad. Quite the opposite, actually." My hand slides up her thigh a fraction of an inch. Ivy's throat bobs as she swallows.

I'm staring at her lips again. I can't stop myself. They're so red, they look stained, as if she's been sucking on a strawberry lollipop. Against her alabaster skin and her dark hair, it makes them almost too irresistible to kiss.

I've had a thousand women like her sister. Gorgeous, tall, thin, blonde, and boring.

But I've never had a woman like Ivy. My eyes drop down to her chest, and I wish my face was buried between her tits again. Sweeping my gaze back up to her face, my heart starts to hammer.

I need to kiss her again. I need to taste those lips. I need to feel her body melt into mine, and feel those delicate fingers clawing at my scalp. This morning, she woke something up inside me that won't go away until I have her.

"How's your head?" Ivy asks, jarring me away from my thoughts. She points to my bandage.

I shrug. "It's fine. I'm tough."

Ivy laughs, and I grin. Her dimples make me want to cup her cheeks in my hands and make her laugh some more. But Ivy's laughter fades quickly, and she stares out at the lake again.

"What's Argyle like?"

"Have you ever been to the Bahamas?"

She shakes her head. "I've never left Farcliff."

"Even with your sister being so famous?"

Ivy smiles sadly. "When Mama got sick, I had to stay back

to take care of her. Dad was the one who went with her. Even now, as my sister's personal assistant, I don't travel. I guess I just got used to staying back. I'm a homebody."

"Hence the baking."

"Muffins make better friends than people, anyway." She giggles again, shaking her head. "But maybe that's why my body isn't as perfect at Margot's."

"Your body is perfect."

Ivy's eyes swing over to mine, and those irresistible lips call out to me again. I want to feel her body arch against mine again, and kiss every inch of her snow-white skin. Even if there are cameras around, and even if the boat is packed with people who might catch us.

Right now, I don't care.

I just want her.

Need her.

Lust leaves a sweet taste on my tongue as desire starts to pulse through my body. Ivy's eyelashes flutter as she blinks up at me.

I reach up to tuck a strand of black hair behind Ivy's ear and angle my head toward hers. Ivy's breath catches, and her tongue slides out to lick her lips. The air between us tenses.

The waves lap against the boat, and its gentle rocking seems to slow. Ivy's eyes widen, and her gaze drops to my mouth.

The addiction swirling in my veins screams for her. She's my poison and my antidote. She's everything I need, and I already know she'll have the power to tear me apart.

But before I can kiss her, the yacht lurches as the engines splutter. A loud scream sounds out from below, followed by a splash, and Ivy's head snaps toward the front of the ship.

"Margie!" she whispers. Her whole body tenses.

Panicked shouts come from down below, and the yacht lurches again. An airhorn sounds.

Ivy pushes my hand away and scrambles to her feet. Before I can blink, she's taking off down the stairs toward the bow of the boat.

15

IVY

I TAKE the steps two at a time on my way down to the main deck. I fly around the corner, almost tripping over a step on my way to the sun tanning area. The boat lurches, and I catch myself on the railing. A messy lump is stuck at the base of my throat. I try to swallow, but it makes me want to throw up.

The captain cuts the yacht's motors, and then starts them again as the ship starts to move back. Screams are coming from the front of the yacht.

I know Margot has fallen into Farcliff Lake. I could hear it in the scream from the upper deck, and I can sense it in my bones.

That would be fine—I took a dip in Farcliff Lake just this morning—except for the fact that Margot can't swim. She's always been terrified of water, and no matter how much Mama urged her to learn, she always refused.

And because Margot is Margot, my parents complied.

Prince Beckett is standing at the bow, stripping his shirt off. What is it about these Argyle men and their perfect bodies? Both Princes look like they've been carved from marble. Beckett's eyes are wide as he stares out into the cold, dark water.

I know exactly how cold it is. I was in it this morning.

I rush to the railing. Prince Beckett hesitates as he looks down at the dark water. Even in summer, the water in Farcliff Lake is freezing.

My sister is thrashing. She's farther away from the yacht than I'd have expected. We must have drifted away from her. As I watch her for a second, I realize that even with the engine idling, we're slowly moving farther apart.

Scanning the deck, I spot a ring buoy hanging on the railing. It only takes me a second to grab it and fling it over the side of the boat.

It lands thirty feet away from my sister.

"Swim to the buoy!" I scream.

My sister lets out a gargled scream. Her arms flail, splashing into the water as her head dips under. The panic in her face makes my stomach clench. Beckett is still frozen near the railing, yelling at her to swim to the life buoy. Everyone is crowding around, but no one is doing anything.

Beckett grabs onto the railing, and I can see him willing himself to jump in.

But he doesn't.

Why isn't anyone *doing* anything?

It's hard to take a full breath. My muscles are spasming, and every second that ticks by makes the panic ratchet higher. Guests are screaming. Staff is scrambling to drag the life buoy back to throw it closer to her.

Everything is taking far, far too long. Margot's head dips under water, and I feel like I'm going to puke.

I can't wait any more.

Fully clothed, with my phone, wallet, and keys still in my back pocket, I swing one leg over the railing.

"Ivy, no!" I hear Prince Luca's voice behind me, but I ignore it.

Unlike my sister, I know how to swim.

I swing my other leg over the railing and grip it so hard the tips of my fingers go numb. With a deep breath, I leap off the side of the boat. My arms windmill, my legs kick the air, and I go flying into the ice-cold water of Farcliff Lake.

Again.

And again, I'm not ready for the cold that shocks my body. As soon as I hit the water, my arms and legs feel like they're made of lead. Everything is heavy, slow, and difficult.

As soon as I'm in, I kick as hard as I can to break the surface again. With a gasp, I gulp down a breath of air and try to ignore the thickening of my blood in my veins.

The screams of the people on deck sound faint to my ears, and I scan the surface for my sister. Her thrashing is weaker. She looks at me, and I can see the whites of her eyes.

The terror in her face is palpable. It skims on the surface of the water and slams into me like a tidal wave, leaving an acrid, sharp taste on my tongue.

"Hang on!" I yell, kicking my legs and swimming freestyle toward her. It doesn't take long. Within a few strokes, I'm beside her.

"Ivy," she pants, before letting out a scream. Her arms wrap around my neck and she pushes me under in her panic, kicking me in the gut.

I swallow a mouthful of lake water, thrashing away from her and breaking the surface again.

"Calm down," I scream, trying to dodge the arms that claw at me. Her nails leave sharp, red marks on my arms as she reaches for me again. Another scream escapes her lips.

She's panicking. I can't reason with her, and if I let her get close to me when she's like this, she'll drown me.

Time for some tough love.

I'm able to tread water as I grab her wrists, but the panic is making her too strong. She thrashes against me again, pulling me under. This time, I close my mouth and avoid tasting Farcliff Lake again. With a powerful kick, I break the surface again and clamp my arms around my sister's torso.

She yelps, fighting against me as I try to save her life.

Finally, I'm able to spin her around and wrap my arm around her chest.

"Will you stop moving?" I yell, louder than I intended.

Margot's breath is ragged. Her nails dig into my arm as I start kicking my legs to get us closer to the boat. With a loud smack, a ring buoy lands two feet away from me. Turns out the crew are better at throwing these things than I am.

With one more kick, I reach the buoy and hook my arm into it. Margot tries to move.

"Don't you dare," I hiss. "Stay limp."

She whimpers, leaning into me. I tighten my arm around her chest and hold her close as the crew starts pulling us back toward the yacht. I let them drag us, holding onto my sister as hard as I can.

My heart is racing. I close my eyes for a moment, opening them to look up at the clear blue sky. A few wispy white clouds float across my field of vision, oblivious to the trauma that my sister just put me through.

I could have lost her.

I should never have been upstairs with Prince Luca. Margot needs me. I should have been close.

Letting out a breath, I hold my sister to my chest. Her heart hammers against my arm as I hold her, and I sense her pulse slow down a tiny bit as we get closer to the boat.

The yacht's crew drop a Jacob's ladder over the side of the vessel. It lands with a slap beside us, and I look at my sister.

"You think you can climb that?"

Her face pinches and her hands tremble as she reaches for the first rung.

"Just hang on, we'll pull you up!" someone calls out from above.

I lean on the ring buoy and nod to my sister. "Hold on tight."

"I'm too weak."

"You can do it, Margot," I say, helping her grab onto the ladder. Her legs kick out behind her and I get another heel to the gut, grunting in pain.

But my sister succeeds in clinging onto the ladder, and I let out a sigh of relief.

The crew start to heave her up. She's trembling, closing her eyes as they lift her up to the deck. As she gets to the top, half a dozen arms reach out to grab her and pull her to safety. Blowing the air out of my lungs, I shake my head.

She's okay.

The ladder comes back down with another smack, and I glance up. Not one head pokes over the railing, and I can hear voices grow more distant as they bring Margot inside. I sigh, gripping the ladder as tightly as I can. I start a slow ascent, trembling as the adrenaline in my body begins to fade. I stumble on a rung about halfway up, and then take a deep breath to steady myself.

Glancing back up, my chest stings. Not a single person stayed back to help me. Everyone was so preoccupied with Margot that they left me here to struggle on my own. I blink back tears, mad at myself for caring.

Of course no one stayed. Why would anyone stay for me? Why would anyone care about Margot's strange little sister? Why would anyone care that I just jumped in to save my sister's life?

Pausing on the ladder again, I take a deep breath to steady myself. The muscles in my arms and legs are screaming, small spasms making it hard to climb up. I bite down on my bottom lip until I taste the coppery tang of blood, and then continue my ascent.

I climb up a bit farther, fueled by my anger. Tears blur my eyes and I take a deep breath before I reach the top, knowing that climbing over the railing when I'm wet, slippery, and emotional will be a difficult undertaking.

I don't have time to compose myself, though, because two thick, strong arms reach down and pull me up the rest of the way.

Prince Luca's warm, broad chest greets me next, and he carries me over the railing to the safety of the yacht. He wraps a towel around me, holding me close as he strokes my head.

"You okay?" His voice is soft. It doesn't have the mocking edge that I've gotten used to.

I nod into his chest, trying to hide my sniffles. "I'm fine. Thank you for helping me on board."

Instead of moving away, the Prince just stands there and holds me. His body is so warm. So safe. I close my eyes, leaning into his chest and inhaling the scent of his skin. I'm trembling now, cold from the water and the shock. Wiping my teary eyes, I pull away and glance toward the cabins.

"Where's Margot?"

"She's fine. She's being taken care of." The Prince hasn't let go of me. His hands are on my shoulders, grabbing the towel that he wrapped around me earlier. His brows are drawn together, and he stares into my eyes, shaking his head. "You scared me."

I'm not quite sure how to respond, so I don't say anything. I stare at his lips, so full and kissable that it should be illegal.

The Prince's hand drifts to my cheek. He tucks a strand of hair behind my ear.

His face angles down against mine, and those stupidly kissable lips brush against my mouth. In an instant, I forget about the cold water in the lake. Heat ignites in my veins, and I tremble against the Prince's strong arms. I tilt my head up, deepening our kiss as my hands wrap around his waist.

Neither of us notice the speedboat that pulls up beside our yacht. We don't see the half-dozen photographers snapping photos of us until one of the crew members shouts at them to leave. Only then do I pull away from the Prince, my cheeks burning.

I glance over my shoulder at the retreating speedboat, and my stomach drops. They definitely saw that kiss—but the only question is whether or not they know who I am.

I gulp. "I should go find my sister."

Prince Luca's eyes linger on me, and I wrap the towel around me more tightly. He motions to the interior deck, and we walk over together in silence. Every single guest is inside, most of them lounging on the sofas and at the bar. There's commotion down the hallway towards the bedroom cabins, and I know that's where Margot was brought.

My heart is in my throat. I can feel the Prince beside me, every heartbeat sending a pulsing desire through me.

It's wrong, wrong, wrong.

He's promised to my sister. *She's* the beautiful one. *She's* the model, the actress, the socialite. *She's* the one that the paparazzi want to see him with.

Not me.

But the Prince's hand drifts to the small of my back as we enter the main salon, and a shiver of heat curls in my stomach. I shouldn't want him this much.

He shouldn't want *me* at all.

Margot's fall in the lake should be a sign for me. It's the universe telling me that I need to stay away from Prince Luca. That he belongs to her. That I don't deserve someone like him.

That I need to be by her side.

The Prince walks down to the cabins at the back of the boat with me, where there's still commotion and people milling around.

When we get to the main cabin, Prince Beckett is pacing back and forth. He sees me, and immediately throws his arms around me.

"You saved her." His voice is muffled into the towel around my shoulders.

I stiffen, not quite sure what to do. That's two members of the royal family that have had their arms around me today.

When he pulls away, I notice Prince Luca's eyes blazing at his brother. I clear my throat, and then duck into the cabin. Margot emerges from the shower with steam billowing around her. Her face is lined with worry, and she drags her feet with exhaustion.

When my sister sees me, her lower lip trembles. She sighs, shaking her head. "I'm sorry, Ivy."

"Don't be."

"I shouldn't have done that. I was trying to get a photo, and then the boat lurched..." She cringes, shaking her head.

Margot walks up to me and wraps her long, graceful arms around me. I lean against her, sighing.

For a second, it feels like the old Margot. Before the crazy fame, before this PR relationship with Prince Luca, before Mama died. The haze in her eyes is gone, and she smells like she used to when we were kids.

"I was so stupid," my sister says, sniffling. "I don't know what I would have done without you."

"Someone else would have jumped in." My voice is flat and emotionless. I feel drained.

She shakes her head. "They didn't. This is why I need you around, Ivy. You're the only person I can trust."

I swallow back the bile that rises up in my throat. Trust? She can't trust me. I've betrayed her in the worst possible way. I've kissed the man she's supposed to be dating—twice.

Margot nods to the bathroom. "You should take a hot shower to warm up."

I blink back tears and nod to her, slumping my shoulders and heading for the bathroom.

16

LUCA

WHEN MARGOT WALKS out of the cabin wearing fresh makeup and a dazzling smile, everyone on the yacht swarms around her. They coo as she smiles bashfully, hugging her white bathrobe to her chest and shaking her head in mock embarrassment. The actress somehow manages to make a terrycloth bathrobe look expensive and stylish.

Everybody in the room laps it up, eyes drawn to her like moths to a flame.

Everybody—except me.

I hang back, glancing over her shoulder to see if I can spot her sister. The cabin door behind her closes, and Margot walks out to the main salon area. A waitress hands her some water and a snack, which she accepts with a smile.

She drinks a sip of water, but she puts the cheese and crackers down on a table without touching them. Her face looks relaxed, almost slack, and her eyes are hooded.

An itching sensation crawls up my spine. I know that look on her face, and it makes me want to reach into my pocket, take a painkiller, and join her in numb bliss.

I pat my breast pocket, but before I slip out my pill bottle and swallow one down, I think of Ivy. I think of her smell, and her touch, and the way her lips feel when they're pressed against mine.

I don't want to numb that. I want to feel that fully and completely, with my mind clear and my body awake.

My eyes drift back to the cabin door, which remains closed. My chest tightens. It's Ivy they should be swarming around, not her sister.

Ivy was the brave one. All Margot did was fall in.

Another actress sits beside Margot, pulling a phone out and angling it toward the both of them for a selfie. Margot poses and then laughs, lapping up the attention. Beckett sits near her, his eyes glued on her pretty, blonde head.

It disgusts me.

Where's Ivy? We should be celebrating the woman who jumped in to save her sister, not the one who fell overboard for a few likes on social media. I stare at the closed door again, but Ivy stays behind it. I gulp as worry knots my stomach.

Grabbing a bottle of water and a sandwich, I start stalking back toward the room. I glance once more at the group as a strong, bitter taste coats my mouth.

This is the woman that I'm supposed to pretend to like? One that leaves Ivy behind right after she saved Margot's life? One that takes a selfie and laughs with her friends while her sister suffers?

It's repulsive.

I'm not perfect—I have my own issues with my family, especially Theo and Cara—but family always comes first. *Always.* I wouldn't have come to Farcliff for this stupid trip if I didn't care about my family. I wouldn't have agreed to this publicity stunt. I wouldn't tolerate Beckett's insufferable moods around Margot if I didn't care for my family.

I did it because Theo asked me to, and because it was good for the family.

I throw Margot one more hate-filled glance, only to see her staring back at me. She inclines her head ever so slightly. Her eyes soften, and a flash of pain passes across her face. She blinks as if to say, *thank you.*

Thank you for checking on Ivy, when I need to be out here to keep up appearances.

At least, that's what I think her look says. It's gone as quickly as it appears. Her face snaps back to normal, and she laughs at something my brother says. She titters as another man compliments her, batting her eyelashes and probably making his cock hard as rock. I frown as I walk back to the yacht's main cabin. Maybe there's more to Margot than I assumed. Maybe she *does* care about her sister, but she knows that she needs to be out here.

It's her job.

Still, it makes my stomach churn. I'm glad no one follows me down the hallway. Knocking softly on the door, I lean my head against the frame.

"Poison?"

Pausing, I hear nothing.

I knock again.

Still no response.

"Ivy?"

A tiny, faint sniffle sounds through the thin wooden door, and I take that as my cue to enter. Ivy is crumpled on the bed, curled up in a tight ball as she cries into the pillow. Kicking the door closed, I drop the sandwich and water on the bedside table and scoop her into my arms.

Leaning back on the headboard, I cradle Ivy close to my chest. I rock her back and forth, stroking her hair. She stiffens momentarily. I lay a soft kiss into her black hair, and she sobs into my arms. Ivy melts into me, every part of her trembling.

My heart squeezes, and I wish I could take her pain away. Seeing her hurt makes my blood run hotter. It makes me itch, makes my body burn up—and not in a way that a pill can take away. I tighten my hold on her, caressing her cheek with my hand.

Sniffling, Ivy wipes her nose on her terrycloth bathrobe and pulls away. "I'm sorry, Your Highness. This is embarrassing. What are you doing here?"

"I was worried."

"About what?"

"About *you*." Stroking her cheek, I force her to look at me. Two different-colored eyes stare back at me, and the air is sucked out of my lungs. A tear streaks down her cheek. I wipe it away with my thumb.

I want to give her the world.

Ivy shakes her head and wipes her eyes again. "I don't even know why I'm crying. It's just scary, you know? I could have lost her."

Ivy leans against my chest, and I hold her close. It feels good to have her in my arms. It feels right. I don't remember the last time I held a woman like this—or the last time I wasn't itching to reach into my pocket for a joint, or a pill, or something to numb the pain.

Ivy's fingers curl into my shirt and she lifts her head again.

"You're wearing a shirt."

"I can take it off, if you prefer."

She laughs, showing off dimples on her perfect, soft cheeks. Shaking her head, she sighs. "You're such a dog." Her eyes lift back up to mine. "Shouldn't you be out there with my sister?"

"She's got plenty of people taking care of her."

"But you're supposed to be...you know..."

"What?"

"You're supposed to be together."

"Are we?"

"Isn't that what your people and her people have been planning since the beginning of time?"

"My people don't control me," I answer. I stroke Ivy's cheek, and the feeling of her skin against my hand makes my heart thump.

Ever since the second she yelled at me for eating her cinnamon buns, I've wanted to ravage her. I've wanted to taste her lips, her skin, her honey. More than just that—I've wanted to feel her body grinding against mine and plunge myself deep inside her.

I can't wait any longer. I need her like I need air.

Cupping Ivy's cheek, I watch as her breath hitches. Her eyes drop to my lips, and her fingers sink into my chest. My heart thunders, sending pulsing heat to every extremity. With her across my lap in nothing but a bathrobe, it's becoming hard to contain myself.

"Poison," I say softly, stroking her lip with my thumb.

She closes her eyes. "Yeah?"

I drag my thumb across her lips, and they part ever so slightly. Caressing her full, red pout with my finger, I watch as her tongue slides out. It swirls around the tip of my thumb and I release a breath.

"You're driving me crazy," I growl.

Her eyes open again, and another jolt of electricity courses through me. She wraps her lips around my thumb and kisses it gently. The pulse in her neck goes *thump, thump, thump.*

When she pulls her lips away from my thumb, I miss

them. Her eyebrows twitch together, and she tilts her head, studying me.

"Why are you here?" she asks again.

Instead of answering, I put my free hand on her knee. Her soft, silky skin feels incredible. I inch my fingers up under her bathrobe and watch as Ivy's eyes widen. Her breath is shallow as she leans into me, curling her fingers into my shirt.

When I touch my lips to Ivy's, she lets out the softest, sexiest moan I've ever heard. Her kiss is hesitant, uncertain— and nothing at all like she usually is. I swipe my tongue across her lower lip, groaning as I taste her once again. I kiss her slowly, meticulously, not wanting to miss a single detail of her perfect mouth. I want to sear her taste into my memory and imprint myself upon hers.

Ivy trembles, parting those soft, red lips for me so I can deepen our kiss. I slide my hand up her thigh as my heart races in my chest. She whimpers, leaning into me as my other hand tangles into her black locks. Pulling her closer, I groan as she finally starts to kiss me back with the intensity that I want.

The intensity that I *need.*

My fingers sink into her thigh as my cock hardens in my pants. She shifts her weight, grinding against it ever so slightly as she scrapes her teeth across my lower lip. I growl. Her tongue swipes over mine, and my cock throbs against her. Another soft moan slips through her lips, and I swallow it whole.

Nipping at her bottom lip, I kiss her harder. I want more. I want it all. My hand slides farther up her thigh as she hooks her arm around my neck. Her moans are driving me wild. Sitting across me sideways, she grinds her hips against my hardened cock and the movement is almost too much to bear.

But when I slide my hand higher—high enough to know

that she's not wearing panties—Ivy pulls back. Her chest heaves as she wipes her mouth on the back of her hand.

She sucks in a trembling breath and shakes her head. "We should stop."

"Why?"

Frowning, she turns her head to look at me. "Well, for one, you're promised to my sister."

"I'm not promised to anyone." I catch her hand in mine, laying a soft kiss on the sensitive skin on the underside of her wrist. Ivy closes her eyes for a moment as a trembling breath slips through her lips. Her ass grinds against me, and I throb.

"Please, Your Highness..."

"Luca."

Ivy's eyes open, both colors shining bright as she stares at me.

I nod. "I want you to call me Luca."

"Luca," she whispers.

Ivy sucks her lush bottom lip between her teeth, and my cock strains against my pants. Does she know how sweet and innocent and completely fuckable she looks right now?

Slowly, softly, I run my thumb over her thighs. I close my eyes for a moment, imagining what it would be like to lay her down and spread those thighs apart. How she would taste. How she would moan. How she would come.

Ivy leans against my chest, swinging her legs over onto the bed so she's laying on top of me. Her back is against my chest, her ass still pressed firmly into my crotch.

Every tiny movement she makes sends electric sparks coursing through my veins.

The air is heavy between us. The yacht sways gently from side to side, and I wrap my arms around Ivy's body. Her head nestles in beside my neck, her body molding perfectly against mine.

"Your Highness…" she whispers, closing her eyes for a moment. "Luca."

"Tell me, Poison." I pull her closer as my heart thumps. Leaning back against the headboard with Ivy on top of me is the best place I could ever be.

17

IVY

I feel dizzy.

I *thought* I'd kissed guys before. I thought I knew what it was like to feel turned on.

I was wrong.

The Prince's touch is unlike anything I've ever experienced before. His hands are warm, strong, and they send and electric current jumping through my veins. My breath hitches, and I run my fingers up his forearms. Prince Luca's skin is an art canvas, and I focus on the tattooed designs to try to calm my racing mind.

With his arms wrapped around my waist, I lean my back against his chest and let out a sigh.

Am I doing this right now? Am I going to let the Prince be my first?

I can't. I'm not ready.

Yet, when Prince Luca's fingers slide down to my thighs, all I want to do is spread them for him. His whole body is cradling mine.

My mind screams at me: *Stop! He's supposed to be dating your sister.*

My body doesn't listen. Still leaning against his chest, I reach down to the terrycloth bathrobe ties. Slowly, shyly, I pull them apart.

The Prince's heart thumps against my back. His hardness digs into my ass, and I grind myself into him almost involuntarily.

When I pull the lapels of the bathrobe open, letting it fall to the side, the Prince lets out a groan.

"You're gorgeous," he breathes, sliding his hands over my stomach. The tips of his fingers sweep up to touch the crease between my breasts and my ribcage, and heat sparks between my thighs.

The Prince's touch is gentle, yet strong. His fingers sweep over my breast, teasing my pebbled nipples as he exhales deeply. When he tweaks my nipples between his fingers, a zing of heat flashes through my body.

A rumble passes through his chest and I melt against him, wanting nothing more than to feel his hands on my body.

It's screaming for him. Every nerve ending in my body cries out for his hands, his mouth, his cock. I've never felt anything like this before.

The ache.

The need.

The lust.

I gasp when the Prince pinches my hard nipples between his fingers. Palming my breasts, he wraps his strong arms around my body as I lay splayed out on top of him. Every movement his hands make sends me into another tailspin of desire.

When his palms slide over my stomach, I lean my head into his neck and release a slow breath. The tips of his fingers tease the edges of my lips down below, moving to the inside of my thighs. He sweeps his hands up, brushing the wetness gathering between my legs.

Gently.

Softly.

Torturously.

I moan, lifting my arm to wrap it behind his head and burying my face in his neck. Luca lets out a chuckle, pulling my thighs apart with his hands. I comply, spreading myself for him.

The tips of his fingers tease my slit again, and heat roars through my stomach. I can feel the pulse thundering in my center, and I do my best to find the words I want to say.

Yes, I want you. Be my first. Make me yours.

I gulp. Is that what I want? It feels deliciously wrong to think those thoughts, and my body screams at me to speak them out loud.

I can't. This isn't right. I should go.

The words stick to my throat, and all I can do is melt into the Prince's body. His hands grip my thighs, spreading me wide, and my body grinds against his.

I never thought I'd be turned on by the feeling of a man's erection against me. I've felt them before, in nightclubs, when men drunkenly rubbed up against me. It's always felt disgusting and wrong.

Not now.

Now, the feeling of the Prince's length against me is making my head spin. There's a deep, aching neediness inside me. An emptiness I've never felt before.

I dig my fingers into the nape of his neck as he moves his hands up to brush my slit.

"Your Highness..."

"Luca," he corrects. His voice is gruff. Commanding.

"Luca," I sigh. "I've never... I'm..."

The words stick in my throat. His hands are so warm, so strong. He moves his palm between my legs, rubbing the heel of his hand over my bud as his fingers slide between my legs. I gasp, trembling against him.

"You're what?" he asks, sliding his hand back and forth. The tips of his fingers slide back toward my ass, and another shiver rocks through my body. The friction of his palm against my clit makes my head spin.

I bite my lip, wanting to scream. The Prince moves one hand up to my breast, cupping it and teasing my nipple as his other hand slides between my legs.

I'm shaking. Sparks fly in the space between my legs, and the air in the cabin is charged with so much electricity, it feels like every hair on my body is standing on end.

"I'm a virgin," I whisper.

He stops. My cheeks burn. His hand stays still between my legs. I'm too nervous to move, even though all I want to do is grind myself against his hand.

"You're a virgin?" Luca asks, his shallow breaths tickling my ear.

I nod, biting down on my lower lip. The Prince's cock throbs against me, growing even harder.

We stay completely still, and I'm not sure what to do. My pulse is still thundering. My body is screaming for him. The wetness between my thighs would be embarrassing if it wasn't so hot.

Luca's lips dip down, kissing the sensitive skin behind my ear. His teeth drag across my earlobe, and I let out a soft moan. The hand he has on my breast moves gently, brushing my pebbled nipple and sending sparks flying across my skin.

I move my hips, pushing myself back against him.

He groans, his breath tickling my neck. I shiver, spreading my knees wider.

I want him to rub me, to touch me like he was doing a moment ago. A heavy, hot ball of desire sits in the pit of my stomach, and I need him to touch me. I need him to set it free.

"I don't know if I'm ready to go all the way," I whisper, even as my hips grind against him.

The Prince groans, moving his hips along with mine. "We won't, then," he growls.

"But I want..." I trail off. My cheeks burn, and I can't find the words.

I want you. Your hands. Your tongue. Your lips. I want to taste you, and see what it looks like when you come.

The words die on my lips, and my blush deepens.

"Tell me," he commands.

My voice isn't functional, so I drop my hand between my legs, resting it on top of his. I push down, guiding Luca to pleasure me. He groans, the sound sending another wave of heat rushing to my toes.

Dragging his fingers through my wetness, the Prince brings them up to circle my clit. I buck against him, trembling as he touches the sensitive bundle of nerves. His cock throbs against my ass, nestling between my cheeks. With his length behind me, and his hand in front of me, I feel like I'm losing my mind.

Gently, Luca moves his fingers around my bud. He drags them through my wetness, absorbing every shiver, every tremble, every whimper that I emit. When he drops his fingers to circle my opening, I lick my lips and lean back into him.

"Have you ever had fingers inside you, beautiful?" he asks, his hand teasing my opening.

I release a breath, needing him to slide them inside.

"Answer me," he growls.

"Only my own," I admit.

His length throbs against my ass, and another wave of shivers tumbles through my body. I let out a whimper of disappointment when he takes his hand away from me, sliding it up my stomach and over my breasts. He grinds his cock against me, groaning.

"You're so fucking beautiful, Poison," Luca says into my ear. His hands trace my breasts, teasing my areola, before running them down my sides and resting his palms on the crease of my thighs. I arch my back, dying for his touch. He tortures me, sliding his hands to my inner thighs without touching my sopping wet slit.

"Please," I beg, breathless.

"I want you, Ivy," he says.

"You have me."

"All of you." His hand slides between my legs and fire floods my veins. "I want to be the first and only cock you feel inside that tight, perfect pussy of yours."

My cheeks burn. Is it wrong that it turns me on to hear him speak like that?

The Prince moves his fingers through my wetness, and my body is bathed in flames. I grind against his hand, needing more, more, more.

"Promise me," he whispers in my ear. "Promise me I'll be your first."

"I promise," I whisper.

Luca slides his finger inside me, curling it against my walls and sending waves of lust crashing through my veins. I moan, bucking against him as his other hand moves to my clit.

My fingers claw at him, reaching back to dig into the nape of his neck. My need for him becomes frantic. Animalistic. Wild.

My hips move of their own accord. I'm not in control of my own body anymore. All I know is the Prince's hard, thick cock is pressed against my ass cheeks, and his hands are working magic between my legs.

I've never felt anything like this. He squeezes his arms around me, holding me tight to his chest as I grind and buck against him.

The Prince groans, circling my throbbing clit with one hand while the fingers of his other hand push deeper inside me.

Then, he stops.

His hands move to my thighs, and he growls against me.

"Luca..."

The Prince chuckles, sliding his hands toward my center again. I'm aching in a way I've never felt before. The need I feel for him is indescribable. It's all-consuming.

This time, when he touches me, he doesn't stop. His hands work magic over me, touching me until the ball of heat and pressure in the pit of my stomach grows bigger.

Then, it happens.

I explode, splayed on top of Prince Luca. I angle my hips toward him, needing more of him inside me. I'm not in control of my own body anymore. I grind against the movement of his hands as my orgasm crests, crashing through me as it breaks every wall I've ever built up inside.

I pant, breathless.

Everything is hot and cold. I want more. I press my hand against his, pushing his fingers deeper inside me, gasping at the feeling of it.

The Prince moans into my shoulder, biting down on my skin as I ride his hands. He grunts, rubbing his cock against me faster, harder.

I squeeze my eyes shut, wondering what it would feel like

to have it inside me. The thought sends another wave of fire roaring through my center, and I know I'll keep my promise.

He'll be my first. I'm his.

Completely.

Prince Luca stiffens behind me, and I feel his cock throb through the fabric that separates us. He lets out a grunt, holding me close. I know he's coming.

The thought of him orgasming in his swim trunks as he grinds against me makes my whole body burn with delicious, tingling energy.

Prince Luca groans, sliding his hands over my stomach again as he kisses my neck. He takes my open bathrobe and closes it over my body, hugging me tight as I twitch and sigh against him.

I'm not sure how long we lay there. Long enough so that when a knock sounds on the door, I jump off the Prince with a yelp, tumbling to the floor of the cabin.

"Ivy! Are you okay?" Margot knocks on the door again.

I tighten my bathrobe belt with shaking hands, climbing up to my feet. I glance at the door. "I'm fine!"

"We're docking in five minutes. The car is going to pick us up so we can go home and get cleaned up. Are you okay in there?"

"I'm fine! Be right out!" Does my voice sound fake? Why did it go up so high?

I steal a glance at the Prince, who's straightening his shorts and combing his fingers through his hair. I suck a breath in through my teeth, squeezing my eyes shut for just a second.

What. Just. Happened.

I think he put a spell on me. There's no other explanation for what just occurred. Two days ago, I wanted to kill him. Now, I was practically ready to give him my virginity?

Scratch that—I *was* ready. More than ready. I wanted him inside me in a way I've never felt before.

What the hell is wrong with me?

I put my palms to my face and blow out a breath. This is wrong. So, so wrong. He's supposed to be dating my *sister*.

Not for real—not really. But still.

Prince Luca stands up and takes a step toward me. All I can do is stare at him. I'm under his spell again, my blood pulsing through every inch of my body. Heat circles my stomach and pings between my thighs. When he reaches me, the Prince sweeps his hand around my back and dips his head down toward mine.

He kisses me again, and I give in to what my body wants. I angle my lips against his, parting them to let him taste them. His stubble scratches my skin, and his fingers slide back to cup the nape of my neck.

Luca's lips are soft—softer than I would expect. His hand on my lower back pulls me toward him, and I melt into his arms.

This is what I want. I can tell myself that I shouldn't, that I can't, that it's wrong—but I'd be lying to myself. It *can't* be wrong to feel like this. My head spins, and I give myself over to the Prince's kiss. A moan slips through my lips, and Luca's arms hold me tighter.

I never want it to stop. My body is on fire, screaming for him so loud I can't hear anything except my own desire. His lips taste like honey and sin. His hands feel possessive and hot as they pull me close.

Then, the yacht thuds against the dock, and we fall apart.

My chest heaves, and I lift my eyes up to his.

"Your Highness..." I bite my lip.

"You taste even better than I thought you would." The Prince's voice is low and his eyes are hooded. "I can't wait to taste all of you." He's still standing so close to me that I can feel the heat of his body and smell the scent of his skin.

I close my eyes for a second, shaking my head. "I have to go."

When I open my eyes back up again, Prince Luca is wearing a roguish grin. His eyebrow quirks, and he dips his chin down.

"I'll see you soon, Poison."

I desperately want him to lean down and kiss me again. The space between my thighs aches for him, and my heart thumps in my chest.

He doesn't, though. Instead, the Prince ducks his head and exits the cabin.

I let out a breath as I watch him disappear through the doorway. A quiver of excitement passes through my stomach, and I try to dispel it with a shake of my head.

I shouldn't be excited about this. I shouldn't want more.

The Prince is not for me. He's *royalty*. He's promised to my sister.

But Holy Farcliff, does he know how to kiss. How to touch.

And the feeling of him orgasming against me...

I touch my fingers to my lips, and I can still feel the whisper of his kiss.

I gather up my wet clothes as well as Margot's. My keys and wallet are soaked in the back pocket of my jeans, and my phone is somewhere at the bottom of Farcliff Lake. Then, with the bundle of wet clothes in my arms, I head out to the main deck.

My sister smiles at me, and I sweep my eyes around the gathered celebrities for any sign of Prince Luca.

A pang of disappointment passes through my chest when I don't see him. Painting a smile on my face as my cheeks burn, I join my sister and walk down the passerelle to the pier.

A mass of reporters is waiting there for us, flinging questions at Margot as she smiles and waves. Cameras flash so bright and fast that I have to shield my eyes, trailing behind my sister like a lost puppy. We duck into a waiting SUV, and the driver takes off toward our house.

My head is still spinning. A few minutes ago, the Prince's hands were *inside me*.

Margot lets out a heavy sigh. "That didn't go as planned."

"No," I agree, glancing out the window. My cheeks are red-hot, and I'm afraid that if I look at my sister, I'll say something that I shouldn't. What happened between Prince Luca and me should stay on that boat, hidden away from everyone.

Margot's hand covers mine. She squeezes gently. "Thank you for jumping in, Ivy. I'm sorry I scared you."

Turning my head to look at my sister, my chest squeezes. A boulder lodges itself in my throat, and my emotions swirl messily inside my chest.

Right now, my sister doesn't have the glow that seems to always radiate from her. Her makeup is mussed, and her hair is stringy. There are lines on her face that I've never noticed before.

She looks...*human*.

My chest tightens, and I try to swallow. "I'm just glad you're okay."

The words sound forced, even though I mean them. I'm completely frazzled. I don't know what to think. Margot's hand stays on top of mine, and a pang passes through my chest.

I shouldn't have done that with the Prince. I shouldn't enjoy his advances. His kiss. His touch.

But *not* enjoying them seems as impossible as not needing food.

Leaning toward my sister, I lay my head on her shoulder. She angles her cheek against my head, and we sit there quietly until we make it back home. I blink back tears, shame burning my throat as I think of what happened today.

I was blinded by my attraction to the Prince, and he knew it. I don't know why he continues to pursue me like he does, but I must amuse him in some way. I have to find a way to resist it—to resist *him*.

Margot needs my support, and today was proof. Even after nearly drowning, she had to pretend like everything was okay. She had to do her job and be the star. She provides for me every day, and how do I repay her?

By hooking up with the guy who's supposed to be her boyfriend.

When we pull up to our mansion, I tell myself that I won't let it happen again. I won't let Prince Luca's spell enchant me like it did today. I won't kiss him, or touch him, or fantasize about him at all.

That promise I made to him?

I'll break it.

He belongs to my sister—even if it's all fake.

18

LUCA

I watch Ivy and Margot leave the yacht from one of the cabin windows before turning to the bathroom to clean myself up. My heart is still thumping wildly as I think of Ivy's body on top of mine.

Her soft, untouched body.

A shiver of pleasure runs through me, and I know that thought shouldn't turn me on as much as it does. My thoughts circle in my head, though, always coming back to one thing: Claiming Ivy.

Being her first. The only man to feel her, worship her, love her the way she deserves.

When I disembark the yacht, Beckett stares at me with dark eyes.

"Where were you?"

I arch an eyebrow. "Why do you care?"

"Do you not care that you're supposed to be dating one of the hottest chicks on the planet?"

"Not particularly, no." I start walking toward the waiting royal car, with two bodyguards flanking me on either side. Beckett rushes to catch up.

"You're so ungrateful. Always have been."

"What the fuck is that supposed to mean?"

Beckett huffs, shaking his head without answering.

"Are you the patron saint of hot chicks, now?" I ask, leveling him with a stare. "Why do you give a fuck about my fake relationship with some boring-ass model?"

"She's not boring," he snaps.

"So, *you* date her."

"I would, but that wouldn't exactly be what was arranged, now, would it?" He shakes his head. "Typical."

I shrug, nodding to one of the bodyguards as he opens a car door for me. I pause before sliding in, glancing at my half-brother.

"Let me ask you something, Beckett. Would it bother you more, or less if I *was* into her?"

His eyes darken.

I chuckle. "Thought so." I slide into the car and nod to the driver. I don't have the time or the energy to deal with Beckett's jealousy. Even when we were kids, he was like this. Always feeling inadequate and walking around with a chip on his shoulder.

We share the same mother. He's my brother. Why can't he see that? Why does he always have to think that things are done to spite him, instead of realizing that he could have whatever he wants, if he just reaches out and grabs it?

Sure, my father, the King, could be a bit of an ass toward Beckett. I'll admit that. Still, Beckett walks around like the world owes him something. It's irritating.

He's welcome to fuck Margot if he feels like it. Fuck if I care. I have other things on my mind. Namely, a black-haired beauty with different-colored eyes.

When we arrive at the castle, I hop up the wide marble steps with a smile. Before I can make it to my chambers, though, I'm called over to one of the formal reception rooms.

Prince Damon is there, and he strides toward me with his hand extended. He shakes my hand firmly, smiling at me.

"Prince Luca," he says with a nod. "I was hoping to run into you."

Damon gestures to a long, overstuffed sofa, and I take a seat. His wife, Dahlia, is there as well. She smiles to me, offering me a glass full of amber liquid. I accept it with a nod.

Prince Damon sits down across from me, leaning his elbows on his knees. "Dahlia told me you'd be willing to accompany us on our mental health campaign. I'm thrilled."

His smile is wide and open. Princess Dahlia slides her hand onto his shoulder, flicking her blue-tipped hair over her shoulder with her other hand.

I nod. "I'd be happy to."

Unlike the first time Dahlia asked me to participate, this time I mean it. The more time I spend in Farcliff, the better. I have some unfinished business with Ivy.

Damon grins. "Good. We're starting the tour here in Farcliff, with a three-day conference in the convention center. It'll be in three weeks' time, and from there we'll have an eight-week itinerary that will take us around the Kingdom. We'd love for you to make a keynote speech. Of course, our royal speech writers are at your disposal, but we were hoping you'd be able to open up about your recovery."

"Let me know the itinerary, and I'll do my best to help."

Dahlia smiles, clasping her hands to her chest. "Thank you, Your Highness."

"Call me Luca, please."

She smiles wider, nodding. "Luca."

I down the rest of my drink, loving the burn of the liquid as it passes down my throat. Excusing myself, I slip out of the room. I cast one last glance behind me, catching a glimpse of Damon sliding his hands over his wife's body. He cups her ass and kisses her tenderly, and a twinge of jealousy tugs at my heart.

I want that. I thought I'd have it with Cara, but I was wrong. When I found out that she married my brother, I was so consumed by hatred and heartbreak that I forgot what it felt like to want a woman. *Really* want a woman.

The way I want Ivy.

Now, that desire is roaring back to life with a vengeance.

My steps are light as I walk through the castle, nodding to the staff as I cross them. There's a persistent smile on my face, and a deep excitement welling up inside me.

I want to see Poison again. Feel her again. Taste her again.

I know she'll be here tomorrow morning to work in the kitchens, but I'm not sure I can wait that long. There's a lightness in my heart that I haven't felt in a long, long time. Maybe not since I was a kid, before the accident that tore my world —and my spinal cord—apart.

That lightness evaporates in an instant when I hear soft footsteps behind me. I smell Cara's sweet scent before she calls out to me, and bitterness coats my mouth. My heart jolts when I feel a small hand on my arm.

"Luca," Cara sighs. "Please."

I stop in my tracks, stiffening. I keep my eyes forward, not wanting to stare into her beautiful face. I know what I'll find there—lost dreams and broken promises. I'll stare at her lips and know that I can never taste them again.

Even though I want Ivy—even though she awoke something inside me—Cara's grip on my heart is still tight. Her claws are dug deep into my flesh, making me drag my shattered heart behind me like dead weight.

I inhale. "Please, what?"

"Look at me."

"I can't."

"I'm sorry."

"Are you?" I snap.

Silence hangs between us, and I still can't look at her. What would it accomplish? If I look at her, I don't know what I'll do. Push her away? Snarl my teeth at her? Kiss her?

She still has a hold on me, even though she's married to my brother. She still makes me feel like laughing and throwing up at the same time whenever I stare into her face. She still smells like heaven and flowers and candy.

Cara. My queen, my first love, my first heartbreak.

"I want us to be friends," she says softly, twisting the knife in my heart once more.

"We'll never be friends." I jerk my arm away from her. Then, I turn to look at her.

I knew I shouldn't do that.

Deep, brown eyes stare back at me, full of memories I'll never live again. Emotions erupt inside me, warring for a place in my heart. I hate her, but the way she looks at me makes me miss everything we had together.

"Do you remember when you told me you'd wait for me forever? That you'd be by my side?" My voice sounds strangled. My chest is hollow.

Cara sucks the inside of her cheek, and I remember what it was like to kiss her. I still remember how she tastes, and the face she makes when she comes.

I wonder if my brother makes her come like I used to.

Blinking the thought away, I stare at the woman who ground my heart to dust. Surprisingly, the tension around my chest eases slightly. I notice lines on her face that I hadn't seen before. The dimness in her eyes. The curve of her shoulders as she drops her head.

Cara sighs. "I thought you wouldn't come back, Luca. You kept pushing me away." She reaches to touch my arm. I don't flinch away, and I'm surprised when her hand doesn't shock me.

The feeling of her fingers on my arm doesn't send heat coursing through my veins, and it doesn't put another dagger in my heart.

I feel nothing.

"You thought I was broken," I say.

"No, I..." Her eyebrows draw together. "I wanted to come to Singapore, but you kept telling me to stay away. It was hard, Luca."

"You thought I'd never walk again, and you couldn't bear to be attached to someone damaged."

"That's not true." Cara shakes her head, her brown curls trembling around her face. "Theo and I were both so heart-broken when you left. We were so worried for you... It brought us closer. You were gone so long, and when you stopped answering my calls..."

She trails off, her hand squeezing my arm.

I purse my lips, nodding. "I was gone a long time getting my body stitched back together, Cara. You could have jumped on a plane and seen me. You could have moved to Singapore with me. You could have tried harder." I shake my head, scoffing. "I'm glad I could play Cupid for you."

Shrugging her hand off, I turn on my heels and walk away. I let my feet carry me all the way to the garages, where an attendant drops a set of keys into my hand. I get into a car and drive myself out of the castle grounds. I need to put some distance between Cara and me. I need some space from her —from her body, her stare, her voice.

I don't know what to think. Feeling her touch made me feel surprisingly detached, but there's still the memory of my heartbreak that clings to our interactions. It's almost as if I *want* to hurt. I *want* to be angry. I *want* to want her...but I'm not sure if I really do.

My foot is heavy on the accelerator, speeding through the unfamiliar streets of Farcliff City. I've spent the past year away from Argyle, and right now, I have no desire to go back. I like the unfamiliarity. I like the strangeness of the world away from home.

I like the distance between me and the woman that I loved. The woman that doesn't love me back.

Maybe she never did.

It's only when I turn onto the road leading up to the LeBlanc mansion that I admit to myself where I'm going. I stop the car a little ways away from the driveway, hesitating.

I shouldn't be here. Does it matter if I am, though?

I get out of the car, slipping the keys into my pocket. The air is crisp, and my footsteps are silent as I make my way up the well-lit driveway.

Too well-lit. I step off the asphalt and onto the grass, slinking near the tall hedges that line the property. My eyes drift up to the multitude of windows that stare back at me, and I already know who I'm looking for.

Poison Ivy. The addictive, intoxicating girl who succeeds in making me feel alive again.

The one whose touch sends pleasant shivers down my spine.

The one who promised herself to me.

Even though my life has been a trail of broken promises, there's something about Ivy that makes me think she'll keep hers.

Maybe it's desperation. I can't bear the thought of another man touching her, when I know she could be mine.

I know that her room is at the back of the building from

the time I spent in it the first night I met her. I make my way around the side of the building, grinning when I see her Vespa. It's forest green, and I wonder if she chose it to match her name. Her helmet is hooked onto the handlebars, and I lean over to sniff it.

I know it's weird, but it smells like her, and it calms the thumping of my heart.

My footsteps are silent as I make my way around the back of the building. It's hard to tell which window is hers. Most of them are dark. I circle the building, ducking under a well-lit window and listening for voices inside.

My heart races when I hear Ivy's voice, and I lean against the building for a moment, just to listen.

19

IVY

"I CAN'T BELIEVE you kissed the Prince." Georgie shakes her head, grinning. "I'm proud of you. You do all right, for a virgin."

"Not a virgin for long, I bet." Giselle winks.

"Stop it." I blush. I told the twins about the kiss, but I didn't have the nerve to tell them about everything else.

"What?" Giselle laughs. "Hey, come on, I didn't mean it in a bad way. You deserve a little nookie."

Georgie throws her arm around my shoulder and pulls me close. "You know we love you."

"I know. It's just... I don't know. I'm nearly twenty-one, and I've never had a boyfriend. Not even close! Don't you think that's weird? Like there's something wrong with me?"

"I can say for a fact that there's nothing wrong with you, Ivy," Georgie smiles. "Nothing serious, anyway."

I wipe my hands on my apron and let out a heavy sigh. "You know the worst part?" I say, dropping my voice and glancing toward the stairs. My sister is in her room, and I don't want her to hear this.

"What's that?" Giselle tilts her head.

"I was ready to do it with him."

"*Do it,* do it?" She grins.

I nod. "Right there on the boat. I wanted to."

Georgie laughs. "You should've."

"That's terrible advice." I shake my head, tossing a tea towel onto the counter.

"Isn't that the reason you keep me around? Bad advice and ill-advised encouragement?"

I laugh, shaking my head. Georgie flashes a smile at me and wraps me in a hug. "Don't worry, Ivy. It'll happen when it happens. You don't have to force it, and you don't want to do anything you'll regret."

"I know. I just... I don't know. It feels like a big deal to lose my virginity, but it also feels like I just want to rip it off like a band-aid. I just want to get it over with."

"Imagine if you'd lost your virginity on a luxury yacht with the visiting Prince of Argyle," Georgina giggles. "That beats my first time with Tim Monkford at the back of the bleachers in eleventh grade."

I smile, shaking my head. Biting my lip, I take a deep breath. "What does it feel like?"

"Sex?"

I nod. "Does it hurt?"

Giselle shrugs when I look at her. "Don't look at me. You know I'm not into dudes. My one and only experience with a penis was enough to scar me for life," she shudders.

I laugh.

Georgina grins, shaking her head. "It might hurt the first time. Sometimes it does hurt, but in the best way possible."

"I'm nervous." I turn on the faucet to start the dishes. I've just put a batch of muffins in the oven, and I can already smell them as they bake. It's comforting to be back in my kitchen, and I need to do something with my hands. I wash my mixing bowl slowly, replaying today's events over and over.

The Prince's gaze, his lips, his touch. My orgasm, and the way his cock throbbed when he came. I close my eyes for a moment, letting the warm water run over my hands.

I feel Georgie stiffen beside me, and I look over at her.

"Did you hear that?" Georgie's ears perk up as she glances at the window. Giselle nods.

I follow their gaze, but I can't see anything, until a shadow passes across the window. A *large* shadow. In the shape of a man. My heart starts to thump, and I gulp.

"Don't you have security?" Giselle hisses.

I shake my head. "Margot sent them away. Said she wanted to be alone tonight."

Georgie puts a finger to her lips, nodding her head toward the door.

I nod, wrapping my fingers around the rolling pin on the counter. I follow my best friends to the back door of the house. Georgie scans the room and goes to the fireplace to grab the fire poker and little shovel. She hands Giselle the shovel.

I nod to the twins and gently unlatch the back door.

My heart is in my throat. This is stupid. The best course of action would probably be to lock the doors and call the police.

I blame the twins. They've always been a bad influence on me. Both of them run into their problems head-on, bulldozing any obstructions in their path. Their parents ran the Grimdale Diner until they died, and the seven kids took over, working day in, day out to keep it afloat.

They haven't accepted anyone's handouts like I've done with Margot. They've worked for what they have, and they don't take anyone's shit.

Georgie's lips tug into a tiny smile, and my heart thumps. Her blue hair is thrown up in a messy bun, and she grabs the hood of her black sweater to throw it over her head. Giselle's lips are set in a thin line.

"You go this way," Giselle whispers. "We'll circle around the front. I think he's just around the corner."

I nod, and the twins disappear. They're so quiet that even I can barely hear them—but maybe that's because the only thing I can hear is the rushing of my blood in my ears.

Every step I take toward the edge of the house makes my throat tighten. I grip my rolling pin with both hands, closing my eyes for a moment to compose myself.

Whoever the intruder is, he doesn't stand a chance against Georgie, Giselle, and me. He's probably some paparazzi sneaking around the bushes, not respecting my sister's privacy. She's been locked in her room since we got home, and I can only imagine how tired and traumatized she is.

Whoever this douchebag is, he deserves to be beat over the head with a rolling pin and assorted fireplace equipment.

I count to ten, and open my eyes again. My knuckles have turned white from gripping the rolling pin so hard, and I inch my way to the edge of the mansion.

Poking my head around the corner, I see the slumped outline of a man leaning against the wall of the house. He has his head in his hands.

Retreating, I gulp down a breath. I stare at our backyard, gathering every last ounce of courage I have.

How do I let the twins get me into these situations? He could be armed! He could be dangerous!

I poke my head around the corner again, seeing movement on the other end. Georgie is there, ready to pounce. With a deep breath, I step around the corner.

Georgie must see me, because she lets out a battle cry. High-pitched and completely terrifying, she sounds like an ancient warrior trilling her tongue as she charges. I see her silhouette brandishing the poker high above her head as she sprints toward the man. Giselle isn't far behind, letting out a battle cry of her own as she takes off.

I don't have time to think or hesitate anymore. I just act.

When I let out a scream, the man is already turning to face the twins. Georgie's pouncing on him, swinging the poker wildly as he tries to dodge her attack. He shouts wordlessly, and I scream in response.

I bring the rolling pin down on his back as hard as I can —so hard the man grunts and falls to his knees.

"Fuck!" he grunts, and my stomach drops. I know that voice.

The Prince.

Georgie runs for another attack, swinging the poker wildly as Giselle runs to tackle him. She's lost the shovel somewhere in the bushes. Georgina brings the fire poker down on the Prince's head. He swears again, shielding himself with his arms as Georgie winds back. Giselle rolls off the Prince, crouching into an attack stance.

"Stop!" I cry, running at Georgina at full speed. I tackle her to the ground, and the fire poker goes flying off to the side. We land on the ground with a thud, and Georgie groans.

I roll off her, tossing the rolling pin away as I grunt, half-dazed from the tackle. Giselle stares.

Lifting my eyes to the Prince, I see him clutching his head as he leans on the wall. He lets out a low groan as he swings his eyes to me. Even in the darkness, I can feel the heat of his gaze.

"Coming to your house is dangerous, Poison."

"Maybe you shouldn't be sneaking around the shadows like some kind of home invader," I snap. I push myself to my feet.

Before the Prince can answer, my pocket starts beeping. I pull the timer out of my apron and pick up my rolling pin.

"Muffins are ready."

"So, you knew I was coming? I thought you said you wouldn't bake for me until hell froze over."

Georgie groans. "You must be Prince Luca." She picks up the fire poker, holding it across her body and taking a step toward the Prince. "Ivy told me you were an arrogant asshole."

"You girls don't have any respect for royalty," the Prince says.

Giselle snorts, rolling her eyes.

"Is that what you call yourself?" I retort before spinning on my heels and walking to the back door. "I thought royalty was supposed to act more proper than you do." The three of them trail behind me, Georgie and Giselle standing behind the Prince as if they're prison guards. They're both still gripping the fireplace tools with both hands, snarls marring their faces.

My heart is doing a funny kind of flip as I make it to the sliding glass door at the back of the house. My hands tremble as I slide it open, and I stand aside to let them pass.

The Prince nods to me as he steps through the door, and my panties are immediately drenched.

Damn it.

Giselle scowls. "I don't like him," she whispers.

"I heard that," the Prince responds.

"Good," she snaps.

Georgie grins. Giselle arches an eyebrow, and her twin shrugs in response.

"I don't mind him. He took the attack like a champ," Georgie says, covering her smile with her hand. "Come on, Giselle, you have to admit he's not that bad."

Giselle grunts, staring after the Prince suspiciously.

The three of us head to the kitchen. The Prince leans against the counter, his eyes following my every movement. I pull the muffins out of the oven, touching them to check for doneness. I put them on a cooling rack, keeping my back to the Prince.

He groans, and I glance over my shoulder to see him rubbing his shoulder where I whacked him with the rolling pin. His white bandage is bloody, and I wonder if Georgie managed to hit it with the poker. I walk to the freezer and pull out a bag of frozen peas, tossing it across the kitchen to him. He catches it against his chest, grunting in thanks.

I'd help him ice his shoulder, but I'm scared of getting too close to him. The memory of his touch is still branded on my skin, and I'm not sure I'll be able to resist him if I get too close.

Being near him feels like standing at the edge of a bonfire. The blaze is hot enough to burn.

So, I keep my distance. I turn back to the muffins, adjusting them and re-adjusting them on the rack. Georgie nudges me with her shoulder.

"You okay?"

I nod. "I'm fine."

She steals a glance at the Prince, and then gives me a loaded look. Her eyebrows wiggle, and I stifle a laugh. Putting a muffin on a plate, I turn to the Prince and present it to him.

"Your Highness," I say, extending the muffin toward him.

His lips curve into a smile, and his eyes flash. He inclines his head as he accepts the muffin, and a tremor passes through my stomach.

Not for the first time, I'm glad the twins are here—I'm not sure what I'd do if they weren't.

20

LUCA

I WISH Ivy's friends weren't here. I know exactly what I'd do if they left.

I'd sweep my hands around her waist and crush my lips to hers. I'd sit her on top of the kitchen counter and pull those ripped jeans off her perfect legs. I'd finally taste her cunt, licking up her juices and devouring her until she came, right here in the kitchen.

But I can't, because we're not alone. I take a bite of muffin and close my eyes as the taste hits my tongue. Ivy is so good. Groaning, I take another bite.

"You should open a bakery," I say.

Ivy and her friend exchange a glance, and Ivy's cheeks flush.

"That's what we've been telling her," the blue-haired girl says. She shakes her head, nudging Ivy with her shoulder. The girl's eyes turn to me. "I'm Georgie, by the way."

"Luca," I nod.

"This is Giselle," she says, nodding to her twin.

Georgie looks between me and Ivy, and a small grin

stretches over her lips. She nods to the two of us. "We'll see you tomorrow, Ivy. Nice to meet you, Your Highness."

"Wait," Ivy says, opening her eyes wide at her friends.

Georgie just winks, and the twins disappear through the door. Ivy's shoulders fall, and I take another bite of my muffin. She turns to me slowly, dragging her eyes back up to mine.

"We're alone," I say, wiping a crumb off my lip.

"My sister's upstairs."

"I'm not here to see your sister."

"Why are you here, then?"

I put my plate down, and take a step toward Ivy. Running my fingers over her cheek, I let a smile drift over my lips. "Why do you think I'm here?"

"You enjoy being attacked with a rolling pin?"

"Only if you're the one doing the attacking."

There it is—that sexy little blush that drives me wild. Ivy's face angles away from me, and I drag it back to face me with the tips of my fingers. Leaning down, I brush my lips over hers. I kiss her gently, tentatively, feeling her melt into my body.

Her arms hook around my neck as I deepen the kiss, kicking her legs apart. I push her back against the kitchen island, dropping my hand between her legs.

She's hot, and I can only imagine how wet she is under those faded, ripped jeans of hers. I tease her through the fabric, dragging my fingers over her and claiming her lips with mine. She moans, gripping onto my shirt and pulling me closer.

Ivy's movements are jerky, almost unsteady. Every time I touch her, she seems so responsive it makes my cock throb. I can only imagine how she'd feel if I was touching her bare skin again.

Reaching my fingers up to the fly of her pants, I unfasten the button and slide the zipper down. Ivy pants, staring up at me with wide eyes. I stare from one eye to the other—from blue to green and back to blue again. Slipping my hand under her panties, I feel her nails dig into my shoulders.

Poison is so, so wet. I groan, my mouth watering at the thought of tasting her. My lips fuse to hers again, and I slide my hand further through her honey.

Ivy whimpers, bucking her hips toward me and kissing me frantically, her legs trembling as I drag my fingers over her bud.

When I touch it, twirling my fingers around the sensitive bundle of nerves, Ivy flinches. She puts her hand on my chest and pushes me away, panting.

"Wait, stop," she says.

I frown, pulling away. "Did I hurt you?"

Ivy shakes her head. "It's not that."

"Tell me." I tuck a strand of hair behind her ear, leaning down to kiss her red lips again. Her mouth lingers on mine, and she drags her fingers through my hair.

When I pull away, Ivy's eyes are wide. Her bottom lip trembles until she sucks it in between her teeth.

"What's wrong?" I ask softly.

"I can't... I can't do this with you."

"What do you mean?"

"I mean it's wrong, Luca." She fastens her pants, stepping away from me.

Fuck, I love how my name sounds coming from her mouth. I shake my head. "It could never be wrong."

"My sister..."

"You sister has everything handed to her," I say. "Why not do something for yourself, for once?"

Ivy's cheeks turn bright red and she averts her eyes, shaking her head.

Catching Ivy's hand in mine, I pull her close to me again. My fingers slide over her jaw and I tilt her face up to mine. My heart thumps, and my mouth grows dry.

I'm addicted to her. I already know it. Kissing her is better than the pills I pop multiple times a day. Sucking on her bottom lip is better than all the weed in the world. Drinking her up does more for me than any alcohol ever could.

She's my poison, and I'm not ready to let her go.

"Maybe we can just take it slow," she says, dragging her eyes up to mine.

Hope flames to life in my chest. I'll go as slow as she needs me to. I nod, nudging the tip of my nose against hers.

"As slow as you want."

"And I don't want anyone to know. Not until I find a way to tell my sister."

"Deal." I whisper, pressing my lips to hers. "Not a word."

Ivy wraps her arms around my neck and melts into me, only pulling away after a few, long moments.

I stare into her eyes as my heart thumps. "I guess I should go," I say.

"I guess you should."

Ivy walks me to the front door. She glances at the stairway before giving me a quick kiss, and then I walk back to my car.

I'm not sure what this accomplished besides giving me blue balls and a few extra bruises on my back, but I feel lighter than I did before.

THE NEXT MORNING, I look for Ivy in the kitchens. She sees me through the window in the pastry room door, and a quick smile crosses her lips. I walk away as a thrill passes through me.

For the next three weeks, that's what happens. Every morning, I look for Ivy in the kitchens. Sometimes, she's able to sneak away with me. A couple of days a week, she has time to spend an hour with me before she has to go home to work for her sister.

I get her a new phone, because I can't bear the thought of not being able to talk to her whenever I want.

"I was kind of enjoying the freedom of having no phone. No social media, no tabloids—just peace," she smiles.

"You can still have freedom, but I want to be able to take you out without stalking through the castle like a maniac."

Ivy laughs, pressing her lips to mine. "My maniac."

I kiss her every opportunity I get, but I don't do much beyond that. Every time her lips touch mine, my need for her grows. She runs her hands over my body, moaning when I touch her, but we only go as far as she wants. We take things slow.

Discovering intimacy with her is something I never thought I'd experience. Every time I make her come, usually in some dark corner of Farcliff Castle, her eyes are so full of lust and wonder that it makes my whole body throb. The first time I taste her pussy, I nearly come in my pants.

Taking things slow is not something I'm accustomed to. Discovering someone's body one inch at a time is not something I've done before. Opening up to a woman day by day, hour by hour, kiss by kiss—that's as new for me as it is for Ivy.

I like it. Everything is heightened. I find myself wanting to take things slow, even though I want all of her at the same time.

Ivy's skittish, though. She jumps at any sound and is

always scared of getting caught. A part of me wonders if she wants to take it slow because she still feels guilty about sneaking around with me, when I'm supposed to be with Margot.

As the days pass, I look forward to seeing her. It's the best part of my day. When she leaves, usually around eleven o'clock or noon, I'm already dreaming of the next morning.

The tension in my body dissolves, and I find myself taking fewer and fewer painkillers. I only smoke weed at night, right before bed. It's a habit, more than anything.

Then, one day, I take nothing at all.

Throughout those three weeks, I accompany Margot to official events. I typically ignore the media, but I see a few headlines about our budding relationship. I scoff, shaking my head.

If only they knew.

Whenever I'm planning to be out in public with Margot, I make sure to spend extra time with Ivy that morning. I make sure she knows that Margot is just a job. I never kiss Ivy's sister—not since that first night. I put my arm around her, and smile for the paparazzi, but I make sure Ivy knows that she's the one that matters to me.

After three weeks, Cara and Theo leave to rejoin Dante in Argyle. Beckett stays behind for an extra week, and a part of me thinks it's because he wants to spend time with Margot.

Not that I care.

When I bid my King and Queen goodbye, Cara's eyes are searching. Theo's eyes are suspicious. Beckett glances at me, and he looks angry.

I have no darkness in my heart toward them. I say good-bye, and all I'm looking forward to is seeing Ivy the next morning.

. . .

THE FIRST DAY of the mental health tour with Damon and Dahlia, I deliver a keynote speech to a large crowd. When I'm done, Dahlia has tears in her eyes. She throws her arms around me.

"That was beautiful, Luca. You're inspiring."

"Not sure about that," I respond with a smile. "I had a team of doctors and surgeons and physiotherapists around me twenty-four-seven. They're the inspiring ones."

After the event, my heart feels light. For the first time in a long time, I feel truly free. Free from the burden of my accident, from the torture that I went through to recover, from the demons that plagued my mind for years.

Maybe, I'm free from Cara.

I drive straight to Ivy's house, because I know I need to see her. She opens the door for me, glancing around to make sure no one followed me there before laying a soft kiss on my lips. It's become hard to contain my desire for her. With every touch, I need her more.

"I wasn't expecting you here tonight," she says, closing the door behind me. "How was the speech?"

"You're asking that like you haven't already YouTubed it," I grin.

Ivy blushes, smiling. "How do you know me so well already?"

"What did you think of my speech?"

"It was gorgeous, Luca. I'm glad you decided to do this tour and share your story."

"I had a good excuse to stay," I respond, wrapping my arms around her. Ivy glances at the staircase, and I know she's worried about Margot seeing us. It's not too hard to hide at the castle—there are lots of empty rooms and secret corners. No one bothers me.

Here, though, I can tell Ivy's on edge. She takes a deep breath. "Let me show you something."

My girl slips her hand into mine, dragging me toward the back door again. Ivy glances at the stairs again when we walk past them, and then squares her shoulders and steps outside. We walk around the huge pool that dominates their backyard, over to a cabana on the far side.

Ivy opens the door and flicks the lights on to reveal a comfortable pool house. There's a daybed in the corner and an entertainment area with a bar across from it.

Ivy waves to it. "Help yourself."

She walks over to a desk in the corner, flicking on a lamp and pulling out a thick folder. I walk up behind her, inhaling the scent of her hair as I cage her against the desk.

With a soft moan, she leans into me before turning back to the folder. When she flicks it open, I see sketches, floor plans, logos. She even has a menu planned out, with special occasion recipes for holidays.

"This is my bakery," she says simply.

I take a step so that I'm beside her and sit down on the desk chair. Flicking through the files, my eyebrows arch. "You've really thought this through."

Ivy nods. "I've been planning it for years."

"*Spoonful of Sugar*," I read, running my fingers over a page full of hand-drawn logo designs.

"You like the name?"

I nod, smiling. Ivy points to one of the sketches. "That's the logo I would choose, if I were starting a bakery."

"So why haven't you done it?"

"Because my sister needs me," she answers simply, turning to look at me. "I owe her everything, and it's my job to protect her."

"It's your job to protect *you*," I answer, stroking the side of her thigh with my hand. Even through her jeans, the feeling of her body sends heat zipping up my arm. "You need to think of yourself once in a while, too, Ivy."

Ivy sighs, flipping through the pages in her folder. A wistful look crosses her face, and she pinches her lips together. She steps away from me slightly, just as she always seems to do when we get too close to each other.

"Do you regret what's going on between us?" I ask. My voice sounds pinched, and I'm almost afraid of her answer.

Ivy snorts. "No. I don't think I could regret it if I tried."

"So why are you fighting it?"

"It feels like I'm betraying Margot by spending time with you."

I don't know what to answer to that, so I don't say anything. I understand being torn about family—it's how I feel about Theo and Cara. They're my King and Queen, and I owe them my life and my recovery, but they've also caused me more pain than I can imagine.

Ivy lets out a sigh and shrugs. "But on the other hand, maybe you, Georgie, Giselle, their brothers, and every single other person who knows me is right. Maybe I need to live my own life." She lifts her gaze to mine, sucking her bottom lip between her teeth.

My eyes drift down over her body—so curvy, so womanly, so fucking perfect. How could she be untouched?

Letting my fingers drift up her sides, I brush my thumbs over the curve of her breasts. She sucks in a breath, sliding her hand up my forearm. Even a gentle touch sends my body into overdrive.

Contrasted against the nothingness that I felt when Cara touched me, I know that what's going on between us is real.

I want to give her pleasure like she's never felt before. I

want to see her face when she feels a cock inside her for the first time.

But not like this. Not splayed out in a tiny pool house, where anyone could walk in.

I want to treat her like a princess, and make sure that she wants it as much as I do. When I finally have her, it'll be on top of a king-sized bed, with down pillows under her ebony hair, and silk sheets for her to twist her fingers into.

I stroke her face with my fingers, and Ivy blinks as she stares at me.

"You know how I'm a virgin..." she says, reading my mind. "Is that... Is that a problem? I know we've been taking it slow. Is it too slow for you?"

I smile, leaning over to kiss her. "Nothing about you is a problem, least of all the fact that you're a virgin."

"It's not that I don't want to," she stammers, gulping. "I just... I don't know. It's just never happened."

"You don't have to explain yourself to me."

"You make my head feel all messed up, Your Highness. Luca. I..." Ivy closes her eyes for a moment, and then finally lifts her gaze up to meet mine. "I just need time."

I nod. "You've got all the time in the world, Ivy. I'm not going anywhere."

"You don't think I'm a freak?"

"I do, but not because you're a virgin."

Ivy laughs, swatting my chest. She pulls me to the daybed, and we lay down together. I wrap my arms around her, trailing my fingers through her hair. Having her in my arms feels right, and I already know I'll go as slow as she wants me to.

21

IVY

I WAKE up at dawn with Prince Luca's arms still wrapped around me. Sitting up in the day bed, I rub my eyes and groan at the stiffness in my body. There's a chill in the pool house. I shiver.

The Prince roughs his hands through his hair, making it stick up in all directions. He yawns before smiling sleepily at me.

He's never looked as handsome as he does now. Unkempt, sleepy, and completely mine.

Blinking at the rays of sun that are poking over the horizon, I let out a happy sigh. Standing up and stretching my arms over my head, a twinge of excitement pokes my stomach. I glance at Luca, and then pull my shirt off over my head.

His eyebrows jump up, and his hand instinctively moves between his legs.

Without saying a word, I unclasp my bra and let it fall to my feet. The Prince's eyes sweep over my chest and he lets out a soft breath. When my hands move to my pants, the Prince's throat bobs.

He looks at me like he's never seen anyone as beautiful,

his gaze sending sparks flying across my skin. Truthfully, I've never felt as beautiful as I do now. To have a man like him looking at me like that... It's not something I ever thought I'd experience.

I unfasten my jeans, pulling them down along with my underwear and kicking both garments off. I stand up again, naked.

I'm not sure where this confidence came from, but it's too late to turn back now. I've never been naked in front of Luca, and doing it now makes me feel incredible. Powerful. Sexy.

"Ivy..." The Prince sighs, his eyes sweeping up and down my body. His hand rubs between his legs, and I smile, blushing.

"I'm going for a swim."

I can feel his eyes on me as I walk out of the pool house, sending waves of heat down to my core. When I jump into the pool, even the cold water doesn't cool me down.

Prince Luca makes me want to be naughty. He makes me *ready* for everything. It's like he's unlocked a part of me that I didn't even know existed.

The fact that he hasn't complained about my boundaries makes me feel even more comfortable with him. Over the past three and a half weeks, I've never felt pressured or embarrassed around him. I've always felt like I'm in control of what happens, and that he respects my desires to take it slow. It makes me want to give myself to him... I just need to find the courage to do it.

Dragging my fingers through the water in the pool, I turn back to look at the pool house, gasping when I see the sight before me.

Prince Luca's naked body fills the doorway. A flush creeps up my neck as my gaze drops down between his legs, where his hand is wrapped around his very thick, very long, very beautiful cock.

Would that thing even fit inside me?

"You're killing me, Poison," he breathes, glancing at the big house. He slides into the water with me, inhaling sharply at the cold. I swim over to him, hooking my arms around his neck and my legs around his waist. I can feel his length pinned between us, and it sends a shiver of excitement through me.

The Prince closes his eyes for a moment, letting his hands drift down my back under water. With my face nuzzled into his neck, I gather the courage to ask him something that's been on my mind since I felt him come in the yacht. Something we haven't done, even in the dark corners of the castle when we feel each other up.

"Luca," I say softly.

"Yeah, Poison?"

"I want to see what it looks like when you come." My voice is barely a whisper. My lips brush against his neck when I talk, and for a beat, I'm not even sure if he heard me.

The Prince's hands tighten around my waist. "You want me to masturbate in front of you?"

I nod, not trusting my voice to answer. His hardness throbs between us, and the Prince's hand slips forward to rest against my chest. He pulls away from me, forcing me to look at him. His fingers caress the base of my neck as he searches my face.

I can feel my face heating up, and I'm pretty sure my skin is fire-engine red.

The Prince exhales, shaking his head. "That's probably the hottest thing anyone has ever said to me."

22

MARGOT

THE CEILING FAN GOES AROUND, and around, and around. I haven't slept. As the first rays of sunshine start to pierce the sky, I roll onto my side and stare at Prince Beckett's sleeping shape.

I shouldn't have slept with him. I know I shouldn't have.

But I'm weak, and I was lonely. After watching Prince Luca's keynote speech for the mental health tour, I felt empty. Prince Luca was distant, as usual, and he left me as soon as he could. His disinterest stings, as pathetic as that is to admit.

Then, Beckett showed up at my house. Am I going to say no to a handsome Prince who shows up at my doorstep with a nice bottle of wine?

Apparently not.

Sighing, I rub my eyes with the base of my hands.

I know why I did it—I'm slowly spiraling out of control. It's because of that little white envelope at the back of my closet, behind a stack of old sweaters that I haven't worn in years.

It's still sealed, and it still tortures me.

Maybe sleeping with Prince Beckett was a way of trying to

distract myself. I'm looking for something that will make me feel good.

The thought almost makes me laugh, but I don't want to wake him up, so I bite down on my bottom lip to stifle the sound.

Of course it didn't make me feel good. I haven't had an orgasm in three years—not with a partner or by myself. There's something in my mind that stops me from being able to let go.

Maybe I'm just broken.

Prince Beckett groans, sighing softly in his sleep as he shifts in bed and turns toward me. His eyes stay closed, a soft snore escaping his nose.

I can't take this anymore. When the envelope first arrived, I was too scared to look at the results of the test. I lied to Ivy, telling her it was negative. I've been living in denial for months, and it's making me do stupid things like sleep with a Prince that I don't really care about, and be needy with Ivy when I know she needs space.

It's time for me to face my fears.

I need to know.

Slipping out from under the covers, I tiptoe to the closet and reach up behind the stack of sweaters, feeling around until my fingers brush the sharp corner of the envelope. I pull it out, hands trembling, glancing up at the door of the walk-in closet.

Beckett's still snoring.

If I hesitate, I won't be able to do this, so I just bite down on my hesitations, take a deep breath, and tear the test results open.

The envelope drops to the floor as I take the single sheet of paper out, unfolding it as my heart races.

This is it.

My future.

My life.

My eyes are filling with tears, and I can't make out the blurred words on the piece of paper. I suck a breath in through my teeth, blinking a few times to clear my vision.

It'll be negative. It has to be. This has all been blown out of proportion. I've been silly. Everything will be okay. It'll be negative. Negative. Negative.

Blink.

Wrong.

Positive.

I frown, shaking my head. Then, I read the letter over from the beginning, hoping the word will have changed by the time I get to it.

It doesn't.

Positive. Positive. Positive.

Every letter of the word is like a bullet piercing my chest. Standing in my walk-in closet, I grow roots. I can't move.

I'm going to die.

The first tear falls from my eye and lands on the test results. The sound of my tear hitting the paper is as loud as a gunshot to my ears, forcing me to crumple the sheet and stuff it into a boot in the corner of the closet.

I suck in a breath, but I can't get enough air.

I can't breathe.

Stumbling out of the closet, I claw at my throat as my vision starts to cloud. My body is clammy and my hair is stuck to my head, and Prince Beckett snores louder.

I'm unsteady. I bump into my bedside table as I try to walk past, knocking a glass of water to the floor. It crashes down and Beckett jumps awake.

I stumble, trying to make my way to the bathroom.

"Margot?"

I turn to him, mouth open, but I can't breathe.

"Are you okay?"

My hands go to my throat. I manage to swallow, sucking in a labored breath. "Help," I croak.

"What's wrong?"

"Panic." I inhale. "Panic."

"Panic? What does that mean? Panic attack?"

Falling to my knees, I squeeze my eyes shut and try to regain control over my body. What was it my therapist said? What do I do in this situation?

I can't remember. I can't think. My thoughts are fragmented.

"Hold on," Prince Beckett says, scrambling to get up and head to the bathroom. "Do you have medication? What do you need? What do I do?"

I crawl on the floor, propping myself up against the wall. My hands find the windowsill and I pull myself up, glancing outside.

I frown when I see Ivy, naked, leading a man into the pool house. He's also naked. My nose touches the window as I squint at them, trying to make sense of what I'm seeing. He has his back to me, and then disappears into the building.

"Oh, fuck, no," Prince Beckett says behind me.

Turning to look at the Prince, I see his eyes blazing and his lips turned down at the corners. His face is dark. Black. Angry.

I squeeze my eyes shut and shake my head.

I'm seeing things.

Ivy doesn't have a boyfriend—never has. She's the pure one of the two of us. The one who stayed back to take care of Mama. The one who takes care of me.

She's the one who deserves this big house and all this

money. She's the one who holds me together every time I feel like I'm coming apart at the seams.

Why would Prince Beckett care if Ivy's seeing someone? *Breathe.*

I suck in some air.

I'm positive for Huntington's disease. I'm going to die.

My thoughts swirl. My fingers dig into the window ledge and vaguely, I sense Prince Beckett moving away from me. I stare out the window, trying to focus on something other than the constriction of my lungs and the racing of my heart.

There's no evidence of Ivy and the man. Shadows on the pool deck make it look like there are wet footsteps leading from the pool to the small outbuilding, but when I blink, they turn fuzzy.

I'm seeing things.

There's nothing there.

Ivy doesn't have a boyfriend.

Prince Beckett shifts behind me, and I wait to feel his hand on my shoulder, his arms around me, his voice in my ear.

I need comfort.

I need *love.*

Instead, I yelp when something sharp pinches my arm. My eyes widen as I see Prince Beckett with a syringe, pushing some liquid into my body.

Trying to scream, nothing comes out. I try to move, but my limbs are too heavy. Words escape me. My vision blurs.

The last thing I see is Beckett's ugly snarl as he removes the syringe from my arm.

23

IVY

Luca spreads a towel out on top of the daybed and then lays back on top of it. Our bodies are still dripping with water from the pool, and goosebumps erupt all over my skin.

I don't know if it's the cold, or the sight of Luca's body that does that to me.

His eyes are hooded as he stares at me, opening an arm toward me. I snuggle in beside him, my eyes taking him in. All of him.

We don't say much. The air between us is heavy, and a bundle of excitement grows in the pit of my stomach.

I nestle my head on his shoulder and watch as he wraps his hand around his thick cock. My fingers go on an exploratory mission of their own, trailing down his chest and tracing the outline of his abdominal muscles, and finally coming to rest on his thigh.

Without a word, the Prince releases his grip on his shaft as an invitation for me to touch it. It surprises me how smooth and velvety his skin is. My fingers barely reach all the way around, and my mouth goes dry.

It's definitely going to hurt if he puts it inside me.

Gulping, I dispel the thought. Instead, I move my hand up and down his hardness, watching. His abs contract as I move my hand. With my head on his chest, I can hear his pulse speed up. With one hand wrapped around my body, the Prince makes me feel safe and comfortable beside him.

His other hand moves on top of mine, wrapped around his cock.

My heart stutters.

Heat floods my insides. My cheeks are burning, and my eyes are glued to the movement of my hand. The tip of his cock seems to grow right in front of me, and I suddenly have an irresistible urge to taste it.

When a bead of precum appears, I can't resist.

I shift my weight and lean over his cock, taking it between my lips.

The Prince lets out a low growl, his hand splaying across my back as I kneel over him. I tremble, spreading my lips wider to sweep my tongue over his tip.

It's salty, but not unpleasant.

I always thought going down on a guy was degrading. I thought it was a bit gross, and I didn't understand the appeal. I never thought I would enjoy it. I never realized that it could make me feel this powerful, this sexy, this completely in control.

Prince Luca—strong, muscular, hyper-masculine—melts like butter in my hands. He moans as I move my mouth over his head, curling his fingers into my back.

I take more of him into my mouth, closing my eyes and relishing the taste of him. Heat pools between my legs, and I moan with him.

This isn't degrading. It's sensual and sexy. Giving the Prince a bit of pleasure after what he's done for me over the past three weeks makes me feel good.

I *want* him to come. I want him to feel as good as I did. I want to do this for him.

A grunt escapes the Prince's lips, and I feel his cock throb. Lifting my head up, I glance at Luca.

"Are you close?"

He nods, his lips parting as if he wants to speak, but can't. His face is completely relaxed. He blinks slowly, dropping his gaze to my swollen lips. He moves his hand over mine again, and we slide our hands over his shaft together.

Then, it happens.

My lips part and my breath catches as I watch the white, sticky seed shoot out of his cock. He angles it toward himself so that it lands across his chest and stomach. Again, and again, and again, his cock throbs under my hand and covers him in cum.

I watch as it pools in the valleys between his abs. A streak of it dribbles down over his side, and I move to stop it with my finger.

Before I know what I'm doing, I lift my finger to my mouth to taste it. Meeting the Prince's eye, he lets out a growl and shakes my head.

"You're killing me."

"Salty. A bit bitter." I wrinkle my nose. "Not great."

He sighs, leaning his head back on the pillows. I grab another towel and hand it to him, watching in fascination as he wipes himself clean.

There's a funny mix of curiosity and desire swirling inside me. It turns me on to see him like this—completely satisfied because of something I did—but not in a burning, needy way. It's like a deep, steady thrum inside me. I snuggle in beside him, leaning my head on his shoulder.

He kisses the top of my head, wrapping his arms around me.

"Did that satisfy your curiosity?" I can hear the grin in his voice.

"Yes, thank you."

"Always happy to oblige."

I giggle, feeling my cheeks heat up. I'm not embarrassed. I'm just blushing because I never could have imagined that sex could be like this—comfortable, sexy, and fun.

When my alarm goes off on my phone, I groan.

"I have to head to the castle for work," I say.

"I'll drive you."

I glance up at the Prince's face. He leans toward me and lays a soft kiss on the tip of my nose, smiling.

"Are you sure that's a good idea?"

"What do you mean?"

"Us, together, driving into the castle grounds?"

The Prince's lips pinch, and he shrugs. "I don't care if it's a good idea or not. I don't care if people see us together, Ivy. I'm with you. No one else."

"How would I get home? I think it's better for me to take my scooter."

"As you wish," he says, forcing a smile.

I've said something wrong. I feel closer to the Prince than ever before, but it still feels like there's a distance between us that I can't bridge.

Of course there's a distance between us—he's royalty, and I'm a pastry chef. This is going nowhere, and we both know it...

...but that doesn't mean I can't enjoy it for a little while, does it?

Standing up from the day bed, I stretch my neck from side to side, gather my clothing, and get dressed. The Prince wraps his arms around me again, laying a soft kiss on my lips.

"When can I see you again?" he whispers.

A smile tugs at my lips, and I shrug. "Probably in about an hour at the castle."

My heart flutters as he brushes his lips against mine, and then I watch him walk out of the pool house with a smile on my face.

When I make it back to the house, everything is quiet. My stomach grumbles, so I inhale a bowl of oats. I lean against the marble counter, letting my mind drift over the events of the past few weeks.

In a little over three weeks, I've gone from only having experienced sloppy, drunken kisses, to nearly going all the way with Prince Luca.

A persistent smile tugs at my lips, and I grab a banana out of the fruit bowl on the counter. Turning the coffee machine on, I sing to myself and float through the kitchen, buoyed by my happiness.

He wants to see me again. I want to see *him* again.

Against all odds, I've found a guy who's choosing me over my sister, and not the other way around. He looks at me the way guys usually look at her, and it makes me feel powerful, and sexy, and completely overwhelmed. Even when he goes out with her, I no longer feel jealous. I see the way he puts his arm around her as if she were his sister. Nothing at all like the way he touches me.

I trust him completely.

The coffee machine gurgles, and I glance at the staircase that leads up to the bedrooms. As I think of my sister, I hear a loud thump.

Frowning, I leave half of my banana on the kitchen counter and step lightly toward the stairs. I pause at the bottom, craning my neck to try to hear any noise.

There's shuffling, and maybe a muffled moan.

I frown. My heart starts to thump, and alarm bells blare in my ears.

Something's wrong.

I grip the staircase railing, simultaneously wanting to fly up the stairs and too terrified to move.

"Margot?" I call out, my voice shrill in the empty house.

No response.

A lump forms in my throat, and I try to shake the dread that creeps into my heart. A black hand squeezes my lungs, pushing all the air out of me. It's hard to take a full breath.

One step at a time, I make it up the stairs. I walk to Margot's room, placing my ear against her door.

"Margot?" I repeat, tapping my knuckles against the wood.

Again, nothing.

My heart bounces against my ribcage. Fear ices my veins, and I squeeze my eyes shut to compose myself.

She's just sleeping. The thump I heard was something falling off the bed, or her fist hitting the wall in her sleep. The shuffling and moaning was a bad dream.

Everything is fine.

Yet even before I push the door open, I know that everything isn't fine.

Far from fine.

Everything is about to fall apart.

24

LUCA

WHEN I GET BACK to Farcliff Castle, I make my way back to my chambers and flop down onto my bed. My body is still buzzing from what happened in the pool house. For the first time in years, I'm not waking up with debilitating nerve pain.

I can walk. I can move. I can laugh, and talk, and feel Ivy's hands on my body without feeling like I'm lying on a bed of pins and needles. I haven't needed a painkiller in days. I haven't smoked in over a week.

Turning my head to the side, I see a fresh bottle of painkillers on my bedside table.

The doctor must have brought it while I was out.

I take the little white bottle in my hands, turning it around and listening to the pills rattle inside. These pills have been everything to me. They've blanketed me in a haze of numbness for the past five years. They've been my crutch ever since my body failed me.

At first, painkillers helped me live. They helped me learn to walk again, and made it possible for me to live my day-to-day life.

Now, I realize that I've been relying on them for something different.

It's not physical numbness I've been chasing. It's the chemical haze in my mind that has attracted me. I shake the bottle again, sighing.

If Ivy can make me feel brand new again, why do I need these?

Maybe the doctors are right, and a lot of my nerve pain is psychosomatic. It's created by my mind—not my body.

At first, when the doctor told me that the pain might be in my head, I was deeply, deeply offended. How dare he tell me that I'm imagining it? How dare he insinuate that my body was healthy, when I couldn't even lay in bed without feeling like my spine was being torn apart by a giant's hands?

I realize now that the doctor may have been right.

It's not that I was imagining it, it's that my mind was sick —not my body.

Now, I'm pain-free. Without drugs. Without pills, or weed, or alcohol.

Without Cara.

It hits me like a bolt of lightning. Over the past three weeks, I've thought of Cara less than I did in a single day over the past five years. I haven't felt like gouging my eyeballs out with my own fingernails, or tearing the skin off my flesh one strip at a time.

To put it simply, I haven't cared about her at all.

Blowing the air out of my lungs, I swing my legs over the side of the bed. I take the bottle of pills over to the ensuite bathroom and unscrew the top.

Frowning, I notice that the seal is broken.

Underneath the cotton ball at the top of the bottle, I pour out a couple of pills into my palm.

Staring at them, something stirs in the depths of my chest.

You should take a couple, for old time's sake, a voice croaks in my head. *Chase the numbness once more. Feel nothing today, and then tomorrow you can give it up. You can stop anytime you want —why not enjoy it one last time?*

The thoughts seep into my bloodstream, and I stare at the pills. My hand begins to shake.

Just one won't hurt. Dump the rest.

I pour the contents of the bottle into the toilet before I change my mind, and then turn my attention to the six pills that remain in my palm.

They feel heavy. All I have to do is angle my palm downward, and they'll tumble into the toilet with the others.

But I don't.

I stare at them, listening to the voice in my head.

Come on, it says. *It'll be fun. Get high. Get numb. One last time.*

I realize I'm trembling. I look up and see myself in the mirror, shocked at what looks back at me. The hollowed-out cheeks, the dark eyes.

Is this what I look like?

As I stare at myself in the mirror, I know what the voice is. It's addiction.

It's evil, insidious addiction, clinging to me like a monkey on my back. It has its claws sunk deep into my flesh—so deep, in fact, that I thought addiction was a part of me.

The real me.

I close my fingers over the pills, averting my gaze from the mirror.

I'm not an addict. I'm in pain. I had a spinal injury. They told me I was paralyzed. I need these pills.

Need, need, need. I need them now.

Opening my hand back up, I stare at the little, round, white pills. I flip one over, noticing a 'T' imprinted on the side. Has that always been there? I bring it closer to my face to inspect it, but the closer I bring the pills, the more I want to take them.

The voice in my head screams.

Yes, yes, yes. Take them. Take them now. Get high.

I can't resist any longer. I throw them into my mouth and close my eyes.

Did they always taste this bitter? For just a second, the pills sit on my tongue. Their coating starts to melt in the heat of my mouth, and I know that sweet release is only a few minutes away.

A sweet release that I haven't needed at all.

A sweet release that isn't so sweet when it ends.

A sweet release that isn't a release at all. It's a prison that I've built for myself, one pill at a time.

Strength wells up inside me from somewhere I didn't know existed. It starts in the depths of my chest, bubbling up through my veins and pushing the voice out of my head.

Leaning over the toilet, I spit the painkillers out and flush the toilet in one frantic, panicked motion. I pant over the bowl, watching the pills swirl away.

Spitting into the rushing water, I let a string of drool fall down from my lips. My chest heaves and I squeeze my eyes shut. Tears drip into the toilet bowl, and I fall to my knees.

My tongue feels numb. A bitter coating covers my mouth, and I spit into the bowl again.

I don't remember that feeling with the pills before. Is it because I kept them on my tongue instead of swallowing them down this time?

Reaching for the pill bottle, I read the label.

They're the same painkillers I've been taking for months. I run my fingers over the seal, remembering that it was broken.

Shaking my head, I lean back against the bathroom wall.

It doesn't matter if they were the same pills or not. They're gone now.

I probably never noticed the bitterness because I was taking them all the time. I toss the bottle into the trash and lean my head back against the wall...

...and I think of Ivy. She's the only poison I need. The only poison I want rushing through my veins is her.

Letting out a breath, I squeeze my eyes shut.

A prickling sensation starts in the tips of my fingers and the soles of my feet. I groan, slumping onto my side on the bathroom floor.

You should have taken them. You were stupid, stupid, stupid. Now, you have nothing to dull the pain.

Sucking a breath in through my teeth, I push myself up and stand. Stripping down, I walk into the shower and turn the water on as hot as it'll go. I wash myself and think of Ivy until the prickling sensation goes away, and the voice quiets down.

When I walk out of the shower, steam billows around me and fogs up every surface in the bathroom. Wiping my hand across the mirror, I stare into my own eyes again.

Clear.

My heart feels calm. I look down at the empty pill bottle, discarded in the trash can, and a smile drifts over my lips.

The fog in my own mind has cleared. With a towel hanging around my hips, I walk out into the bedroom and stare out at the bright sunshine streaming through the window.

For the first time since as long as I can remember, the monkey isn't on my back. Addiction's claws aren't embedded in my flesh.

I'm free.

25

IVY

MARGOT'S FACE is a scary shade of grey. White, frothy spittle gathers at the edges of her mouth. Her hands are curled near her chest where she lies at the foot of the bed. Drag marks in the rug make it look like she's crawled there from the window.

I freeze.

It's only for a second—less than a second, even—but it feels like an eternity. I stand at the door to my sister's room, trying to make sense of the scene before me.

My blood turns cold. There's a tingling in my lips, and I lose sensation in the tips of my fingers.

Then, a scream sounds, and after a moment, I realize it's coming from me.

I dive toward Margot, grabbing her shoulders and screaming her name. I slap her face—harder than I intended—and her head lolls to the side.

My throat is raw. My stomach has dropped so far down I almost expect to see it in a bloody heap on the floor.

Sheer, white terror grips my chest, like barbed wire tightening around my lungs. I scream again, scrambling to find my phone. I realize it's downstairs in the kitchen, and despairs starts to tear me apart.

I scan the room, but the edges of my vision are going black.

That's when I remember to take a breath.

I suck in some air through gritted teeth, teetering onto my feet as I look for my sister's cell phone. Lunging for it, I grab it from the bedside table. It slips through my fingers and goes flying across her rug.

"Hang on, Margot," I rasp, crawling to the phone.

My fingers tremble so hard, I misdial the emergency number the first two times I try. Finally, it rings. I hold the phone between my shoulder and my ear and scoot back to Margot, cradling her head in my lap.

A calm, female voice comes on the other side of the line. Her words sound hazy, like she's speaking to me from far away. All I can see is Margot's skin, grey and listless, and the way her eyes are rolled back in her head.

Somehow, I manage to tell the emergency services where I am. I think I put Margot on her side, following the woman's instructions.

It's a blur.

All I know is that when the paramedics burst through the room, Margot still hasn't breathed.

The paramedics ask me a thousand and one questions, and suddenly my sister's bedroom is a flurry of activities.

"Jim," one of the paramedics says to the other, holding up a syringe and a little bag of powder. I frown, staring at the two items.

A syringe.

Whitish-brown powder.

A syringe.

Whitish-brown powder.

My eyes flick from one item to the other, not understanding what I'm looking at.

"Heroin. Might be laced with something," the man says.

Jim, the other paramedic, nods. "OD. I'll get the naloxone." His hands move as he speaks, pulling out a sterile syringe from a pocket of his bag.

"OD?" I repeat. "Heroin?"

What the hell is going on?

The paramedics brush me out of the way with surprising gentleness, and I stand by the wall to watch them work. I have to look away when they inject my sister with the drug, lifting her shorts up to deliver it to the muscle of her outer thigh.

"What's that?" My voice trembles as I squeeze my eyes shut.

"It reverses the effect of opiates," Jim answers. The two paramedics work on my sister, speaking to each other in curt, professional voices.

It's a normal day for them. Work. Another day on the job.

Me, on the other hand?

My world is shattering all around me. It's like someone taking a sledgehammer to a snow globe, pulverizing it into a million pieces as I watch.

Opening my eyes again, I see one paramedic put his fingers to Margot's neck, listening for a pulse. He looks at his coworker and nods.

"Got it."

Jim looks at his watch. "Three minutes until the next injection. Let's get her on the stretcher." He looks at me. "Ma'am, would you like to ride with us?"

I nod, unable to speak.

This isn't real life. This is a dream. A nightmare. This isn't happening.

Everything is a dream. Ever since the very first night Margot went to the castle, I must have been asleep. This can't be real.

Heroin?

My sister?

As the paramedics carry her out of the room, her body firmly strapped to a board, I glance around my sister's room. The paramedics have taken the bag of drugs with them. Whether it's as evidence or just to be able to identify the drugs at the hospital to treat Margot, I'm not sure.

The rest of her room looks normal.

This is wrong. This isn't her. Something else happened.

I stumble on the steps on the way down. My legs are heavy. My tongue feels too big for my mouth, and I'm having trouble seeing straight. When the paramedics motion to the back of the ambulance, I stumble on the way up and smack the side of my head on some equipment.

"Oopsie-daisy," Jim says, pulling me into the ambulance. "Sit."

Oopsie-daisy?

He gives me a piece of gauze and instructs me to hold it to the side of my head while he clicks a seatbelt over my lap. Then, he and his partner secure Margot into the ambulance, and the sirens go on.

Jim sits beside me, peeling the gauze off my face. I stare at Margot, seeing nothing.

The paramedic's touch is gentle as he cleans the wound on my forehead, patching it up with a small bandage.

"Shouldn't need any stitches," he says with a sad smile.

"What's going on?" My voice doesn't sound like my own. It's scratchy, like my throat has been ripped to shreds from the inside. I motion to Margot, shaking my head. "What's... How..."

Tears sting my eyes, and I don't have the energy to brush them away.

"Your sister overdosed," Jim explains. "We've been seeing more and more of these in the past few weeks. Fentanyl has started making its way into the heroin supply in Farcliff. We think it's coming up through the border with the U.S."

"My sister doesn't do heroin," I spit, even though the evidence in front of my face suggests otherwise. I shake my head. "She doesn't."

Jim lets out a sigh, patting my knee. The ambulance lurches as we speed through the streets.

Tears fall from my eyes, but I don't feel them. I don't sob. The only reason I know I'm crying is because the tears drip onto my lap, my hands, my arms. I hug my stomach, staring at my sister.

Jim's watch goes off, and he swipes a sterile wipe on Margot's leg. Then, in a practiced movement, he injects her thigh again.

"What's that?" I croak.

"It's the same drug we used earlier. It doesn't last forever, so we need to make sure her heart keeps beating until we get her to the hospital."

We have to make sure her heart keeps beating.

Because she took heroin.

Laced with fentanyl.

And overdosed.

Closing my eyes, I try to keep the bad thoughts at bay. The whispering, evil voices that tell me I should have seen it. I should have stopped it. I should have known.

The voices that tell me I was too busy worrying about my virginity and the Prince to notice my own sister was in trouble.

The slithering, hissing voices that tell me it's my fault. If I wasn't so jealous of her, I would have seen the signs. If I didn't resent my own sister so much, I could have saved her.

If I wasn't so selfish, I would have seen this coming.

When we stop outside the hospital emergency department, I follow the paramedics inside and shield my eyes against the glare of the fluorescent lights.

The smell of rubber, sanitizer, and that unique smell of hospital hits me. A nurse puts her hand on my arm and says kind words, but all I can hear is the voice that tells me this is all my fault.

26

LUCA

BREAKFAST IS SERVED in the casual dining room at Farcliff Castle. 'Casual' might be the wrong word for it. I'm greeted by a long banquet table laden with silver platters, piled high with all manner of treats and delicacies. There aren't as many priceless paintings on the wall as the formal dining room, though, and the chairs are more comfortable.

When I walk into the room, Beckett's head whips toward me.

"L-Luca," he stammers, unable to contain his shock.

I arch an eyebrow. "Surprised to see me?"

Scanning the long table, I look for the special cinnamon buns with little chunks of apple in them. Not seeing them right away, I walk the length of the table.

Beckett's eyes follow me. "I wasn't expecting to see you this morning."

I glance up at him. "No?"

His face looks dark. His eyes are nearly black.

I look away from my little brother, not wanting him to dampen my spirits. I don't have time for his moodiness this morning. I'm too happy for that.

Not seeing the cinnamon buns, I opt for some scrambled eggs. I nod to the chef in the white hat, standing behind a portable stove. He cracks a couple of eggs and starts whisking them with a pair of chopsticks right in the pan.

Beckett appears by my side. "How are you feeling?"

His eyes search mine, and unease crawls up my spine. I turn away from him, ignoring the sour taste that coats the back of my throat.

The chef hands me a plate of steaming scrambled eggs, which I accept with a nod.

Beckett's eyes follow me as I find a seat at the edge of the room. Finally, when I refuse to meet his gaze, my brother stalks out of the room with his shoulders hunched.

I shake my head, turning back to my eggs. At least he's leaving Farcliff tomorrow. I won't have to deal with his moods and irrational jealousy about Margot LeBlanc.

When I look up again, Prince Damon is standing in front of me. He's wearing a broad smile. The Prince sits down across from me, stretching his legs out and sipping a cup of coffee.

"I've organized a tour of the hospital for today, if you'd like to join. We'll start in the pediatric ward. Dahlia and I would love to have you around—the kids at the hospital might be a good audience for our tour. They tend to be a little more forgiving than adults."

I nod. "Sounds good, Your Highness."

"I think we're on a first-name basis now," he grins. Damon turns his head when Dahlia enters the room, and his face lights up. "Got to go," he grins. "I'm giving Dahlia some bike riding lessons this morning."

"She doesn't know how to ride a bike?"

"Don't ask," he grins. "The car will be ready at noon to take us to the hospital."

Watching them leave, something tugs at my chest. It's the same thing that always happens when I see Damon and Dahlia together. A hint of jealousy and longing. I want what they have.

I know exactly who I want it with.

After breakfast, I wander down to the kitchens. Glancing inside the dessert room, I frown when I don't see Ivy. The head chef pushes the door open and bows to me when he spots me.

"Have you seen Miss LeBlanc?" I ask.

George shakes his head. "*Non*, Your Highness." His French accent gives his voice a musical lilt. "She didn't come in for work today. Her *téléphone* number isn't working, either."

I frown, nodding. "Thanks."

The sour taste in my mouth gets stronger, and a chill passes down my spine. I try to ignore the tingling in my hands, and the feeling that something is very, very wrong.

DAMON IS RIGHT—KIDS are a good audience. When I tell them the story of my accident and my recovery, their eyes are wide as saucers and their lips drop open. One little boy's hand shoots up in the air.

"Yes?" I ask, nodding to him.

"Did you lose feeling in your legs?"

"Everything from the waist down," I nod.

"Did you pee your pants?" He tilts his head, and titters escape a few of the children. The boy's friend nudges him.

I smile sadly. "Sometimes."

All the kids' eyes widen. "Really?"

I nod. "I had to wear a device called a catheter, or a little tube that helped me pee. With the doctor's help, I was able to regain control of my urge to pee. Let me tell you, that almost felt better than learning to walk again," I grin, glancing at Damon and the staff. Damon smiles at me, nodding.

The children giggle, and one little girl walks over to wrap her little arms around me, planting a sloppy kiss on my cheek. My heart melts.

Our visit to the pediatric ward reminds me how grateful I am to be able to walk again. In all my weeks and months of focusing on Cara and everything I've lost, I'd forgotten what I've actually gained.

My health. My mobility. My ability to control my own bladder.

Ivy.

I thought my time in Farcliff would be a quick, painful stop on my way home to Argyle. I thought it would be torture to pretend to be polite to these people, all the while watching my brother parade his new wife around in front of me.

In reality, my visit to Farcliff has been incredible. I've realized that Cara's betrayal isn't as crushing as I thought it was. I've overcome so much already—why would I let one woman tear me down?

Thinking of Cara turns my mind to Ivy. That's another surprise that came with Farcliff. I thought, at best, I'd have some fun with Margot LeBlanc. It would be good for my public image to get people to stop talking about Cara, and to start talking about another woman. I thought, selfishly, I could make Cara jealous.

I never thought I'd meet someone I actually care about.

A smile drifts over my lips as I think of her smile, her snark, everything about her that makes me feel alive again.

Then, just as my heart starts to thump, Ivy turns the corner in the hospital.

Her tear-streaked face is pale, with big splotches of red on her skin. She has a bandage near her temple. Her eyes are hazy, and her hair is a bird's nest. She's wringing her hands, keeping her eyes trained on a door just behind me.

I stop in my tracks, and the two bodyguards assigned to me pause.

"Sir?" one of them asks.

I ignore him. "Ivy?"

When she turns her head to look at me, her gaze knocks me back. Her eyes, usually so bright, are full of darkness and pain. She puts her hand to her neck, curling her fingers as if she's trying to claw her own throat out. Her mouth opens in a silent cry, and my whole body turns cold.

Something's very, very wrong.

"Ivy," I repeat, taking a step toward her.

She inhales then. It's a deep, shuddering breath that makes my blood turn to ice. As I take another step toward her, Ivy collapses into my arms with a sob.

"Margot," she says between rattling breaths. "It's Margot."

I clutch her to my chest as my heart cracks. The pain in Ivy's face is unbearable.

"Where is she?"

Ivy nods to the door, wiping her face with her hands. She takes a breath, glancing around at the royal procession. Everyone has stopped to watch, from the hospital staff, to the bodyguards, to Damon and Dahlia.

Ivy's face reddens, and she ducks her head. "I'm sorry," she whispers, and disappears through her sister's hospital room door.

27

IVY

MARGOT'S ROOM IS DARK. The doctors gave her a sedative, so she's lying in the bed, immobile. I sink into a chair next to her and let my tears fall from my eyes.

She's out of danger now, but her bloodstream was full of powerful drugs.

I never saw any of it.

Never guessed that she was using.

Never wondered if she was unhappy.

Never asked her if she was okay.

I mean...heroin?! Who...?

I shake my head.

Guilt and shame churn in my stomach until I feel like I'm going to throw up. I've been so busy feeling sorry for myself —so busy being jealous of my sister's supposedly 'perfect' life —that I haven't even seen how much she's suffering.

More recently, I've been too busy being a horny, hormone-addled mess with love goggles on to notice that she was spiraling.

How long has she been using? People don't just start with

heroin. She must have done lots of drugs in the past couple of years. How did I miss it?

Turning my head when the door opens, I see Prince Luca in the doorway. He steps inside without a word, closing the door behind him.

Kneeling in front of me, the Prince wraps his arms around my waist and pulls me into his chest. I melt into him, allowing myself to cry for just a little bit longer.

Luca doesn't say a word. He just holds me until I can take a full breath again.

"Are they waiting for you?" I ask, nodding to the door.

Luca shakes his head. "I sent everyone away. I'm staying here with you."

"Luca..."

"Stop. Stop pushing me away. Stop telling me that we can't be together. You need me right now, and I'm not leaving your side."

He holds my cheeks in his hands, staring deep into my eyes. His thumbs brush the last of my tears away, and I nod gently.

"Okay," I whisper.

Luca sits in a chair and pulls me onto his lap. I lay my head on his shoulder, and I tell him what the doctors said. I tell them about the drugs they found in her system. Heroin, and the one that they think caused her to overdose, fentanyl.

"I've heard of fentanyl," the Prince says, stroking my hair.

"What is it?"

"It's a synthetic opioid. Really strong, and really, really dangerous. In Argyle, it's becoming a serious problem. Dealers are mixing it with cocaine, heroin, methamphetamines, you name it. They're making it into pills." He shakes his head. "People overdose often. Your sister isn't the only one."

"How do you know that?"

The Prince lets out a sigh. "I've taken my fair share of drugs—including opioids. When the doctors wouldn't give me enough morphine to dull the pain, I looked elsewhere." He kisses my temple.

"You took fentanyl?" My throat tightens at the thought of the Prince ending up in my sister's position. My body stiffens.

He shakes his head. "No, thank goodness. At least I had a bit of sense left in this thick head of mine."

Relaxing into his chest, I let out a sigh.

The Prince stays with me for hours, stroking my head and holding me until we both doze off in the chair. A nurse unceremoniously wakes us up as the sun goes down.

"Visiting hours are over, folks," she says, checking Margot's IV bag and marking something down on a chart.

"I want to stay." My voice is strangled.

The nurse lets out a sigh and turns to face me. "I'm sorry, sweetheart. You can't."

Prince Luca squeezes my hand, and we both stand up. He puts his arm around my shoulders and leads me out of the room. When we get to the lobby, tears fill my eyes.

"I can't go back to that house, Luca. I can't. I know I'll just be seeing visions of her on the floor. Her skin grey, her lips blue..." I shake my head. "I can't."

"Come on," he says, leading me out of the hospital. "I'll take you to the castle."

I don't have the energy to think about the ramifications of that. The tiredness has settled deep in my marrow, and I let the Prince lead me to his car.

I could blame tiredness completely, but the truth is that it feels good to lean on him. I've always been the one to provide support for my sister, for my mother, even my father at times. I've always been the strong one.

Now, I don't feel strong.

I need help.

With Luca's gentle touch, his kind eyes, and his warm embrace, I know I can't resist him—and I don't want to.

THAT NIGHT, when I climb into Prince Luca's bed, I'm worried he'll want to have sex. He emerges from the bathroom and slips into bed beside me, but his hands don't wander. He wraps them around me and kisses the top of my head.

He knows I can't have sex with him right now.

Even in the morning, when I wake up to his erection poking me in the back, he just lays a soft kiss on my forehead and rolls over to get up.

We spend a week like that as Margot recovers in the hospital. Prince Luca becomes my rock, and I lean on his support more than I ever imagined I would. His kisses are soft, and tender, and his touch is nothing but loving.

By the end of the week, when the haze of panic and sadness starts to lift, I look at him with new eyes.

He's not the rough, sexy, irresistible man I thought he was. He's rough, and sexy, and irresistible, of course—but that's not everything he is. He's caring. Thoughtful. Supportive. His strength gets me through one of the worst weeks of my life, and every time he drops me off at the hospital and drives away to deal with his own responsibilities, I miss his presence beside me.

Margot doesn't speak much. She avoids my gaze, and her eyes are dim. Her skin, usually bright and glowing, is sallow and sunken.

I spend every day with her, even though she tells me I don't need to. By the end of the week, Margot is strong enough to sit up and move around on her own.

On the day she's going to be discharged, my beautiful, bright sister looks at me with a determined set to her jaw.

"The doctor told me about a facility in the countryside. It's kind of like rehab, except mostly just a therapy retreat. Since I'm not a regular user, they recommended I go there."

My heart flips. "Really?"

Margot nods. "I need help. I don't even remember anything about that night. The doctor said that can happen with trauma and overdoses, but... I don't know. I have a bad feeling." Her face darkens, and she shakes her head. "I need to get out of Farcliff."

"I'm proud of you, Margot."

She gives me a tight smile. "I don't deserve you."

Throwing my arms around my sister, I nuzzle my head into her neck. I blink back tears, because I don't want her to see me cry right now. I need to be strong for Margot, too.

"No word from Dad?" she asks when I pull away.

I shake my head. "I left a message at his house in the Bahamas, but they said he's on a cross-Atlantic sailing trip."

"Figures," Margot grins. "It's just you and me, then. As usual."

"Wouldn't have it any other way."

That night, Margot and I go home. It's the first night that I sleep in my own bed in over a week. I toss and turn all night, missing the weight of the Prince's arm across my body.

The next day, I drive Margot to the facility. It's about halfway between Farcliff and Westhill, the country castle where Prince Gabriel stays most of the year. Margot will spend ninety days isolated from everything and everyone, working on herself. She'll have no access to internet, and only have dedicated phone call times when we can talk.

It'll be a detox from drugs, alcohol, and every vice, but

also from the fame and scrutiny that crushes her on a daily basis.

My sister looks scared, but she puts on a brave smile and wraps her arms around me. "Thank you, Ivy. I'm sorry for causing you pain."

"Stop it," I say, sniffling. "Just get yourself better."

Margot nods. Her long hair is tied back in a ponytail, and her face is free of makeup. She looks tired, yet gorgeous. My sister turns away from me and follows one of the center's staff down a long, carpeted corridor. I watch her disappear, feeling equally devastated and proud.

Devastated, because my sister isn't the person I thought she was, and because I was too self-absorbed to see that she needed my help.

Proud, because my sister was able to walk into this facility with her head held high. She's facing her demons head-on, without hesitation.

Would I have done the same?

I'm not sure.

I drive back to Farcliff in silence, drumming my hands on the steering wheel. When I get home, I swap the car for my scooter. I need to feel the air whipping around my face, and the freedom of having two wheels underneath me.

I drive aimlessly through the Farcliff countryside until the sun starts to go down. When I make it back to my own house, I feel calmer than I have since this whole ordeal started. I park my scooter on the side of our mansion, and jingle my keys in my hand as I head toward the front door.

Prince Luca is sitting on my front porch. He lifts his head and smiles at me, relief evident on his face.

"I was worried about you," he says, wrapping his arms around me. "I missed you last night."

"Me too." My voice is muffled in his broad chest.

"I have a surprise for you."

I pull away to look at the Prince's face.

Luca's eyes glimmer, and he nods to the driveway. "Come on. I have something to show you."

28

LUCA

I T TOOK a lot of string-pulling to get this surprise organized in just one week, but seeing Ivy in pain was enough motivation for me to do it.

I drive through the streets of Farcliff City toward the main shopping district. Parking the car on a side street, I produce a blindfold and dangle it in front of Ivy.

"Put this on."

"I'm scared," she grins, taking the blindfold. "What are you planning?"

"Just put it on," I laugh, taking the silk blindfold from her and securing it around her eyes. I jog around the front of the car and open the door for her, helping her out.

Leading her down the street, I take a set of keys out of my pocket, jingling to tease her. Ivy titters, squeezing my hand. Then, I unlock the back door of the shop. Ivy stumbles over the threshold, but I catch her before she falls. Taking her hand, I can't keep the smile from my face. I lead her down a narrow hallway and into the main kitchens.

Ivy's pulse is hammering. I can see it thumping in her

neck as I stand behind her, wrapping my arms around her waist.

"You ready?" I whisper in her ear.

Ivy bites her lip. "I'm not sure." She smiles, and my heart does a flip. I've seen far too few smiles from her this week.

Hopefully this surprise will remedy that.

I pull the blindfold off her head and take a step back. Ivy pauses, looking around the room. Gleaming stainless steel counters stare back at her, complete with a row of brand-new ovens, industrial stand mixers, molds, pans, bowls, utensils, and everything else that she could possibly need to start her bakery.

Ivy's jaw drops. She spins in a slow circle, taking everything in, and finally letting her gaze land on me.

"What is this place?"

"This is *Spoonful of Sugar*."

Ivy frowns. "What?"

I laugh, kissing the tip of her nose. Nodding to the swinging door, I guide her out into the shopfront. I start pointing. "This is where you'll display all your incredible baked goods. That's where customers will walk in. This is where you'll take their orders, and that's where they'll pay."

Ivy's breath hitches. Tears cloud her eyes as her fingers come up to cover her mouth. Her eyes drift up to the sign above our heads. I've had it commissioned with the logo she sketched.

"Luca," she whispers.

"It's yours, Ivy." I wrap my arms around her shoulders. "The lease on this place is paid for three years. I was hoping it would be fully finished, but the painters are in next week, and the main sign out front is still being manufactured. I just got impatient and I wanted to show you right away. I have some tables and chairs on order, as well, and they're arriving in three days. I figure it'll take us a few weeks, maybe a month, to get this place finished and get the menu finalized so you can open." I go to the cash register and pull her folder out from the shelf underneath. "I hope you don't mind, I broke into your pool house and borrowed this."

"My dream folder."

"Your reality folder," I grin. "I haven't purchased any ingredients yet, because I didn't know if you were particular about types of flour and sugar, or whatever." I shrug. "I don't know anything about baking."

Ivy is still standing there, letting her eyes wander over the whole place. Finally, she looks at me and her face breaks into a smile. She throws her arms around my neck. I stumble back, catching myself on the display case as I laugh.

"Luca! Oh my goodness..." Ivy pulls back, threading her fingers through my hair. "This is the most amazing thing anyone has ever done for me. I don't deserve this."

"Stop." I shake my head, tightening my grip on her waist. "Stop right there. You deserve every bit of it. I haven't known you a long time, but in the time that I've known you, all you've done is live your life for other people. You can't put your dreams on hold forever. You deserve this, and you're going to do an amazing job."

Tears stream down Ivy's face, and I brush them away with the pads of my thumbs. I press my lips to hers, feeling the way she trembles against me. Ivy clings onto me, burying her face into my neck. She sobs, and I just hold her until she starts to laugh, peppering me with kisses as laughter tumbles out between us.

Shaking her head, she leans against my chest and looks around again. "I thought everything was falling apart when Margot got admitted to the hospital. I didn't know what I'd do for the next ninety days. This is beyond my wildest expectations."

"You'd better put those cinnamon buns on the menu."

Ivy giggles, nodding. "I will. I'll call them Luca Buns." She reaches around to grab my ass, squeezing it with a giggle. "I feel like such a horrible person for saying this, but the fact that Margot is away for ninety days makes me feel a bit relieved—like I can throw myself into this bakery without feeling bad about it." With a sigh, Ivy rubs her hands against her face. "That's a terrible thing to say."

"Sometimes, the truth isn't pretty." I wrap my arms around her and pull her in for a kiss. "And sometimes, you have to take care of yourself—that includes your own dreams and your own aspirations."

"You don't think I'm an awful person for being glad that my sister is in rehab—or celebrity therapy retreat or whatever you want to call it—so I can start my own business? Because I feel like an awful person for saying that."

"I think you need to take care of yourself. You're just as important as your sister. You're human, and you're perfect."

My heart thumps when I look into Ivy's eyes. She thinks that I've done all this for her, but the truth is, I did it because she makes me want to do something good. Watching her take care of her sister has made me realize that I've been living my life in my own head. I don't remember the last time I did anything purely for someone else, just for the sake of it.

Ivy makes me want to be better, and seeing the happiness in her face makes it all worth it.

Taking her by the hand, I lead her out from behind the counter. The tables and chairs haven't arrived yet, but I spread out a blanket and pillows that I've prepared. Popping a bottle of champagne, I settle Ivy down on the blanket and disappear into the back.

I grab the picnic basket one of the royal chefs put together from the fridge and bring it out to Ivy. A smile breaks across her face when she sees me carrying the basket, and she shakes her head.

"You really planned this out, didn't you?"

"I wanted to treat you how you deserve to be treated, Ivy. Make you see what I see in you."

Gathering her in my arms, I press my lips against hers. When she lets out a soft sigh, a shiver of excitement passes through my body.

For the past week, I haven't done much more than hold her and kiss her. It wasn't the right time. She needed me to be there for her, to support her and love her—not to pressure her into having sex.

Now, though, in Ivy's new bakery, with the windows covered in paper and our picnic blanket spread out, the familiar desire is rising inside me again. I take Ivy's lips in mine, deepening our kiss as I tangle my fingers into her hair.

When Ivy moves to straddle me, I let out a soft groan.

"You're incredible, Poison."

"I haven't done anything."

I smile, words sticking to my throat.

What I want to tell her is that she's saved me from myself. She's saved me from the same demon that claimed her sister. She's made me realize that I'm incredibly fortunate—not only to be able to walk again, but to be able to give my time and money to people who need it. Whether it's the kids at the hospital, or the people who will come to Damon's tour, or Ivy's new bakery.

She's incredible, because she's been selfless and brave and supportive to her sister.

Now, it's time for me to do the same for her.

29

IVY

THE FEELING of Luca's hands on my body is making my skin tingle. He runs his fingers up under my shirt, sending a trail of sparks flying off my skin. A million tiny lightning bolts follow the movement of his hands, and my heart takes off at full speed.

Even as we kiss, I know I'm going to give myself to him.

Here, on the floor of my new bakery, on a bed of pillows with the Prince of Argyle, I'm going to lose my virginity.

It's perfect, and it feels like everything I've been waiting for.

Luca lets out a low growl, pulling my chest against his. I wrap my arms around his neck and crush my lips against his, feeling the fire ignite in my veins as I think of what I'm about to do. Pulling Luca's shirt off over his head, I trail my fingers over the ridges and valleys of his muscles. I trace the outline of his pecs, running my fingertips over his collarbone.

The Prince leans against the wall and lets out a soft growl. His fingertips sink into my waist. I start to slowly grind my hips against him.

Sucking my lip between my teeth, I force myself to meet his gaze. The Prince's eyes are hooded, promising sin and sweetness.

"Poison Ivy," he breathes. "What are you doing to me?"

"Whatever you want me to," I whisper. My cheeks flush as soon as the words slip out of my mouth. When did I get so dirty?

The Prince doesn't mind, though. Quite the opposite. He lets out a moan, picking me up and flipping me onto my back. My head lands on a pillow and I giggle, wrapping my arms around his neck.

With Luca's legs nestled between mine, he starts to grind against me. Even the movement of his hips is making my body temperature increase. My heart starts to bounce against my ribcage, doing its best to hammer its way out. Every time Luca touches me, I feel like I'm melting in his hands.

Leaving a trail of kisses down my jaw, the Prince brushes his lips over my collarbone. I shiver, arching my back toward him. His hands work to unbutton my pants as his eyes look up to mine.

Luca arches an eyebrow, and he doesn't have to speak for me to know what he's asking.

Sucking my bottom lip between my teeth, I nod my head.

"You want to?" he breathes.

I nod. "Yes."

When he slides his hand into my underwear, we both moan. I buck my hips up to meet his hand, unable to contain my excitement.

Is this how it always is, I wonder? The electricity in the air, the feeling like a spark would set this whole place off?

What's it like for normal people when they make love?

Do they feel this burning ball of heat in the pit of their stomach?

The *need* inside me is something I've never experienced before. I need to kiss him. Bite him. Touch him. I need to feel his fingers inside me. I need to have his cock in my hand.

All my embarrassment evaporates with the Prince. I'm no longer the inexperienced, virgin girl with the hot sister. With Luca, I'm everything. He makes me feel sexy and sensual. He makes me feel completely comfortable to spread my legs for him, like all my dirtiest secrets are exactly what he wants to hear.

I close my eyes, reaching down between his legs to rub his length over his pants. When he slides his fingers inside me, I think of what we did in the pool cabana, what we did on the yacht, what we did in every dark corner of Farcliff Castle when no one was looking...what I've been dreaming of doing with him since the first day I met him.

I never thought I would say this, but I want to suck his cock, even though I used to think it was gross. I want him to eat me out, even though I always thought it would be uncomfortable. I want to feel his hands everywhere, anywhere.

I want his cock inside me.

I want it all.

When he tugs my pants down my thighs, I kick them off and push them out of the way. The Prince kneels in front of me, and I feast my eyes on his rugged, ripped body. When his hands slide over the inside of my thighs, tingles of pleasure chase his touch. He spreads my knees wide, staring between my legs with a look of absolute pleasure on his face.

I blush, but not because I'm embarrassed. I blush because I never want him to stop looking at me like that.

When his tongue slides through my slit, I let out a gasp. I rough my hands through the Prince's hair and grind myself against his face.

I've never done that, either, and for a second I'm worried

I'm being too rough—but the Prince hooks his arms around my thighs and pulls me into him, groaning as I grind into him.

I'm breathless. I squeeze my eyes shut, hanging onto him as he devours me. When he slips his fingers inside me, I explode. I clamp my thighs around his ears and ride his face as the Prince brings me to orgasm. He moans with me, and when it's over, the look in his eyes tells me he enjoyed that almost as much as I did.

As my chest heaves, my eyes drop down to the bulge in his pants. The Prince looks at me, and then hooks his thumbs into his waistband and pulls his pants off.

When his cock springs free, my breath catches.

"You sure you want this?" the Prince asks, leaning over to kiss me. The tip of his cock brushes against me, and a shiver of desire rips through me.

"Yes," I answer between kisses.

I'm sure. I've never been surer of anything.

Prince Luca reaches into his pants and pulls out a condom. I watch, fascinated, as he rolls it onto his length. When he positions himself at my opening, I feel oddly calm.

I thought I'd be nervous right now. Maybe freaking out or afraid of the pain.

All I feel is complete peace.

This is right. This is exactly how it's supposed to happen.

Slowly, gently, the Prince pushes himself inside me. My eyes start to water and I lean into the pillows, squeezing them shut.

"Am I hurting you?"

"A little," I rasp, breathless. "But it's okay."

The Prince's hands caress my body, and he lays soft kisses over my neck as he slides himself inside me. It hurts more than I expected, but I don't want him to stop. I let my knees fall open and sink my fingers into his shoulders. With my nails digging into him, the Prince pushes himself inside me with a groan.

"You okay?" He kisses my earlobe.

I nod. I don't trust my voice. My muscles relax, and my heartbeat slows a touch, and the Prince starts to move his hips.

He grunts, his breath washing over my skin like a hot breeze. I hang onto him, and with every passing second, the pain lessens, until it's gone. In its place is a deep, pulsing heat. I arch my back, mimicking his movements as the pleasure starts to flood my veins.

I moan when he thrusts inside me again, the friction of his body against mine sending pulsing light through my veins.

"I'm going to come, baby," Luca says in my ear. "I'm sorry, I can't last. You feel too good."

"Come, Your Highness." I arch my back, spreading my legs to accept his length. He rocks himself inside me again and again.

I gasp when I feel him come. I didn't think I'd be able to feel it—but I do. His body contracts, and the noises he makes send a shiver of pleasure down to my toes.

When it's over, I'm a little glad it didn't last any longer than it did. I can already tell I'm going to be sore. But the Prince pulls out of me and wraps his arms around me, cradling me into his chest.

"That felt incredible, Ivy," he breathes.

I nod, and a smile drifts over my lips. It did feel incredible —but not because I had a mind-blowing orgasm. I didn't come with him inside me, but it doesn't matter. It feels like we've forged a connection that can't be broken.

We signed that oath on the floor of the bakery that will shape my future.

I'm his, and he's mine.

Forever.

30

LUCA

"Shit. The condom broke." I pull the latex off my cock and reach for a napkin from the picnic basket. Glancing at Ivy, I arch an eyebrow. "You were too tight."

Ivy blushes, glancing down between her legs.

"No blood, either," I note, frowning.

"I broke my hymen riding a bike when I was fourteen," Ivy says, grinning. "Sorry to disappoint you. I promise you were my first."

"Nothing you do could ever disappoint me."

Excitement curls in the pit of my stomach at the thought of being her first. I've never taken anyone's virginity before. Glancing down at Ivy's body, I let my hands wander up to her stomach.

No one else has touched her like this. No one else has been inside her, or felt her the way I have. It feels special, like we share something that no one can take away from us.

Laying back on the pillows, I stare up at the ceiling of Ivy's new bakery. I glance over at her, pulling her in to lay on my chest.

"Did you come?" I ask, burying my face in her hair.

"Once," she says. "When you...did that thing with your mouth."

I chuckle. "When I ate your pussy?"

"Yeah. That."

"Not after?"

Ivy shakes her head. "No, but it's okay. I'm sure it'll happen. I'm just glad to get the first one out of the way."

I smile. "What was it like?"

Even without looking at her, I can tell she's chewing her lip. Ivy takes a deep breath, and then shrugs. "Felt like a big ball of fire was sitting in the pit of my stomach, and all I wanted you to do was be inside me."

"Similar to how I felt, then," I sigh, pulling her close.

THE NEXT FEW weeks are pure bliss. When I'm not doing talks with Damon and Dahlia, I'm at *Spoonful of Sugar*. Ivy stocks the shelves with all the supplies she needs and starts baking as soon as she sets foot inside the kitchen.

"I need to get to know these ovens," she tells me when I ask why she's baking so much so far ahead of the Grand Opening in a month's time.

There's so much to do that I never would have expected. Packaging, labels, business registration, setting up the accounting systems, planning the menu—Ivy attacks it with enthusiasm I've rarely seen before.

George, the pastry chef from the castle, comes to visit one day in the week before the Grand Opening. I had no idea Ivy had made such an impression on him, but he immediately rolls up his sleeves and helps her tweak one of her recipes.

Ivy's cheeks are rosy, her hair is full of flour, her eyes are bright, and she's the most gorgeous woman I've ever seen.

I usually spend nights at Ivy's house, when I'm not traveling for the tour. No one misses me at the castle. Beckett leaves to rejoin Theo, Cara, and Dante in Argyle, and I'm free to do as I please.

Namely, spend every waking hour with a black-haired beauty.

THE MORNING OF AUGUST 1ST, the Grand Opening, Ivy rolls over in bed and plants a kiss on my cheek. It's just over a month since Margot was admitted into rehab, and the past four weeks have been incredible. It's been peaceful, and joyous—and *happy*.

Perhaps most surprisingly, I haven't taken a single painkiller. I've been in pain, of course. Sometimes it's almost unbearable—but I haven't wanted to numb anything. I know that if I take the drugs, it'll dull everything that's going on. The good and the bad.

Ivy tells me my kiss tastes better now that I'm smoking less weed, too. My kiss—and something else she's been enjoying tasting.

She snuggles into me, smiling. "Today is the day."

"What time is it?" I groan, opening my eyes just a slit.

"Four-thirty."

"In the morning?"

Ivy laughs. "Get used to it, buddy. Still happy you set up this bakery for me?"

Wrapping my arms around her, I pull Ivy into my chest. "Always, Poison."

We make love that morning, and I make sure to make her come. The look on Ivy's face when she orgasms with me inside her is something I cherish. I can't stop staring at Ivy's smile, her eyes, the light shining from her. When it's over, she lays back in bed and lets out a sigh. Reaching for her phone, Ivy grins at me.

"*Spoonful of Sugar* has over five thousand followers on Instagram already! We haven't even sold a single pastry yet. There's such a big buzz for the opening. I think all those free samples we gave out have worked." She glances at me, grinning. "And maybe all those rumors flying around that you've been in the bakery have helped, too."

"It's all you," I respond, kissing the tip of her nose.

Ivy leaves before I do, and I take my time getting ready. I don't want to steal her thunder by bringing paparazzi to the bakery, but I want to be supportive of her. Using the back streets, I make my way to the bakery. I pull a hat onto my head and slip some sunglasses on, rounding the corner right as Ivy opens the doors.

A smile drifts over my lips when I see the lineup of people waiting outside.

Ivy is beaming. She's wearing a red ribbon in her hair, and a t-shirt with her new bakery's logo on the front. Sweeping her arm toward the door, she welcomes the waiting customers in. Taking a few steps forward, I shake my head.

When we set up the interior of the bakery, Ivy insisted on having one corner of the room dedicated to social media. I thought it was silly, but she shook her head, and told me that she'd learned a thing or two in her time being Margot's assistant.

She had a swing installed in one corner, with a backdrop wall full of flowers. Lighting was installed especially with selfies in mind. People can sit on the swing with a cupcake in their hand, getting the perfect picture to post online.

I thought it was stupid—but I was wrong.

As I get closer to the building, I can already see influencers with multi-colored cupcakes posing next to the wall.

Ivy has moved behind the counter, and is serving clients with an ear-to-ear smile.

I slip inside the doorway, keeping my sunglasses on. Ivy's eyes lift up to mine, and her smile somehow widens. There's a hum of energy inside the bakery that warms my heart. She's already sold out of her special apple cinnamon buns, and a lot of the muffins and pastries are flying off the shelves.

George appears from the kitchen with another tray of baked goods, beaming at Ivy. Bread is stacked behind her, and the twins Georgina and Giselle are making coffee after coffee after coffee.

My heart feels light.

For the first time in years, I helped achieve something that wasn't for myself. Even the small part that I played in making this bakery come to life makes me feel like I've done something good, for once.

I slip out of the bakery again, and let my feet carry me down the main street. I glance at shops, restaurants, cafes, and I revel in being normal. No one is mobbing me, I don't have bodyguards, there aren't any paparazzi following me around.

I'm happier than I've been in years, and it's all because of Ivy.

31

IVY

AT THE END of the opening day of *Spoonful of Sugar*, my feet hurt, my whole body aches, and I can't keep the smile off my face. When the last customer leaves, I sink down into a chair and let out a sigh.

Giselle grins at me from the other side of the counter. She's leaning against it, her bright orange hair tied in two pigtails, with different silver rings on every finger.

"Not bad, Ivy. Sold out of almost everything except the fig and almond tarts."

"A few loaves of bread left, too," Georgina says, nodding at the baskets displayed behind her.

I shake my head. "If every day goes by like that, I don't know how I'm going to keep up."

"Well, you can always take us on full-time," Giselle grins. "I wouldn't mind working here a few days a week. Those influencers were hot." She grins, wiggling her eyebrows.

"Keep it in your pants," her twin replies, nudging her with her shoulder. "But seriously, we could ask the boys if they want to help out." 'The boys being their five brothers.

I glance at Georgina, arching my eyebrows. "Yeah?"

The twins exchange a glance. "The diner's not doing too well. I'm sure they'd appreciate the work."

My eyes widen. "Are you guys okay? Do you need money?"

Giselle laughs, hooking her arm around my shoulders. "Don't worry, Ivy. We're fine. Just be glad there's seven of us to help you out. Marcus and Mickey have experience in a bakery, and I'm sure Irving would love to expand his milk-shake brand to sell it here. You know we all love to work ourselves to the bone."

"Ask them to come in tomorrow," I say, excited. "I thought I'd have leftover pastries for tomorrow, but I'm going to have to prep a whole new batch."

"That's a good problem to have," Georgie grins. "You deserve it."

"Do I?" I ask, glancing around the bakery. My dream business landed in my lap. In the past month, my whole life has transformed.

A part of me feels guilty for doing this without Margot. She's tucked away in the forest, healing herself, and I'm here profiting off her absence.

She'd be happy for me, though. I know she would.

"Holy shit," Giselle says, staring at her phone. "You're trending, Ivy."

Turning her phone toward me, she shakes it from side to side.

"I am?"

I pull out the phone that Luca bought me, scrolling through my social media. I haven't had time to look at it all day, and my eyes nearly bug out of my head.

I have *thousands* of notifications. I've been tagged, reposted, liked, followed—you name it. *Spoonful of Sugar* is *everywhere*.

"Whoa."

Georgie squeals, jumping up and down. She hops over the counter, rushing toward me to wrap her arms around my shoulders. "Congrats, babe."

"Definitely ask your brothers if they want work," I laugh. The three of us glance at each other, and laughter starts bubbling up inside me. I throw my arms around my two best friends, still in shock over what my life has become.

"I'd better get to work," I say, wiping the tears of joy from my eyes.

"I'll help," Georgie nods, pulling an apron off a hook on the wall. "Let's prep."

THE GRAND OPENING of *Spoonful of Sugar* marks a huge change in my life. For the next sixty days, my life is complete bliss. I get up early, give Prince Luca a kiss on the cheek, and then bake for a few hours before the doors open. Every single day, we sell out of almost everything. Every single night, I work late, prepping for the next day.

I'm in my element.

For the first time in my life, people are congratulating *me*. They're flocking to *me*, not my sister. I don't love being the center of attention—but boy, do I love my pastries being in the spotlight. For once, it's not pictures of Margot that I see online. It's pictures of cinnamon buns and muffins and Danishes and tarts.

George ensures that I sign an ongoing contract with the castle, so that when he leaves to go back to Westhill Castle, the royal family will have a well-stocked breakfast and dessert table.

With the royal contract alone, *Spoonful of Sugar* can support itself.

Luca is supportive, loving, and attentive. His generosity with his time and love surprises me, and I lean on him more than I thought I ever could. It feels good to have someone by my side. I didn't realize how lonely I was until I met him.

He officially visits the bakery two weeks after it opens. With his presence comes even more media attention, and the major news outlet run a story on the opening of the bakery.

With the profits from the first couple of weeks, I'm able to hire the twins permanently, and get their brothers to help out, too. I expand the menu to include Irving's unforgettable milkshakes, and the added exposure gives the diner a bit of a boost, too.

As the days go on, tiredness sinks deep into my bones. I blame it on the late nights and early mornings. When I throw up a few mornings, I blame it on the stress. I have a lot on my plate. My body is used to working hard, but not this hard. I'm sure it'll adjust.

So, I just get to work. Week after week, I ignore the changes that are happening in my body. I gain a little weight, and I blame that on all the tasting and testing I do in the bakery.

When the first two whirlwind months of *Spoonful of Sugar*'s life comes to a close, I turn my attention to my sister. She's due to get out of rehab soon, and I'm giddy at the thought of showing her what I've accomplished.

I can't wait to see the look on her face when she sees the bakery—she's always talked about how much I should open my own shop.

I know she'll be happy for me...

...right?

THE DRIVE over to the therapy facility dampens my spirits

slightly. I drum my fingers on the steering wheel, chewing my lip as I wonder what will be waiting for me. I've spoken to Margot on the phone once a week, when she was allowed outside contact, but I haven't seen her in three months.

The leaves have started to change, and I'm sure it'll only be a few weeks until the first snow. It's nearly October, and I can't believe how much things have changed since that day in late May when I first met the Prince.

Now, I'm picking my sister up from an intensive therapy program.

Will she have changed?

Will she be happy?

Will she be healthy?

I park the car outside the facility and get out. A cool breeze whips around me as I walk toward the door, remind me that it's autumn, and it's about to get a lot colder out. I hug my arms to my chest and speed up, pushing the door and loving the relief of warmth inside the building.

Margot sits on a sofa with her hands folded on her lap, waiting. Her face breaks into a smile when she sees me. Her skin looks clear and bright, and her eyes look like her own again. Without the heavy makeup she used to wear, she looks like the sister I've been missing.

She's gained some weight, and she looks good. Healthy.

Tears fall from my eyes as I wrap Margot in a tight hug.

"It's good to see you," I say, staring into her eyes.

My sister smiles, nodding. "You too, Ivy. I've missed you." There are lines around her eyes and she looks wearier than she used to, but her gaze is clear.

"I have a surprise for you," I say. "But it's not urgent. If you want to go straight home, we can do that and leave the surprise until tomorrow."

"You know the curiosity would kill me." She laughs the

musical sort of way she used to, before there were always cameras stuck in her face. Before she became closed off and anxious all the time.

I thread my fingers through hers and bring her outside, but the flash of a camera makes my heart sink.

"Don't you have any fucking decency?" I shout at the paparazzi hiding in the bushes. "For fuck's sake."

Dragging my sister to the car, I get in as quickly as possible and drive off.

"They're animals, those reporters," I grunt, staring in the rear-view mirror.

"Just part of the price you pay for fame," my sister says with a sad smile on her face. "I signed up for this. I'm sorry to put you through it, too."

I shake my head. "I owe you a lot, Margot. More than I could ever say."

Squeezing my sister's hand, my heart feels at ease. With Margot back, it feels like my life is complete. Now, we can go back to normal. We can both live our lives to the fullest, and we can both be happy. Maybe Margot will help out at the bakery, or maybe it'll become a new hub for us to hang out.

Excitement and nervousness war in my chest as I drive toward the bakery.

When I park the car in downtown Farcliff, I glance at my sister. "You ready?"

She grins. "I'm not sure."

Nodding toward the main shopping street, I exit the car and hook my arm in hers. We walk slowly, and a hum of excitement builds in the pit of my stomach. It's early afternoon, so the bakery won't be jammed with people. Still, as we walk up, I can see a steady stream of people walking in and out.

I nudge my sister, unable to contain my excitement. "Look," I say, pointing.

She frowns, tilting her head. "What am I looking at? A bakery?"

"Not just *a* bakery, Margot. *My* bakery. Don't you remember *Spoonful of Sugar*? You came up with the name!"

Shock paints itself on my sister's face, and after a long couple of seconds, she rearranges her features into a smile. "Wow!"

It sounds fake. My heart starts to thump.

"You're not happy about this." I shouldn't have brought her here. It's too much of a shock. She just needs normalcy, not a brand-new business for me to deal with. I should never have brought her here straight from the facility.

"I am!" She smiles again, but it looks too forced to be real. "I'm really happy. Of course I remember the name. Wow— how did you manage to do this?"

"I had a little help." I open my mouth, but I don't want to tell her about Prince Luca. One shock is enough for the day.

When I bring her inside the bakery, a murmur sounds through the customers inside. One influencer, busy taking selfies by the flower wall, lets out a yelp.

"Margot LeBlanc!"

To her credit, Margot slides right back into her old persona. She smiles at the influencer, and hooks her arm around the girl's shoulders. They take a picture together, and the influencer runs off with her nose close to her phone screen, excited to post whatever picture she's managed to take.

Margot's eyes scan everything. She finally looks at me, shaking her head.

"This is incredible, Ivy. Really, really great."

This time, her smile seems genuine. Maybe knowing that

her presence still has the same effect on people bolstered her confidence, and now she's able to be happy for me, too.

Or maybe the shock has worn off, and my sister is back to herself.

"I guess I'm going to need a new PA, huh?" She wraps me in a hug, squeezing tight. "I'm happy for you, Ivy."

In that moment, I think she means it.

For a few hours that day, I'm completely, utterly happy. I have my sister back. I have a boyfriend who cares about me. I have a new business that's been successful right out of the gate.

It doesn't feel like anything could ever go wrong.

32

LUCA

THE PAST THREE months have lulled me into a false sense of security. That's the only explanation I have for not noticing the paparazzi following me to the bakery.

It's become Ivy's and my evening ritual—I pick her up when she's done closing up, and we head back to her place together. By that time of day, she's tired and happy, and ready for some food, a foot rub, and maybe an orgasm or two.

Today is a bit different. The tour with Damon and Dahlia has wrapped up, and Theo asked me to come back to Argyle. I leave in a couple of hours, so I'm just coming by to say goodbye to Ivy.

I walk in the back door of the bakery to find Ivy finishing up the last of her tasks for the day.

She smiles at me, leaning her head toward me for a kiss. As soon as she wipes the last counter down, she lets out a sigh.

"Margot saw the bakery."

"You brought her straight here?"

Ivy nods. A bright, happy smile stretches across her lips. "She really liked it."

I slide my hands around her waist, nuzzling my face into her hair. Ivy lets out a soft sigh, hooking her arms around my neck. We sway back and forth for a moment, and then I lay a soft kiss on her neck. I trail my lips up her jaw and over her mouth.

"Don't go," she sighs.

"I don't want to."

"Duty calls?" She lifts her eyes up to mine.

I nod, nudging her nose with mine. "I'll be back in two weeks."

"Miss you already."

I press my lips to hers. Our kiss starts slow, and then slowly becomes more frantic. Within moments, Ivy is clawing at my pants, pushing them down to my ankles. She sits up on one of the stainless steel tables, wrapping her legs around my waist.

I groan, shaking my head. "You're incredible, Poison."

Her eyes darken, and a sinful smile tugs at her lips. "Will you fuck me, Luca? I won't get to feel you for two whole weeks."

I've never had such a strong, visceral reaction to someone saying simple words to me. My whole body arches toward her, as if every single cell in my body is screaming *yes, yes, yes.*

We don't even have the time to remove any other clothing. Her dress gets flipped up to her waist, her panties pushed to the side, and I'm inside her. We claw, bite, rip, grunt, and explode together.

I'm breathless. Ivy is smiling, her hair falling out of her bun in all directions. She lets out a sigh, pulling her dress back down and shaking her head.

"I love the way you do that to me."

Catching her chin in my hand, I kiss her perfect lips. "And I love *you,* Poison Ivy."

Her eyes widen. "What?"

"You heard me."

"You love me?"

"Desperately."

She sucks in a breath, and for a horrible second, I think I've made a mistake by telling her how I feel—but that feeling evaporates when she throws her arms around me and crushes her lips against mine.

"I love you too, Your Highness," she says against my lips. "Luca. My Prince."

I groan as my heart thumps against hers, holding her close to my body.

"Let's get you home before I sit you up on that table again and fuck you senseless."

"I mean, that doesn't sound too bad, either," Ivy grins. How she's gone from a shy, uncertain girl to the vixen before me is a mystery, and one that I'm happy to accept.

I think I'm in a rose-colored haze when we exit the bakery, because again, I don't look for photographers. I don't even think about them.

I just walk Ivy to the passenger's side of the car and cage her against it, kissing her viciously. My cock is hard again already, and she reaches between me to feel it, giggling in that sexy way that only she has.

We kiss like no one's watching—like I'm about to bend her over the hood of the car and start round 2...

...until I hear the familiar sound of a camera shutter clicking.

The haze dissipates in an instant, and I'm on high alert.

"Fuck," I whisper.

Ivy's eyes are wide. She ducks into the car as the photographer comes closer, and I rush to the driver's side. We screech out of the parking lot, and Ivy rubs her hands over her eyes.

"Oh, no."

"It's okay," I say, sliding my hand over her thigh. "It's fine. I want people to know."

"I was hoping I could tell Margot myself..." Her eyebrows arch, and she cringes.

"She'll understand."

"It's a lot to take in on the day you get out of an isolated retreat."

"Maybe they won't publish the photos right away."

My thoughts flick to my own situation, when I learned that Cara had shacked up with Theo the day that I got out of the hospital in Singapore. Shame coats the back of my throat, and I shake my head.

It's not the same. I was never with Margot—not really. I kissed her once. It was all fake.

Sliding my hand over Ivy's thigh, I give it a squeeze and flash her what I hope is an encouraging smile. "It'll be fine, Poison."

She nods. "I hope so." Her fingers thread into mine as she stares out the window.

My chest squeezes, and I force myself to take a full breath. I have to believe my own words. It'll be fine. Margot will understand. Nothing bad will come of a few paparazzi pictures. It's nothing new, and nothing I can't handle.

But judging by the look on Ivy's face, she's not as used to them as I am. She's used to being in the background. Used to seeing her sister's face in the tabloids—not her own.

I stop the car outside Ivy's house, and she gives me a sad smile.

"I don't want you to leave."

"Do you want me to come in? We could tell your sister together."

Ivy shakes her head. "I'd better do it on my own. It'll be better that way."

"You sure?"

Ivy nods.

I kiss her gently. "I'll be back soon. Theo said he has something to tell me, and he wants to do it in person."

Ivy leans over the center console to give me a kiss. We linger there until I pull away.

"I have to go. The jet is waiting for me."

Ivy sighs, kissing me one last time. "See you soon."

She waves at me as I drive away, and I feel like we've turned a corner. Even if her sister is surprised, it doesn't matter. Ivy and I can brave the media and go public with our relationship. I can tell my family, her family, the entire world that she's the woman for me. I can hold her hand in public and call her mine.

Even if she's worried about Margot, I know that this is a good thing.

Just me, and Ivy, and our love.

Or at least...that's what I hope is going to happen.

THE FLIGHT from Farcliff to Argyle is just over three hours. My home Kingdom is an island nation, just south of the Bahamas. As soon as we land, I glance at the palm trees and let a smile drift over my lips.

I can't wait to show Ivy my home.

Leaning my head against the private jet's window, I look at the tarmac and let out a sigh. The flight crew flips the staircase down and nod at me as I disembark. A royal car is waiting to take me to the palace.

Inhaling the tropical evening air, my heart beats easier. Soon, I hope to show Ivy what Argyle is like. I hope to take her here and introduce her to my family, and show her all the sights that I grew up with.

It's been five long years since I was here, and I feel like a brand-new person.

When we get to the palace, Theo, Cara, Beckett, and Dante are waiting for me in the formal reception room.

Dante wraps me in a tight hug, spinning me around in a circle. Beckett still looks oddly angry, and I avoid looking at Theo and Cara just yet.

"Easy," I laugh as Dante sets me down. "You'll break my back all over again."

"From what I hear, you're indestructible," he grins. Dante is just as tall as I am, and has obviously spent the past five years in the gym. His biceps are as big as my thighs. He's a couple of years younger than me, and always followed Beckett and me around when we were kids. Now, he looks like he's grown into a man.

My brother claps me on the shoulder, and I do my best not to stumble forward.

Theo and Cara step forward. I haven't seen the two of them in three months, and I wait for the assault of bitterness and emotion that always washes over me when I see them...

...but nothing happens.

The lightness in my heart stays, and my smile doesn't slip.

Striding over to my brother Theo, I extend my hand. Theo looks surprised, but he grabs my hand and pulls me in for a hug.

"Thank you, Luca," he says, his voice muffled against my shoulder.

"For what?"

"For understanding." He glances at Cara, who smiles softly at him.

Now that I'm not clouded by anger, bitterness, and prescription opioids, I see the look they're giving each other. Cara and Theo are in love.

How did I miss this?

They're head-over-heels with each other.

Somehow, I twisted their relationship into something that was done to purposefully hurt me. I made their love about me. My pain. My accident. My heartbreak.

Never once did I consider that it had nothing to do with me. Cara wasn't climbing up the ladder. She didn't do this because I was broken.

She married my brother because she loves him, and he loves her back.

Cara lets out a surprised yelp when I wrap my arms around her. I lift her up off the ground with a laugh, setting her back down and putting my hands on her shoulders.

"I'm sorry I was an ass."

"I'm sorry I hurt you," she replies.

I smile and shake my head. "I hurt myself a lot more than you hurt me."

Staring at my family, assembled in the palace where I grew up, I let an easy smile drift over my lips. My heart beats slowly, and I think of the woman I've fallen in love with.

They're going to adore her.

Waving to one of the staff members, I motion for a special box of baked goods that I've brought with me. The *Spoonful of Sugar* logo is emblazoned on the top of the box, and I flip it open, presenting it to my family.

"A special treat," I announce. These are so much more than baked goods. They're so much more than sweet treats.

They're Ivy in a box. They're the woman I love, neatly arranged in delicious rows of sugar and pastry.

Beckett's eyebrow arches, and he exchanges a glance with Dante.

Dante clears his throat. "We, uh, heard about this." He nods to the box of treats.

"Heard about what?"

Beckett scoffs, shaking his head. "About your hooking up with both sisters, Luca. One wasn't enough?"

I frown, and Dante pulls his phone out of his pocket. He taps the screen a few times, showing me the headline of a gossip magazine.

My stomach drops.

Ivy was right. The pictures were posted right away, and they're all over the internet.

I should have stayed with her.

33

IVY

WHEN I WALK through the front door of my sister's mansion, I feel incredibly tired. My feet hurt, and I swear they're starting to swell. All my shoes are tight.

I trudge over to the kitchen and scrounge for some leftovers, eating them cold as I stand over the sink. I listen for noise, but don't hear anything. Margot must be asleep.

Laying on the couch in the living room, I stare at my phone and try to stop myself from texting Luca non-stop. It feels selfish to want him beside me all the time, but I've gotten used to his presence. I flick the television on, and my eyes glaze over as I watch something I don't care about.

I doze off.

When I wake up, I jump off the couch at the sight of a man in the shadows. Hunter steps forward, his face black with anger.

I'd gotten used to his absence while my sister was at the facility. Seeing his sniveling, sneering face turns my stomach. His eyes are full of fire, and his lips curve downward when he sees me wake.

Grabbing my arm, he pulls me up to stand. "I need to talk to you," Hunter hisses.

I yank my arm away from his grip. "First of all, don't touch me. Second of all, I'm tired, and I just want to go to bed. Whatever you want to talk about can wait."

Margot appears in the doorway. Her face is lined, and she won't meet my eye. She moves to stand next to Hunter.

My heart starts to thump. Something's wrong. Do they know about Prince Luca?

"What game are you playing right now, Ivy?"

I arch an eyebrow. "Excuse me?"

"You're supposed to be supporting your sister, not sabotaging her."

"Sabotaging her? Everything I do is to support her. I was the one to pick her up from the facility, not you, remember? I brought her to the hospital. I put my entire fucking life on hold for her!"

Margot flinches, and shame burns my cheeks.

"That's not what I'm talking about." Hunter's eyes flash, and my anger flares. He nods to the door. "What about that silly bakery, huh? You think that helps Margot? Your face plastered all over the internet trying to leech off her fame."

"*Leech?*"

I don't like Hunter on a good day. And today? Today I can't fucking stand him. I make a mental note to get the locks changed and never, ever give him a key.

Shaking my head, I cross my arms. "Listen, Hunter, I know you think you're the most important person in the Kingdom, but newsflash: you're not. You have no right to shit on me the way you've done for the past few years. You're my sister's agent. You work for her. Nothing more."

Hunter arches an eyebrow, and his eyes turn flinty. He

pulls out his phone, tapping on it a couple of times before turning the screen toward me.

If my cheeks were hot before, now they're on fire. Hunter shows me a picture, and I know exactly when it was taken—just a few hours ago. I have my hand over the Prince's crotch, and our kiss is open-mouthed and downright dirty.

It looks intimate. It *was* intimate. Five minutes earlier, the Prince was buried inside me telling me he loved me.

My heart thumps, and I look away from the screen. Hunter scrolls down, and I see a picture of the Prince kissing me on the deck of the yacht. The headline screams:

Mystery Woman: Identified!

Hunter arches an eyebrow. "You're not even going to try to explain this?"

"What is there to explain?" I growl, taking a step toward Hunter. Margot still hasn't looked at me. Her face is shuttered, and I hate that she hasn't said a word.

"Well, for one, what fucking game you're trying to play here." Hunter points between the photo and me, arching an eyebrow as if it's completely impossible that the Prince would be interested in me.

Pain pierces my heart, because that's exactly what I believed for a long time.

Hunter knows my insecurities, and he digs them out from the depths where they hide.

Squaring my shoulders, I shake my head. I'm not going to let him tear me down like this. The Prince loves me. He told me so. Luca has been the single most supportive, loving person I've ever met. He's made me realize how much I've been ignoring my own dreams.

He's made me feel worthy.

Before tears fill my eyes, I jerk my chin toward the door. "Leave."

"No, I'm not leaving before you explain yourself. Our teams worked very hard on crafting the perfect relationship between the Prince and Margot. She goes to fucking therapy and you swoop in and snatch him away?"

"I didn't snatch anything," I snap. "They were never together."

Margot makes a noise, finally lifting her eyes up to mine. "And whose fault is that?"

I swallow thickly. "We love each other." My voice is small, and suddenly love doesn't seem like enough.

Hunter just laughs, the noise peppering my chest like a million tiny knives.

"Fuck you, Hunter," I snap.

"No, fuck *you*, Ivy," Margot says. "I think it's time for you to leave. You want to be independent? You want to run your own business? So, do it. But you're not riding on my coattails anymore."

I open my mouth, but nothing comes out. Tears sting my eyes.

She tilts her head. "I just saw a poll online, and apparently sixty-eight percent of people think you're prettier than me."

I shake my head as my chest hollows out. "Margot, that's just the internet. It's stupid."

Margot scoffs. "I can't believe I never saw it before, but they're right. You are pretty, with those big, unique eyes of yours and all your multitude of talents. What am I? A washed-up starlet with an anxiety disorder, and—" She stops herself, inhaling sharply.

Hunter's lips twist into a cruel smile. "The articles say his nickname for you is 'Poison.'" He scoffs. "That's accurate. You're nothing but a poison to this family."

How did the media know that?

My thoughts swirl around me, and I blink back a fresh wave of tears. Margot's face is impassive, and Hunter motions toward the door.

"Let me grab a few things," I say, squeezing the words out through my tightening throat. I trudge up the stairs and put my things into a bag, not even sure where I'll sleep tonight. The bakery? Georgina and Giselle's house?

When I go back downstairs, Hunter has his arms around Margot's shoulders. They watch me leave, and the weight of their stares almost crushes me. When I get to my Vespa, I lean against it and let myself cry.

With trembling hands, I dial Luca's number. He answers on the second ring.

"Hey, babe." His voice is like a soothing balm on my aching heart.

"They know."

"I shouldn't have left."

"They kicked me out," I sob. "I'm going to the twins' house. I knew Margot wouldn't be happy."

Luca lets out a string of expletives, saying he'll be on the first flight back. As I cry, I manage to talk him out of it. I know he has to be with his family. We both have our own things to deal with, and I don't want to be the one to pull him away from it.

Luca's quiet for a second, and finally sighs. "Why would they think I would continue pretending to be with Margot after she gets out of the facility, when everyone knows that she overdosed? That wasn't in the contract. I'm with *you*."

I frown, taking a breath as I process his words. My head is a mess. I'm vaguely insulted by what he just said, but I can't figure out why. He wouldn't want to be seen with Margot when she gets out of the retreat?

I shake my head.

It doesn't matter—he's not with her. He's with me.

He just said so.

Still, that familiar protective instinct arches up inside me. "What's that supposed to mean? Why does it matter that Margot left to go heal herself? You should be supportive of her. You should be happy for her. For me."

Luca lets out a sigh. I imagine him raking his fingers through his hair. "I am."

"Didn't sound like it." I stare into nothing, trying to understand why I'm mad. Margot just kicked me out, and now I'm defending her? What's wrong with me?

Maybe it's just the tiredness that seems to be sinking deeper and deeper into my bones with every passing day. Maybe it's the emotion of seeing those pictures online.

Maybe it's the fact that after everything is said and done, I still care about my sister more than I care about anything else. Even when she hurts me, kicks me out, and treats me like I mean nothing to her.

Luca groans on the other side of the line. "I'm with *you*, Ivy. I didn't mean to insult your sister. If I could, I'd jump on a jet and be there first thing in the morning. I love you, Ivy. It's just..."

"Just what?"

"It's just that, you know... Being seen with her *would* have a negative impact on the royal family of Argyle. You understand that, right? It would never be allowed. But it's a moot point, because I'm not with her. I'm with you."

I don't know how to respond.

"So it's okay to be with the sister of someone who overdosed? Wouldn't that impact your reputation, too? Am I soiled goods now, as well?"

Luca takes a deep breath. "I'll deal with my family. They've seen the articles, and they haven't kicked me out." I can hear the grin in his voice, but I don't laugh.

"Too soon, Luca."

"Sorry, babe. I just want to be with you, Ivy. You know that."

I nod my head, sniffling, but a torrent of emotions is coursing through me. I'm being torn apart by everyone in my life.

Luca wants me to forget about my sister and pursue my own selfish dreams. Hunter wants me to be a doormat for him to walk over on his eternal climb up my sister's ass.

But it's Margot I'm most worried about. My sister, who's relied on me since we were little, who has provided me a life I never could have created on my own, who's everything to me, stared at me like she didn't even know me.

I feel stupid for thinking she'd be happy for me. I'm an idiot for thinking she'd understand my relationship with Luca.

How am I supposed to choose between them?

"I got to go, Luca," I say through gritted teeth.

"Call me when you get to the twins' house, okay?"

"I'll text you."

"Ivy..."

"Bye, Luca." I hang up the phone before he can say anything else.

Pain shatters through my chest. How is it that a few hours ago, his voice made me melt, and now it makes me recoil?

I can't get rid of the nagging feeling that my fairytale is coming to an end. It was too good to last. There was too much happiness in a short amount of time, and I can feel it slipping away like sand through my fingers.

Texting Georgina that I'm coming over, I don't even wait for a response. I know it'll be okay for me to sleep there. That's one good thing about having two best friends.

I swing my leg over the scooter, turning the key in the ignition. The scooter roars to life. There's a finality to the sound that I don't expect. I'm about to drive away from my sister. My family. My entire life.

For what? For a man who would toss my sister aside so easily?

I lean into the scooter, speeding down the streets. Even the whip of the air around my face does nothing to calm my nerves.

Something has changed, but I'm not sure what.

34

LUCA

Leaving Ivy behind feels wrong. Every hour I spend in Argyle feels wrong. The elation that I felt when the plane landed has evaporated, leaving a hole in my chest in its place.

Ivy needs me. I should be with her.

Taking a deep breath, I shake my head. She needs time with her sister. There have been huge changes in her life in the past couple of months, and I need to respect the time it takes for her to process things.

If she sounded distant, it's because she needs to come to terms with things. Margot will come around. She has to.

I overanalyze the entire phone call as I make my way to my childhood bedroom. When I walk inside, a wave of nostalgia hits me.

I wish I could show this to Ivy. This room is where I grew up. This castle is my home.

As much as I resented my family sending me away, and as much as I hated the fact that they never visited, I know now that I pushed them away. A lot of the pain that I felt was my own mind. I tortured myself, and now it feels good to be home. The only thing that doesn't feel good is the fact that Ivy isn't beside me.

Cringing at my own comments over the phone, I promise myself I'll make it up to Ivy. I know she cares about her sister very, very deeply—more deeply than I can understand.

Ivy sends me a message to let me know she's safe at the twins' house, and I breathe a sigh of relief.

Before I fall asleep, I vow to return to Farcliff as soon as I can.

THE NEXT DAY, there's a big ceremony to welcome me back to Argyle. I'm surprised to see the crowds that gather in the streets as we drive through. People have t-shirts with my face on them, they wave signs, and scream my name.

Dante grins at me from the seat behind me, shielded from the crowds by dark-tinted windows. He hasn't had his face shown to the public in years. "You're a hero, Luca. We broadcasted a video of your first steps, and the whole Kingdom celebrated for three days.

"It did?" I frown, glancing at him. That was the day I found out about Cara and Theo. I don't remember any celebrations about me.

Was I in such a dark hole that I didn't even realize the impact my story was having?

Dante claps me on the shoulder. "It was a nightmare," he laughs. "We kept trying to urge the banks and schools and garbage men to start working again, but everyone was just too giddy to do anything. The center square became this massive shrine to your recovery."

Since my brother has shied away from the public, he's used his tech expertise to help run the Kingdom. He's the head of castle security, and comes up with lots of the systems that help make Argyle what it is. He's a damn near genius, and almost no one in Argyle even knows.

"They love you," he says.

My heart thumps, and I wave to the crowds. All I remember from that time is pain, and drugs, and crushing betrayal.

I didn't realize that thousands of people cared about me like that. I didn't know that my people were behind me, even if it felt like Theo and Cara had stabbed me in the back.

Dante clears his throat. "This girl of yours..."

I glance at him, stiffening. "What about her?"

"You love her?" My younger brother's eyes search mine. He's always been an expert at seeing through my bullshit, even when we were just little kids.

I let out a heavy breath and lift my eyes to him. "Yeah," I answer simply. "I do."

Dante's face opens into a broad smile. "I'm happy for you, then."

By the time the event is over, it's late afternoon. I check my phone for the first time since this morning, and my heart sinks when I don't see a message from Ivy. I tap a quick message out for her and attach a couple of photos of the Argyle Palace, the city, and the crowds that came out to see me.

Wish you were here, I write.

I stare at the screen for a few moments, and then slip the phone into my pocket.

THE NEXT THREE days continue in a whirlwind of activity. The days are packed with official events, and I'm whisked from one end of the Kingdom to the other. I speak to Ivy in the evenings, and her voice sounds flat and emotionless. It tugs at my heart, and I tell her that I'll be back soon. I count down the days until I can go back to Farcliff.

On my fourth night in Argyle, my footsteps echo as I make my way to my chambers. I haven't heard from Ivy all day, and last night she told me that Margot still hasn't spoken to her. I can feel her slipping away from me, shutting herself off from my love. I need to go back there.

Every echoing footstep in the empty hallways sounds like a hammer pounding the final nail into my heart.

Something's wrong.

I can feel it.

I need to fix it.

When I see that my chamber doors are ajar, alarm bells sound in my head. I slow down, peering through the opening before pushing the door open. It glides silently, and I see a man crouched over my bedside table.

"Who the fuck are you?"

The man yelps, jumping up as pills go scattering across the floor. My eyes widen when I see my half-brother, Beckett, staring back at me.

"Luca," he manages to say as he clears his throat, his eyes bouncing around the room.

I frown. "What are you doing? Is that my medication?"

"I..." He rakes his fingers through his hair. "I got a new bottle off your doctor. I was just checking that you didn't need any more."

I frown. First of all, I don't have a regular doctor in Argyle. I finished my prescriptions from Farcliff weeks ago, and never got a new one. I haven't requested it from anyone, or even mentioned that I needed new pills.

Second of all, why would Beckett care about my medication? I hadn't seen him in five years until we saw each other in Farcliff. Why is he all of a sudden invested in my recovery?

My brother's cheeks grow bright red, and I know he's lying.

"Why are you here?" My voice is hard.

Beckett lifts his eyes up to mine, and the mask on his face falls away. He sneers at me, shaking his head.

"It should have been you in that hospital bed, not Margot."

"What?"

"These pills," he says, sweeping his arm at the floor. "I know you depend on them."

Taking a step, he grinds his heel onto a pill on the floor before kicking the powdery remains toward me.

I let my arms hang loosely at my sides, trying not to betray the tension that snakes through my muscles. I clench my fists and unclench them, looking Beckett up and down.

"I did depend on them," I admit. "But that's because I was a paraplegic and I broke my back. Or have you forgotten that?"

"How could I forget, when it's all anyone ever talks about?" he spits.

Beckett shakes his head, and an ugliness in him shines through. My throat tightens as I look at my brother, my fists clenching once again. I just want him to leave. My emotions are too charged with everything that's going on with Ivy. I need some time to myself to decompress and figure out what to do.

But I'm not going to get it.

Beckett takes another step, and I see a plastic bag of pills on the bedside table. Frowning, I take a step toward them. My half-brother scoffs, grabbing the bag and stuffing it in his breast pocket.

"What are those?"

"Doesn't matter."

"It does matter, Beckett. What the fuck are you doing in here? Are you fucking with my medication?"

"You're just an addict, Luca. The sooner you admit it, the better off you'll be."

Leaning down to pick up one of the pills on the floor, I bring it close to my face. Noticing a T-shaped mark on one side of it, realization hits me like a sledgehammer to the gut.

These are the same pills that were in my room in Farcliff. The same ones I flushed down the toilet.

They're not my painkillers.

Horror churns in my gut as I lift my eyes to my brother. He lets out a bark of a laugh, shaking his head.

"The look on your face is priceless, Luca. Did you finally figure things out?"

"What is this? Are you trying to poison me? Did you poison Margot?"

"I had nothing to do with Margot LeBlanc," he spits.

I stare at the man in front of me, not recognizing any part of him. This is the boy I grew up with. The guy who would tag along when I played, the one who was by my side at every turn, the one that actually spoke to me when I left Argyle to get my surgery.

My *brother*.

And he tried to kill me?

It's too horrific to accept, so I just stare at Beckett. My mind is completely blank. I can't process any feelings or thoughts. A ringing sound pierces my ears, and I blink two or three times, swaying on my feet.

Finally, mustering all my courage, I croak out the one word that screams through my head:

"Why?"

Beckett's eyes turn black. His lips twist, and his gaze pierces through me like a hot knife. "*Why*? You're really asking me that? You're wondering why I'm jealous of the golden boy who learned to walk again? The man who had women falling all over him? The man who overshadowed me every single fucking day of my life?"

Beckett shakes his head, kicking at the scattered pills on the ground.

"You drove yourself to a fucking pill addiction, and people still welcomed you back into the family with open arms. Me? I'm the perfect son, and I'm ostracized. I'm never good enough. I'm just the bastard son of a cheating mother, hated by every one of you fake fucks."

"You know that's not true."

"Stop bullshitting me, Luca. The only way I would ever step out of your shadow is if your shadow didn't exist."

"I should have you arrested."

"Do it," he spits. "It won't change what's happening in Farcliff with your little girlfriend."

My blood chills as Beckett's lips curl into a smile. He arches his eyebrows, and all I can do in response is open my mouth. Nothing comes out.

"You never deserved Cara, or Margot, and you don't even deserve her ugly little sister."

The sound that rips through my throat is inhuman. It tears my vocal cords to shreds as I lunge at Beckett. He snaps his teeth as I crash into him, pummeling my sides with punches as we fall to the ground. Flipping me over, Beckett reaches back and brings his fist down onto my face.

I snap my head away at the last moment, and his blow glances off my cheekbone. Pain explodes across my face, but I grit my teeth and grab his wrist. Bucking him off me, I shield myself against a flurry of blows.

I can't bring myself to hit him. Even as he punches my

face, kicks me in the shin, knees me in the gut. Even as his dead eyes look into mine, I can't hit my brother.

All these years, he felt inadequate. All these years, he thought of himself as less than us.

I never saw it.

Maybe I never cared. I was too invested in my own life—and then, my own pain, my own accident, my own heartbreak. I never stopped to think about my brother.

A punch cracks across my jaw. The metal tang of blood coats my tongue, and I wheeze to get a breath in. I hit Beckett in the gut, wincing as he cries out.

My brother pulls his arm back to hit me, and I know it's going to be over. He'll knock me out, because I can't defend myself. I can't hit him.

Before his fist comes down, though, another arm hooks around his and pulls him off me. He struggles against the guard, screaming and kicking as he's pulled away.

Theo stands in the doorway, wide-eyed.

I roll onto my side, coughing as I wheeze and try to catch my breath. The King watches silently, scanning the room.

"What happened?" he asks.

I shake my head. "I'm not sure. I think Beckett has been trying to kill me. These aren't my painkillers."

Theo lets out a sigh. I glance up at him and my heart falls. He doesn't look surprised—only sad.

He knew.

35

IVY

I NEVER KNEW likes on Instagram could cause such a big rift between family members. My latest post on my bakery account garnered more likes than Margot's last picture, and I can see in Margot's eyes that she's upset about it.

Social media has been her mirror. It's been millions of screaming fans telling her how wonderful she is. All day, every day.

Now, they've turned. She still has screaming fans, but the spotlight has turned to me.

And I hate it.

My sister stands on the other side of the bakery counter, ignoring the adoring fans that snap pictures of her. Her eyebrow arches, and an ugly feeling curls in the pit of my stomach.

I don't like my sister like this.

She looks bitter and tired. She doesn't look like herself.

"You want a cinnamon bun?" I ask, knowing she'll refuse.

"No. I want you to not be so selfish, Ivy. I can't believe you continue to open the bakery every day after Hunter and I spoke to you. I thought you understood."

Her hair is sticking up around her head, and her eyes look hazy. I wonder if she's using again, and then shoo the thought away.

She isn't an addict. She said so herself. We still don't know what happened with the overdose. She thinks she was poisoned, but she won't talk about it.

Nausea rises up in my throat as my gut gurgles uncomfortably. A sharp pang of pain passes through me. I put a hand to my stomach.

Taking a deep breath, I focus on what my sister is saying. "You thought I understood what, Margot? That you don't care about my dreams? That you only care about your own image?" I wince as another pain passes through my gut, glancing at the wide-eyed fans who stare at us. I nod my head to the door behind me. "Let's go in the back and talk more privately."

Margot just scoffs and shakes her head. "You never cared about me, Ivy. You just used me to get what you want—just like everyone else. I just spent three months living through torture, and I come out to find you've abandoned me. I thought I could count on you."

My eyes dart to the people filming our interaction. I gulp. "Margot..."

She shakes her head, spins around, and walks out. My shoulders slump.

Giselle puts a hand on my shoulder. "Don't worry, Ivy. It'll be okay."

Marcus slides a fresh tray of cinnamon buns in the display case before squeezing my other shoulder. "We're here for you, Poison."

I flinch at the nickname, and give him a tight smile.

Grabbing one of the cinnamon buns, I head to the office at the back of the bakery and lock myself inside. Even with my gut cramping uncomfortably, I still tear off chunks of cinnamon buns and stuff them in my mouth.

That's the reason I've never been as willowy as Margot—comfort eating. I always turn to food. This is my second cinnamon bun of the day, and I know it won't be my last.

It tastes bitter in my mouth, and tears start to stream from my eyes.

I can't win. If I keep the bakery open, Margot will take it as a personal insult. Why she can't just be happy for me, I don't know. She's hurting right now, and I'm not there to build her back up like I used to.

But going back to my old life doesn't seem possible anymore. I don't see how I could continue to serve my sister hand and foot when I've seen what life is like when I live for myself.

I lick the sticky cinnamon off my fingers as I chew the last big bite of dough and sit back in my chair. My stomach gurgles violently, and I wrap my arms around my abdomen.

Yet another sharp pain passes through my gut. I groan, leaning back in my chair.

The stress is getting to me.

When another dagger twists in my stomach, I frown. That doesn't feel like stress.

Standing up, I immediately double over as pain shoots through me. Gasping, I clutch the desk. A hot poker jabs my stomach over and over again. I need a bathroom.

Stumbling to the doorway, I tremble as I reach for the door. I'm still chewing, and it feels like glue in my mouth. I can't grip the doorknob properly. My vision doubles, and I blink to try to clear it.

Every breath feels difficult. Another hot dagger slices through my stomach, and I let out a low groan. I try to inhale, but my throat feels tight.

Too tight.

Panic wells up inside me, churning in my gut along with more sharp pains. Finally, I'm able to grip the doorknob and pull it open, but the effort makes me fall to my knees.

At the same time, I try to swallow the lump of dough in my mouth.

Why don't I just spit it out? Why do I try to swallow it?

The dough lodges itself in my throat. A little bit of apple —my signature—goes down the wrong hole.

Black spots dot my vision, and I clutch my throat. I can't breathe. I can't breathe.

I can't breathe.

I WAKE up in a hospital bed with a tube sticking out of my arm. Blinking, I try to bring the room into focus. My head feels hazy.

"Good, you're awake!" a nurse says as she enters the room.

I try to speak, but all that comes out is a gargled groan.

"Shh," she smiles, patting my arm. "You're in the Farcliff General Hospital. You came in after passing out. Your friend Marcus found you and was able to get the obstruction out of your airway."

I nod, trying to swallow. The pain in my throat is intense.

The nurse pats my arm. "You had an accident—your bowels evacuated when you passed out."

My eyes widen. I shit myself?

She continues as if I'm not lying here, dying of embarrassment. "We've determined that you ingested E. coli bacteria and developed an infection. We've given you antidiarrheals, and everything seems to be improving. You might feel weak over the next few weeks, though. You were lucky that your friends brought you in so soon."

I groan, nodding, but I still don't understand.

"And your baby is fine," she adds with a smile.

I blink.

Baby?

"What?"

"We've run some tests, and everything seems to be fine. Of course, we'll have to keep an eye on you in the coming weeks. Who's your obstetrician?"

"Baby?" I croak.

The nurse tilts her head. She frowns at me, and I frown back at her.

"Miss LeBlanc," she says slowly, "were you not aware that you're pregnant?"

If this nurse had told me that I was Tinkerbell's granddaughter, I would be less shocked than I am now.

"No," I say, coughing. "That's not possible."

She takes a deep breath. "Have you had unprotected sex in the past few months? The doctors estimate that you're about fourteen weeks on."

I shake my head, every movement sending pain shooting through my neck. Everything feels heavy. Thoughts move sluggishly through my head as I try to understand what the hell is going on.

Pregnant.

Sucking a breath in through my teeth, I squeeze my eyes shut.

It's not possible. It can't be. The Prince and I were careful. We used protection.

The nurse stares at me, her eyebrows arching expectantly.

I shake my head. "I was careful. We used condoms. I..." My eyes widen as I think of the very first time.

The condom broke.

How did I not think about that? How did I gloss over that fact when Luca mentioned it?

I was too busy thinking about the fact that I'd lost my virginity to even think about the fact that the condom broke. Pregnancy didn't even cross my mind.

My mouth drops open, and horror starts bubbling up inside me. I bring a hand over my stomach, staring down at the pudge around my hips.

I thought I was tasting too many pastries with the bakery opening up. I thought the tiredness was because I was run off my feet.

This whole time...I was *pregnant?*

The nurse pats my arm again and gives me a sympathetic smile. "The doctor will come in and talk to you. Would you like to speak to one of our counselors? It might help you process this. I know it's a lot to deal with, so just try to relax."

I nod, frowning. Relaxing doesn't exactly seem like a viable option right now. My pulse is thundering through my thighs, and I can't make any sense of the thoughts swirling around my head.

I watch the nurse close the door, and my cell phone chimes in my bag. Grunting through my labored movements, I drag the purse over to my bed and dig through it until I find my phone.

There are dozens of notifications. Georgie left me a message saying she left the hospital to go close up the bakery, and she and Giselle will be back later. I sigh, leaning back in my bed.

Then, my phone chimes again. I have an alert set up, so whenever *Spoonful of Sugar* shows up in a news story or is tagged in something online, I get notified.

For the past month, getting those emails has been a source of joy.

Not today.

Dozens Ill. *Spoonful of Sugar* to Blame?

My eyes widen. My hand is trembling so hard I can hardly read the screen, and it takes me three tries to tap the news story to read it. When it finally pops up, I have to blink half a dozen times to clear the haze from my vision.

The headline comes into focus, and a chill courses through my body. My breaths become shorter and shorter as I read the news story. Panic laces my blood. Another headline screams at me.

Spoonful of E. coli: New Bakery Might Be Cause of Outbreak

Over twenty-five people have been hospitalized after eating at the bakery today. They're saying it's caused by a dangerous strain of E. coli bacteria.

I feel like I'm going to throw up. Or maybe poo my pants.

In fact, I know I'm going to throw up—and that's exactly what I do.

All over the hospital room floor.

A nurse bursts through the door at the sound of my retching. I wipe my lips as tears sting my eyes.

"Sorry."

"It's okay, honey," she says, laying some paper sheets on the floor. She presses a button on the wall and hands me a glass of water.

I lay back in my bed as tears fall from my eyes, trying to process everything that's going on. A hospital worker shuffles in and starts cleaning up my mess.

It's too much. My heart starts beating faster, and my hand

begins to tremble. The water sloshes all over my hand as I try to bring it up to my mouth.

Swallowing doesn't work, so I cough all over myself, spilling water down my front. It hurts to inhale. It feels like a giant hand is squeezing my ribcage, and my lungs might collapse.

Pregnant.

E. coli.

Pregnant.

E. coli.

Margot. Hunter. Luca.

Pregnant.

My heart is a runaway train. I can't stop shaking. The nurse is saying something, but it sounds like she's speaking to me underwater. I can't make out the words. I frown as my vision goes blurry. An alarm goes off, and another nurse comes in.

They inject something into my IV, and I slip into sweet, blank oblivion.

36

LUCA

"I NEED TO GO."

"Sit. Down," Theo spits.

"Ivy needs me."

I've read the news reports on the E. coli outbreak, and I have to get back there. I haven't heard from her at all, and even from thousands of miles away, I know she's in trouble.

The King slams his hand on my shoulder and pushes me back into my chair. Pain scatters across my ribcage where mottled bruising is already starting to appear.

Groaning, I lean back.

"What the fuck is going on?" Theo's eyes are blazing. I've never seen him this angry.

"Beckett tried to poison me, that's what's going on."

Theo pinches the bridge of his nose. "You've been back one day, Luca. One day."

"Are you blaming me for this?"

"Why is it that trouble seems to follow you around?"

I stare at my brother, fuming. A part of me agrees with him. Everywhere I go, things seem to fall apart. Isn't Ivy in trouble, too? Deep down, I think that might be because of me.

Shaking my head, I let out a huff. "I haven't done anything wrong, Theo. You know that."

Theo sinks down onto a chair. He lifts his gaze up to mine, and he lets out a heavy sigh. "I know. I'm sorry."

"What are you going to do?"

"I'm not sure. I can't go public with this. If the media catch wind of Beckett's attempts, it'll throw everything we've worked for out the window. All the trade agreements we've just spent the last six months forging will be in jeopardy. Argyle's image is just starting to recover. If the rest of the world finds out that Beckett has done this..."

Theo's voice trails off, and I let out a sigh.

"I won't talk."

"Thank you."

I lean back in my chair, feeling my pocket for my phone. I want to call Ivy to make sure she's okay. She must be dealing with a shit storm of epic proportions with the bacterial outbreak at her bakery. The timing is awful.

Theo clears his throat. "Luca, I..." He keeps his gaze on the floor between us and takes a deep breath. "I'm sorry."

When my brother lifts his eyes up to mine, I know that he means it.

He continues: "I'm sorry about Cara. I never meant for it to happen. It wasn't malicious. We just... We just fell in love."

A couple of months ago, those words would have sent me in a tailspin of prescription drug abuse and depression. It would have sent me searching for a high that I'd never come back down from.

Now?

Now, I get it. You can't help who you fall in love with, even if it's the most inconvenient, unexpected person in the world. I stand up and extend my hand toward my brother.

Instead of taking it, he wraps me in a hug and holds me tight.

When I leave my brother, I take my phone out and call Ivy right away.

"Hey, Your Highness," she answers. I flinch at the formal title.

"Hi, babe. I heard about the E. coli thing. What happened?"

Ivy lets out a sigh. "I don't know what's going on. I follow all the health and safety guidelines. You've seen the bakery. It's clean."

"Did you ever think..." I pause, glancing over my shoulder to make sure I'm alone. I drop my voice. "Do you think maybe someone did it maliciously?"

"What?"

"I don't know the details, but there's been some shit going on here. Beckett..." I pause, not wanting to go into details. "I just think that maybe someone could be trying to hurt you to get to me."

Ivy's quiet for a while, and the silence tortures me.

"I'll be on a plane in the morning and be at your side by the afternoon, Ivy," I promise.

I think she sobs, but the noise is so quiet that I can't be sure. "Luca, I think it might be best if you stay away for a little bit."

My chest feels hollow. "What?"

"Well, if someone is trying to get back at you, isn't it best if we figure it out? If you come back here, it'll only cause more trouble."

"But Ivy..." I choke on her name. Does she not want to see me?

The distance between us grows, and I can almost see the walls she's building around herself. She's lost her sister, her bakery, her life as she knew it. Does she want to get rid of me, too?

She takes a shuddering breath. "Don't you think it's best if we let the dust settle?"

"I think it's best if we're together, Ivy. If we let this tear us apart..." I stop, listening to Ivy breathing.

"Isn't it us being together that started this whole mess in the first place?" Ivy sniffles, and the pain in her voice shatters through my chest.

"Us being together is a good thing, Ivy."

"It doesn't feel like a good thing right now."

She doesn't mean it. She's just talking through her pain and letting it speak for her. She's not saying what I think she's saying.

"Poison..."

"That's an accurate nickname, don't you think? I'm just poison. Everywhere I go, things die around me. Margot, the business, my customers..."

"No." My voice is stronger. "Ivy, come on. Where are you right now?"

There's a pause, and then Ivy takes a deep breath. "I'm at home. I mean, at the twins' house."

The way she says it makes me frown. It sounds like a lie. I chew the inside of my cheek and take a deep breath. "Don't worry, Ivy, it'll all work out."

"Will it, though? You keep saying that, but it just keeps getting worse."

I frown, leaning against the wall in the hallway. Where is this coming from?

"Did anything else happen?"

Ivy pauses long enough for me to know she's choosing her words very carefully.

Finally, she answers. "No."

"I'm coming back."

"Don't." Her voice is strangled, and she lets a sob slip through her lips. "Please, Luca, just let me deal with this on my own. Having you here just brings more media, and it'll make Margot hate me even more."

My chest feels hollow. I run my fingers through my hair, squeezing my eyes shut. "You don't want to see me?"

Ivy's breath is shaking, and the thudding of my blood is starting to grow louder. The edges of my vision are going fuzzy.

This can't be happening. Ivy is everything to me, but she's pushing me away. What am I supposed to do without her?

"Goodbye, Luca," she whispers. The dead air that follows sounds louder than any noise I've ever heard. I stare at the screen, not understanding.

The thudding of boots on the floor makes me turn my head. Three palace guards are rushing toward me. I hold up my hand to stop them.

"What's going on?"

"It's Prince Beckett, sir," the leader says. "He's disappeared."

37

IVY

"You should have told him," Georgina says when I stare at the phone.

"I can't, Georgie. If he comes back here, his reputation will be tainted. I've seen the articles talking about his return to Argyle—that's where he belongs. Being with me will only bring him down."

"Being with you is where he *wants* to be, Ivy." Her eyebrows draw together.

My heart squeezes so hard I feel like I can't breathe. Tears sting my eyes, but I blink them away. I shake my head. "He thinks he wants that. I'll just be a footnote in his autobiography."

"You are the stupidest smart person I know. Did you know that?" Georgie huffs.

I try to laugh, but it just comes out as a bark. I lean back against the hospital pillows and stare at the ceiling tiles. There's a water stain on the one right above the bed, its jagged edges looking as broken as my heart.

"I need to do one good thing, Georgie. You know? If he

comes back here, he'll be dragged into this whole E. coli mess, into the mess with Margot, into my pregnancy. It'll be a scandal of epic proportions. He doesn't deserve that."

"Don't you think he should decide that? Why are you pushing him away?"

I can't answer that question out loud, so I just turn my head away. I'm pushing him away because I love him more than anything else in the world, and I don't want to drag him down into my mess. I've seen the pictures of him in Argyle, smiling at his cheering subjects. I've seen the way his face looks when he's surrounded by his family in his home country.

He looks happy.

Who am I to drag him away from that?

Georgie lets out a sigh. "You didn't even tell him you were in the hospital, Ivy. Don't you think he has a right to know?"

"He said that people might be trying to get back at him, and that's why the bacterial outbreak at my bakery happened." I stare at Georgie, my eyebrows drawing together. "I could lose *Spoonful of Sugar*."

"You could lose *him*."

My heart thumps.

I don't know what to think. I've closed the bakery for the rest of the week. I feel like I've been run over by a truck.

A soft knock on the door is followed by Irving's bearded face poking through. "Hey, Ivy," the twins' eldest brother says with a sad smile. "How are you feeling?"

He comes in, followed by the other six siblings. All seven of them surround my bed, looking at me with sad looks on their face.

Irving lifts a big, meaty hand to reveal a bouquet of flowers. I smile, nodding to the side table in my room. He places the flowers down and squeezes Georgie's shoulder. Glancing at his sister, they exchange a loaded look.

"What?" I ask, looking between Georgie and Irving.

Irving takes a deep breath. "The boys and I cleared out the bakery today. We got rid of all the pastries—both baked and prepped, and threw out any food that might be contaminated. Everything besides salt, basically."

I nod.

Irving clears his throat, staring at his hands. "We noticed the lock on the back door had been tampered with. There were scratches all over it, and the key doesn't fit in it straight."

My heart takes off running, and a machine next to me starts to beep.

"So, Luca was right?" I whisper, glancing at Georgina. "This was malicious?"

Her eyes are wide. She stares from me to her brother, who bites his lip. The five brothers shift their weight, and Georgie and Giselle take one of my hands each.

"I don't know, Ivy. I don't have any evidence of that. But..."

The word hangs between us.

My stomach twists uncomfortably. I move my arm, and the IV tube sticking out of it jabs me uncomfortably. Huffing, I readjust my position and try over and over to get comfortable in the tiny hospital bed.

I feel completely powerless.

"Well, if the E. coli bacteria was someone being malicious, at least that means you know the bakery wasn't unsanitary," Georgie says, arching her brows.

I snort. "Yeah, that makes it so much better." Shaking my head, I sigh. "I don't know what to do."

"Just take a few days to figure things out, Ivy." Giselle smiles sadly at me. "It'll work out."

I nod, not sure if I believe her. How is everything going to work out?

My sister won't talk to me, my boyfriend is better off in his own country, my business has fallen apart. I don't want to wallow in self-pity, but what else is there to do? Unless I know who contaminated my pastries, how can I stop it from happening again?

"I don't want anyone to get sick by eating my stuff," I say, shaking my head. "What if the delivery to the castle had been contaminated? What if I'd inadvertently poisoned the King?"

Tears sting my eyes as frustration and hopelessness bubble up inside me. I let my hand drift over my stomach, staring at my abdomen.

Through it all, as my entire world falls apart around me, I have to come to terms with the fact that there's a baby growing inside me.

I love the love that the twins and their brothers are showering on me. I love having their support. But right now, I just want to suffer in peace. Their presence is stifling, and I feel like I can't think with so many people in the room.

Georgina motions for her siblings to leave the room. She can read my mind. Irving clears his throat and stands up. We say our goodbyes, and I somehow manage to keep it together until everyone but me and the twins are gone.

As soon as the door closes, though, I burst into tears.

"What am I going to do, Georgie?"

"Well, right now, you're going to get yourself better. The doctor said that they'll keep you here until you're clear of the bacterial infection, so you'll stay here until they release you. Then, you'll call that Prince and tell him he's going to be a father. Then, you'll go to your sister and tell her to stop being such a selfish asshole. Finally, you'll go back to that bakery, make some cupcakes, and open the doors."

Giselle squeezes my hand, nodding at me. "She's right."

"Okay?" Georgie asks, tilting her head. Her hair color is fading now, leaving pale blue streaks at the ends.

I gulp. "Okay."

When my friends leave, I lay back on the pillows and let out a sigh. It sounded so easy when Georgie said it, but I'm not sure I'll be able to do any of what she said.

How am I supposed to open the bakery back up when I don't know who tried to poison me? It's not just me that they hurt. It's my customers.

It's my *baby*.

I curl onto my side and let my tears soak into the pillow. It feels good to cry, but when I wipe my face and pull myself together, nothing has changed.

Closing my eyes, I think of the life that's growing inside me.

If I set aside Margot, and the bakery, and even my love for the Prince, all that's left is my unborn child. No matter what, I need to do what's right for my baby.

I wrap my arms around myself and hang onto that thought. Before, I was adrift in a sea of misery. I was lost.

Now, I've found an anchor.

My child.

I sit up in the bed and bring my knees up to my chest. I lean my chin on my knees and sway softly from side to side.

Doing right by this baby will be the one guiding factor that leads me through this mess. What happens with the bakery is irrelevant. What happens with Margot doesn't matter.

Even if she never speaks to me again, and even if the bakery falls apart, I still have to take care of this child. *My* child.

With a sigh, I let go of the panic that's been gripping my

heart. I turn a corner, finding strength inside me that I never knew existed.

I still don't know what I'll do. I still don't know how I'll tell Luca, or what will happen with my sister.

The only thing I do know is that I'll be the best mother I can be.

38

LUCA

I'M GOING to lose Ivy. I know I am. I could hear the distance in her voice—it's getting worse as time goes on. Every day that I spend in Argyle, Ivy slips further and further away from me.

I can't stay here. I have to go back to Farcliff.

It's moments like this that you realize what's important to you. I don't care about Theo and Cara. I don't care about the betrayal that consumed my heart for the past year.

I don't care about Beckett, or his fresh betrayal. His attempt on my life means nothing.

The only thing that matters is Ivy.

My Poison. My antidote. My everything.

Rushing to my bedroom, I start throwing clothes into a bag. I'll jump on the jet tonight. I need to see her.

But Theo appears in the doorway, his eyes flicking to my bag.

"Where are you going?"

"Farcliff," I answer, tossing my toothbrush in my bag.

"Luca, you can't."

"Like fuck, I can't."

"What about Beckett?"

"What about him?" I spin around, staring at the King. Shaking my head, I scoff. "Why would I give him any more of my time? The woman I love needs me, Theo. Surely you would understand that?"

Theo stares at me, his eyes boring into mine. "So, you leaving has nothing to do with Cara? Nothing to do with me?"

I laugh, turning back to my suitcase. "No," I say. "Nothing."

Theo is silent behind me, and I sense his eyes on my back as I move back and forth in the room. The air hangs heavy between us, and I force myself to straighten my shoulders and turn to look at him.

"Do you have a problem with me leaving?"

"I grounded all the planes and closed the ports," Theo says quietly. "I wanted to make sure Beckett didn't make a run for it."

"Are you going to force me to stay?" Anger flares inside me, igniting the fire in my veins. I clench my fists. Everything feels hot. The tips of my ears feel like they're burning.

After everything that's happened between us, is Theo going to stop me from leaving? He stole the woman I thought I wanted, sent me off to get fixed, and never visited me once. Then, once I got better, he used me for his fucking publicity campaign to boost the image of our Kingdom.

Now, he wants to keep me hemmed in here while he looks for the man who tried to kill me, all the while sweeping the whole thing under the rug?

I'm trembling, clenching my fists to stop myself from doing something that will have me arrested for treason.

Theo lets out a sigh and shakes his head. "I'll get the royal jet prepared for you." My brother lifts his eyes to mine. "Thank you for coming back and doing the events over the past couple of days. Thank you for treating me and Cara with respect. You're a better man than I am, Luca."

I shake my head. "I just know what's important."

Theo nods. "You going to bring her back here? I'd like to meet her."

"If she lets me," I smile.

Theo snaps his fingers, and an attendant materializes in the doorway. I turn back to my suitcase as Theo commands the man to prepare the jet.

The tension between my shoulders eases slightly, because I know I'll be by Ivy's side within hours. I'll get to hold her hand in mine and press my lips against hers. I'll touch her, kiss her, breathe her in.

I'll bridge this distance that has grown between us, and show her that I care about her more than anything else in the world. More than my reputation, or my Kingdom, or my past.

She's everything to me.

Even if she wants to push me away, I need to go back to her and let her know how I feel.

MY KNEE BOUNCES up and down the entire flight back to Farcliff. A car is waiting for me at the airport. The driver puts my small suitcase in the trunk of the car and then slips into the driver's seat. He looks in the rear-view mirror and arches his eyebrow.

"Where to, Your Highness?"

I stare back at him blankly. "I... I don't know."

To his credit, the driver's face remains neutral and professional. I clear my throat and give him *Spoonful of Sugar*'s address. While we drive, I dial Ivy's number.

She doesn't answer.

I text her, staring at the screen as I wait for a response.

The sun has long gone down, and I wonder if maybe she's asleep.

When we get to the bakery, the shopfront is dark. I direct him to the back of the building, but the door is locked. There aren't any cars parked here. It's empty.

I sigh, frustrated, and call Ivy again.

Still, no answer.

So I direct the driver to Margot's mansion. I don't know the twins' address or their phone numbers, so the only other person I know is Margot.

When we get there, a chill passes through me. This mansion became my second home while I was in Farcliff, but now it seems cold and uninviting.

Dread twists in my stomach.

Why isn't Ivy answering? She hasn't spoken to me at all since that awful conversation. Does she really want to toss me aside?

Does she not care about what happened between us?

Closing my eyes, I try to talk myself down. It's late. She's probably asleep.

Margot will know where she is. At the very least, she should know where Giselle and Georgina live. I take a deep breath and put my hand on the car door handle, ready to face Margot and her wrath.

As it turns out, though, Margot's wrath isn't directed at me today. The front door of the mansion flies open and Hunter, Margot's agent, sprints out.

Margot isn't far behind, hurling projectiles at him as she screams. One of them hits him on the head, bouncing toward the driveway. I get out of the car in time to see an apple rolling on the pavement.

"I trusted you!" Margot shrieks, her eyes blazing. She

doesn't even look at me. All her energy and anger is directed at her agent. "You bastard!"

"I did it for you, Margot. With the bakery and your sister gone, you'd be able to rebuild your career. But you're too fucking dumb to realize what's good for you."

My eyes widen. Hunter's gaze swings to me, and he snaps his teeth.

Margot trembles, stalking toward him with fury in her eyes. "How *dare* you?"

"Oh give me a fucking break," he says, puffing his chest out but backing away from her. "You never cared about your sister. You just used her, and she used you."

"*Leave*," Margot says. Her voice is low and dangerous. It sends tremors through my stomach, and her eyes don't leave her agent. "I never want to see your face again, Hunter."

"You'd be nothing without me, Margot. You're making a big mistake. You'd still be waiting tables at the Grimdale Diner if I hadn't discovered you."

Margot trembles, staring at her agent and taking one more step toward him. The roar that comes out of her mouth is inhuman. She screams wordlessly as Hunter scrambles away from her, jumping into his car and tearing down the driveway.

Falling to her knees, Margot drops her head in her hands. Sobs shake her shoulders. I rush toward her, putting my hand on her back.

She sniffles, wiping her nose on the back of her hand as she lifts her gaze to mine. "He poisoned them, Your Highness. He said he did it for me. He put my sister in the hospital because he thought that was what I wanted."

A chill runs down my spine. "He *what*?"

The next few minutes are a blur. My heart is in my throat as Margot slips into the back seat of the car with me. Vaguely,

I hear her give the name of a hospital to the driver, and I grip the edge of the seat with my hand.

"Drive faster, damn it!"

I'm hyperventilating, gripping the leather so hard my hands go numb. Margot sits beside me and puts her hand over mine.

For the first time, her touch doesn't make me uncomfortable. It's not the touch of a lover—or someone pretending to be a lover—it's the touch of a friend. Of someone who is hurting just as much as I am.

Her face is white, and runny mascara has left trails down her cheeks. Her long, blonde hair is stringy. She gives me a tight-lipped smile and nods her head.

"It'll be okay."

I inhale, not believing her.

Why didn't Ivy tell me? Why would she hide the fact that she was in the hospital? What if she's not asleep or ignoring me... What if it's worse?

The driver stops outside the emergency department, and I rush through the sliding glass doors. I drum my fingers on the reception desk as the old woman behind it takes an eternity to type Ivy's name in the computer.

Her glasses are perched on the end of her nose. "Let's see, here," she says, staring at the screen.

I want to scream. I want to turn the screen toward me and yell at her to *hurry the fuck up, old woman!*

But Margot puts her hand on my forearm, and I don't say anything. We finally get Ivy's room number, and I take off at full speed. Mashing the elevator buttons, I get impatient and decide to rush up the stairs. I can't stay still. I need to see Ivy, to touch her, to make sure she's okay.

When I get to her floor, I run down the hallway until I get to the very last room. It has floor-to-ceiling windows on either side, encasing Ivy almost entirely in glass. The blinds haven't been drawn, and I can see Ivy's black hair against the white hospital bed sheets. Her face is turned toward me, her eyes peacefully closed.

My heart jumps to my throat and a tear slides down my face.

She should have told me. I should have been here.

A weird mix of love, relief, and anger swirls inside me. Love for Ivy, relief that she's okay, and anger that she didn't tell me she was here.

I push the door open gently and walk to her bedside. Cupping her face in my hands, I press a trembling kiss to her lips.

When I pull back to look at her face, Ivy's eyes open.

A sigh escapes her lips, and a tiny, tired smile stretches across her face.

"You're here," she whispers.

"Of course I'm here. I'll always be here."

39

IVY

"I'm pregnant," I blurt out, opening my eyes wider.

I hadn't meant to say it like that, in the darkness of a hospital room with the Prince leaning over my bed. I'd spent all afternoon crafting the perfect speech to tell him, when I was finally strong enough. But now that he's here, I just had to get it out. I had to tell him the truth.

The Prince freezes, and for a horrible moment, I think I feel him pull away from me. My mind spirals, and all my fears come true. He doesn't want the baby. He doesn't want me. He's going to leave.

Instead, he strokes the side of my face with the back of his fingers as his eyes soften.

"You're...pregnant?" His eyebrows arch hopefully, and a flash crosses his eyes.

I nod, not trusting my voice. When the Prince's face breaks into a smile, my heart erupts. I don't realize how much fear was housed inside me until it's released all at once. My worries fall away, and I cling onto the Prince like the lifeline that he is. He buries his face into my neck as a sobbing laugh falls out of him.

Of course he wasn't leaving me. Of course he wants the baby.

I was a fool to push him away.

I don't even realize tears are falling from my eyes until the Prince brushes them away. He presses his trembling lips to mine, and in his kiss I feel the strength of his love. I hook my arms around his neck and pull him close, deepening our embrace and showing him what he means to me.

When he pulls away, Luca slides his hand over my stomach and leans his forehead against mine. He lets out a shuddering breath, and a tear rolls down his cheek.

"I'm going to be a dad," he sighs.

"And you're...you're happy about that?" My voice squeaks.

Luca chuckles. "Yes, Ivy. I'm happy about it. More than happy. Ecstatic. Over the moon. Head over heels in love with you."

I bite my lip to stop it from trembling. Luca grabs a chair and pulls it toward the bed, sliding his hand into mine. I bring it up to my lips and lay a kiss on the back of his hand, and then nuzzle my face against him. His skin smells so good.

I missed him so, so much.

"I'm here," he repeats, over and over. "I'm here."

We stay there for a long time without moving. Every time he says, 'I'm here,' it loosens some of the tension in my heart. When he presses another kiss to my lips, love fills up my heart so fully that I feel like I'm going to explode with happiness.

In that moment, I realize many things.

I learn that I'm strong enough to do it on my own. Strong enough to rebuild the bakery. Strong enough to carry this child. Strong enough to walk away from my sister if she doesn't want me in her life, and doesn't treat me like I deserve to be treated.

But I also learn that I don't *want* to do it on my own—and I don't have to. In Luca's arms, with few words being spoken between us, I feel the kind of unity and peace that I didn't even know existed before this moment. I let go of the fears that have held me back from loving Luca like he should be loved, and I open my heart to him completely.

The Prince lets out a sigh, and our souls melt together. He pulls away from me, tucking a strand of hair behind my ear.

"I love you, Ivy."

Blinking back tears, I nod. "I love you, too."

It doesn't feel like enough. How can the word 'love' encompass everything I feel for him? I want to tell him that he makes everything brighter. Now that he's here, I'm not afraid. I felt strong before, but he makes me feel invincible.

Instead, I just squeeze his hand and stare into his eyes. A thousand unsaid words fly between us in that gaze, and my heart beats with his.

Behind him, Margot clears her throat in the doorway.

I stiffen. "Margot."

"Hi, Ivy," she says, her eyebrows arching uncertainly. "Can I come in?"

I gulp, nodding.

She takes a hesitant step forward. Her face is drawn, and she wrings her hands in front of her stomach. Her chest rises and falls quickly as her breaths become more staggered.

"Ivy..."

I shake my head. "It's okay, Margot."

"It's not."

"It is. You're my sister. Always will be."

"I was an ass."

"So was I."

Margot laughs, shaking her head. "Stop it. You've always been a saint."

"You don't know the thoughts that have crossed my mind," I smile. A tear rolls down my cheek. "They've been far from saintly."

Guilt crosses Margot's face. She glances at Luca, and then takes a deep breath. "It was Hunter." Her voice cracks when she says his name. "The bacteria in your pastries. Hunter planted it. He thought..." She chokes on the words, shaking her head. "I didn't know. I swear, I didn't know. I'm sorry, Ivy. I would never..."

Shock freezes me for a moment, but my sister's tears make me spread my arms toward her. She buries her head next to mine and sobs, apologizing over and over again.

I pat her head and whisper comforting words until she pulls away.

"I fired him, Ivy." My sister stares into my eyes and lets out a heavy sigh. "I would never..."

"I know."

Luca squeezes my hand, and I reach my other hand toward my sister. She sits on the edge of the bed, staring out of the window as she holds my hand.

With a deep breath, she swings her eyes over to me. "I've always been jealous of you, Ivy."

That makes me laugh. "Me? You're the one who has it all."

She shakes her head. "You're just like Mama. You got her eyes, and her soul. She was the kindest, most thoughtful person in the world. And I'm just like Dad. Selfish, self-absorbed, short-sighted." She sighs. "Except for one thing, I guess," she adds, mostly to herself.

"Don't say that."

My sister gulps. "It's true." She looks at the Prince and then back at me. "I should never have gotten between you two. I can see how much you care about each other. I was scared of being alone."

"It was a weird situation," I smile. "Takes some getting used to."

Margot nods, and tears fill her eyes.

She opens her mouth, but before she can speak, I clear my throat. I glance at Luca, and he gives me the slightest nod.

He knows that I want to tell her about the baby. With just one glance, he understands everything that's happening inside my heart, and is there to support me. It's micro-moments like this that make me appreciate him even more. My love for him multiplies in an instant. I take a deep breath, bracing myself to deliver the next bombshell that will rock Margot's world.

"Margot," I say softly, forcing myself to look her in the eyes, "I'm pregnant."

My sister's eyes widen. She glances from me, to the Prince, and back to me again. She swallows thickly.

I'm not sure what I expect her to say. Congratulations, maybe. Or some platitude that comes to her head. The last thing that I expect her to say are the words that eventually come out of her mouth.

Margot takes a deep breath, blowing it out and then biting her lower lip. She drags her gaze up to mine, her eyes wide and full of fear.

"Me too."

Keep reading for a preview of Book 5: **Wicked Prince**.

Margot has her own story to tell to finish off the LeBlanc sisters' saga...

Don't forget to grab your FREE bonus extended epilogue by signing up to my reader list:

https://www.lilianmonroe.com/subscribe

If you're already signed up, you can follow the link in your welcome email to access the bonus content from all my books.

xox Lilian

WICKED PRINCE

ROYALLY UNEXPECTED: BOOK 5

Previously titled Knocked Up by the Wicked Prince

1

MARGOT

ATONEMENT.

That's what I'm doing when I haul another tray of baked goods into a cooling rack at my sister's bakery. I move to sweep flour off the floor and smile as my sister comes through the door.

"You don't have to do this, Margot," Ivy says. "I have enough employees. You should just relax."

My sister's black hair is pulled into a sleek ponytail. She wipes her hands on her apron, glancing through the front door of the bakery. Chewing her bottom lip, Ivy wrings her hands. "You think people will come back?"

"It's your grand re-opening," I smile. "Of course they'll come back."

"Even after people were hospitalized because of me?"

"It wasn't because of you," I answer, leaning the broom against the wall. I put my hands on my sister's shoulders. "It was my dickhead agent, Hunter. You were a victim of his maliciousness."

"I know, but you know what I mean. People will still

blame me. Hunter hasn't been charged with anything—besides his confession to you, there's no evidence that he was even here."

I smile. "It'll be fine. Word has gotten out that he planted the bacteria. I've been looking at the response online, and it doesn't look like people blame you at all. All kinds of shady stuff Hunter's done is surfacing, now. If anything, the extra publicity will be good."

"Not for the people who were hospitalized." Ivy grimaces, and my chest squeezes.

I try to swallow past the lump that's lodged itself in my throat. "I'm sorry, Ivy."

Her eyes turn back to me, and she shakes her head. "You know it wasn't your fault."

"If I'd been more supportive..."

"You had just gotten home. You're in recovery. You were taking care of yourself after supporting me your entire life. None of this is your fault." Ivy wraps her arms around me, and my chest tightens some more.

Guilt is a useless emotion. It doesn't serve any purpose. It doesn't push me to be a better person, it only drags me down further into my own anxiety. Feeling guilty doesn't change the past.

Logically, I know this, but the guilt persists.

It snakes in and out of my heart, creeping into my thoughts whenever I feel like I'm doing well. Guilt is a group of little gremlins, hiding in every corner of my mind. They poke their heads out once in a while to remind me that I'm a terrible person.

Even when I spend a week helping Ivy out at her bakery, *Spoonful of Sugar*, and endorse her publicly when she announces that she'll re-open it, I still feel bad.

It was *my* agent who poisoned her food. It was my agent who put her in the hospital. It was my agent who tried to ruin her new business.

Guilty, guilty, guilty.

The back door of the bakery bursts open, and Ivy's boyfriend, Prince Luca, comes through. He gives me a broad smile, hooking his arms around both Ivy and me.

"Today's the big day!"

Ivy's face breaks into a grin, and she nuzzles her face into his chest. The Prince kisses the top of her head.

My heart melts. There was a time when I was jealous of Ivy. It wasn't long ago, either—only about four months. They were the darkest days of my life, right before I learned the truth about my diagnosis. Before I hit rock bottom. I saw the relationship budding between the two of them, and I thought it should be me that Prince Luca wanted, not my sister.

I was in a haze of self-medication, depression, and anxiety. My mind was a mess, and it landed me pregnant, overdosing in hospital, and forced to retreat to an intensive therapy course in the middle of the Farcliff wilderness. I was unhealthy, selfish, and wrong.

I know that now, but it doesn't make it any easier.

I reach for my bottle of water on the counter, and my hand shakes slightly. I look at the tremor in my hand, and fear pierces through me like an ice pick. I ball my hand into a fist to hide the shaking. Glancing at Ivy, I breathe a sigh of relief when I see she hasn't noticed.

I reach for the bottle again, knocking it to the ground.

"Shit," I say under my breath.

Ivy laughs, shaking her head. "Always the clumsy one. How your publicist manages to hide that from the public is beyond me."

"She's a magician," I say, laughing nervously as I pick up the water bottle with trembling hands. "Being an oaf doesn't exactly fit with the image of a 'graceful blonde goddess.'" I grin, making air quotes around the last words.

Ivy giggles. I turn away from her, using a precious moment to take a deep breath and compose myself.

Four months ago—on the same day I somehow overdosed from laced heroin, which I don't remember at all—I tested positive for Huntington's disease. It's the illness that killed our mother.

Ivy and I watched her degenerate slowly over the last twenty years of her life, her brain slowly falling apart from the mutated proteins the disease pumped into her grey matter. She died of pneumonia, which ravaged her weakened immune system, but not before her whole personality transformed into something negative, angry, and sometimes violent.

That's the fate that is awaiting me, too—and no one knows, except me.

Ivy doesn't know about the diagnosis, but she does know about my pregnancy. She thinks I'm just a regular old messed-up celebrity. She thinks life will continue as it has been, and we'll all live happily ever after. She's excited that her child will have a cousin to play with.

I'm trying to think like her. I go to therapy twice a week and I'm taking care of my body with yoga and weightlifting. I'm eating healthily and spending more time with Ivy. I don't stare at my social media quite so much. I'm really, really trying. My therapist says I need to forgive myself for my mistakes, and I can't cling onto the guilt that eats away at me.

My hand moves to my stomach, and I draw strength from the life that's growing inside me.

A gremlin pokes his head out from the recesses of my mind, his giggles echoing off my skull.

Guilty, guilty, guilty. Your baby could get the disease, too. Did you think of that when you decided to get pregnant?

Squeezing my eyes shut, I try to talk myself down. The baby was an accident, but also a gift. I wouldn't be as dedicated to my recovery if I didn't have a child to take care of.

I *will* be a good mother, Huntington's or not.

"You okay, Margot?" Prince Luca glances at me, and I realize I'm gripping the edge of the stainless steel counter with both hands. My knuckles are white.

I force myself to relax my shoulders, painting a smile on my face. "I'm fine. Just a little dizzy, is all. Might need a muffin to keep me going."

"I never thought I'd see the day when you actually eat the things I bake," Ivy laughs, grabbing a banana chocolate-chip muffin from a tray for me. "It makes me happy to see you eating my stuff."

"You're a rare talent," I answer, taking a nibble of the muffin and groaning as the taste hits my tongue. "I can't believe I've been missing out on all this goodness just in the name of being skinny."

Ivy grins, then takes a deep breath. Her eyes shine as she stares at me. "Will you come open the doors with me? It's time. I want you beside me."

My heart thumps, and I nod. "I'd be honored."

We open the doors to the bakery together, smiling for the cameras that are waiting to snap photos of us. I hook my arm around my sister's shoulders, pointing to the sign above our heads.

Spoonful of Sugar is officially re-open for business.

This time, I'm happy about it.

The gremlins in my mind are blissfully quiet. The

anxious thoughts that plague me all the time are absent, and I'm truly, completely happy for my sister.

IVY OPENS the front door to our house, and I glance up from my seat on the couch. Melissa, my hair stylist, is working on my blonde hair extensions, moving the wefts up closer to my scalp. She's been by my side for years, and is the closest thing I have to a friend.

"How was the rest of the grand re-opening?" I ask my sister.

Ivy smiles sweetly. "It was great. Lots of press. It meant a lot to me that you were there."

"You're such a star, Ivy," Mel says, tugging a strand of my hair.

I wince.

"Sorry," she says, patting the sore spot. She glances at my sister. "I tried one of your salted caramel brownies today. Oh. My. Lord. Ivy, you're incredible."

Ivy blushes, nodding. "Thank you."

"Let me do your hair this weekend," Mel says. "Take it as payment for all the baked goods you've fed me over the years."

"This?" Ivy says, flicking her black hair over her shoulder. "I don't know what you could do with this."

"Don't underestimate her," I grin, glancing at my hair stylist. "If she can make me into a long-haired blonde, she can make you feel like a princess."

Ivy's smile widens. "Well, okay. I'd like that."

My heart squeezes. Ivy is so...*good*. She's spent her whole life being by my side, not asking for anything. She's supported me through years of fame, never holding my status as a celebrity against me.

Me, though?

I resented her. When she opened her bakery, I thought she was using me and leaving me behind, just like everyone else.

It wasn't until she was hospitalized that I realized what an ass I was being.

The gremlins cackle in my mind, amplifying my insecurities.

You're a horrible person, and you don't deserve a sister like Ivy.

My sister flops down on the couch, letting out a long sigh. "Thank you for your help. I couldn't have re-opened the bakery without you."

I put my arm around my sister's shoulders. "Of course you could've. I didn't do anything except say the truth—that you're the best damn baker Farcliff has ever seen."

Ivy blushes. She's never been good at receiving compliments.

Melissa zhuzhes my hair one last time, and then pats my shoulder. "I've got to go. Keep that wrapped in a silk scarf while you sleep."

I give my friend a kiss on each cheek and watch her walk out through the front door. Glancing at myself in the reflection of the window, I let out a breath.

Melissa makes me look like a movie star, but inside, I still feel broken.

From the seat beside me, Ivy stares at me with those two-toned eyes of hers. One blue, one green. Just like our mother. I hold her gaze for a moment, and then I have to look away. Looking at my sister's face is too much like looking at Mama's.

Thinking of Mama makes me think of her death. Her death makes me think of my own diagnosis.

I wasn't even there when our mother died. I was on a photo shoot for Vogue Magazine.

What kind of person does that? Chooses work instead of family?

The rational part of my brain tries to stop the whirl-wind of anxiety that threatens to drag me down. Logic tells me that it was my father who pushed me to work so much. He would guilt-trip me into taking more jobs, saying that the only way we could afford Mama's treat-ment was due to the money I made modeling and acting.

When you're just a young teenager, and your father says those kinds of things to you, you believe him. Being the main breadwinner for your family at age fourteen has a way of twisting your view of the world.

But even as I say those things to myself, the gremlins in my mind gather together and laugh at me.

Stop making excuses, they sneer. *You're just bad, bad, bad.*

Ivy takes a deep breath, pulling me from my thoughts. "You still don't want to tell me who the father is?"

She nods to my belly. My heart clenches. "It's not important."

"It *is* important, Margot," Ivy says softly. "Does he know, whoever he is?"

I shake my head. Ivy sighs.

I bite the inside of my cheek until I taste blood. I know exactly when I fell pregnant, and I know who the father is: Prince Beckett of Argyle. The man who tried to kill his half-brother, Prince Luca. The man who's currently on the run and has the entire Kingdom of Argyle looking for him.

I found out about my pregnancy when I was at the retreat. The doctor who told me was gentle and kind, but it didn't stop me feeling like the world was ending. Only Ivy and Luca know that I'm carrying a child—and the doctors, of course—and it still doesn't quite feel real.

My pregnancy is more fodder for the snarling voices in my mind.

What if I hurt my baby by injecting my body full of poison before I knew about the pregnancy? What if he or she doesn't develop properly because of what I've done?

What if the baby gets Huntington's?

Taking a deep breath, I reel my mind back in. My therapist tells me to name my anxiety, to treat it like an intruder in my mind. So, I try.

Those thoughts aren't serving me. Instead, I turn my mind inward, to the child growing inside me. Before I found out I was pregnant, I was only in that facility because I thought I needed to be. My anxiety was out of control, and I was afraid I'd do something to hurt myself. I didn't know how I overdosed, but I'm sure it was my own fault.

Guilty, guilty, guilty.

Once I found out I was pregnant, everything changed.

Now, I could never relapse. I could never do anything to willingly hurt my child. Never, ever, ever.

But Prince Beckett...

Maybe we're made for each other.

Bad, bad, bad.

"Have you taken your medication today?" Ivy asks.

I smile at my sister. "It's probably time for me to take it. Thanks for reminding me."

"I can see those wheels turning in your head. You need to stop torturing yourself."

"Easier said than done."

Ivy smiles sadly, wrapping her arms around me. "Everything will work out. That's what Luca always tells me. So far, he hasn't been wrong."

I nod, forcing a smile, but I know the truth. As soon as people find out I'm pregnant and who the father is, my career will be over. I'll lose my endorsements, and I doubt I'll ever land another acting gig.

Then, my body will slowly break down over the next ten, fifteen, twenty years.

I'm staring at the face of the grim reaper.

Everything will most definitely *not* work out.

2

DANTE

As soon as I step off the plane, my teeth start clacking. Cold air whips through my thin jacket and chills me to the bone.

It's not often that I leave the tropical, Caribbean island of Argyle—especially not to come up to somewhere as far north as Farcliff. Nestled between the United States and Canada, just east of the Great Lakes, Farcliff is a stunning country. Lush forests, clear lakes and rivers, healthy wildlife. Farcliff looks like a postcard brought to life.

But damn, it's cold—and it's not even November yet.

A driver is waiting next to a luxury sedan. He opens the back door for me, nodding as I slide into the car. I lean back, thankful for heated seats.

The driver gets in, glancing in the rear-view mirror. "Where to, Your Highness?"

I give him the address that Luca provided and then settle in for the drive. I don't often leave Argyle, so being driven to a strange address in a foreign Kingdom is a rare occurrence for me.

I'm on a recovery mission. Get Luca out of Farcliff and bring him back home.

Since I've always hated being in the public eye, King Theo of Argyle, my brother, has given me different responsibilities. I'm able to stay away from the cameras as long as I deal with most of the day-to-day goings-on in Argyle. That leaves him free to travel to other countries and Kingdoms, work on international relations, and be the face of Argyle.

It helps that I've always been good with computers. I developed a state-of-the-art security system for the Argyle Palace, upgrading everything tech-related on our royal premises. Now that Beckett is on the run, I'm glad that my family is safe. No one except a select few people know that I'm the one behind the upgrades to the security in the Palace.

Anonymity has its advantages.

For one, I don't get mobbed if I go outside the palace gates. I can travel unhindered, and I don't have to deal with lies and stories about me in the media. They call me the 'reclusive prince,' but I don't mind.

I *am* a recluse.

Another advantage is a situation like this one. With our half-brother Beckett on the run, there are precious few people that we can trust. Theo sent me to Farcliff to bring Luca back to our home Kingdom of Argyle. He'll be safer at home.

Luca's girlfriend just re-opened her bakery, but I'm hoping I can convince him to choose safety and common sense. We don't know who we can trust in Farcliff, so it's better if they both come back to Argyle.

Typically, I wouldn't leave my home Kingdom, but things are tense back home, and I was the only one who could make the trip without causing a splash in the media.

Since my face isn't plastered over every media outlet in the world, and few people know what I actually look like, the task to bring Luca home has fallen to me.

I watch the streets of Farcliff whizz by. People walk quickly with their chins stuffed in their jackets against the cold. It's getting dark already, and the days are only getting shorter. I'd rather be on a tropical island, that's for sure.

The driver pulls up outside a tall gate. I can just see the top of a house behind a row of trees. He rolls his window down and reaches for the buzzer, exchanging a few words with a security guard. The gates swing inward, and I'm taken up the driveway to my temporary new home.

Hopefully it has good heating and insulation.

Stepping outside, I nod to the driver as he takes my bag out of the trunk. "I'll take it from here," I say.

"Are you sure, Your Highness?" He hesitates, not wanting to hand the suitcase over.

In Argyle, all the staff in the castle is used to me. I don't like being coddled or treated like...well, like royalty. I dress myself, I drive myself, I do most thing without the help of my staff.

This driver obviously isn't used to that. I smile at him, slipping some money into his hand as a tip before grabbing my suitcase. I packed light, because I don't own any cold weather clothes, and I don't intend to be here long.

If Luca will listen to reason, I'm hoping we can get out of here at the break of dawn tomorrow and be back in the sunshine and warmth by noon.

Easy, right?

Setting my small suitcase on the front porch, I ring the doorbell. I take a step back, clasping my hands behind me as I wait for the door to open.

Light, quick footsteps approach on the other side. The lock slides, and the heavy door swings inward.

My breath catches.

I've seen pictures of Margot LeBlanc. I've seen her in half a dozen films, and I respect her skills as an actor.

But, damn. Cameras do *not* do her justice.

I guess a part of me just assumed that it was Photoshop. I didn't think she'd actually be this breathtaking in person.

Her long, waist-length blonde hair is swept to one side. Bright blue eyes stare back at me, and her full, kissable lips fall open. She drags her eyes down my body and back up again, and I'm surprised at how much I enjoy her gaze.

Heat follows her eyes, sending little tendrils of pleasure snaking through my veins. I let a grin tug at my lips, arching an eyebrow.

Margot's almost as tall as I am, with a thin waist and gorgeous curves. My eyes keep wanting to drop down to her body, but it's her eyes that are magnetic. Deep pools of blue stare back at me.

I clear my throat, but I still can't seem to make words.

This is why I don't go out. This is why I hate the public eye. I clam up.

Margot's face breaks into a polite smile. "You must be Todd," she says. "Thank you for coming on such short notice."

I frown. Who's Todd?

Before I can answer, Margot slides some slippers on her feet and motions for me to follow her. We head around the house, and my eyes stay glued to the movement of her ass. She glances over her shoulder, and my eyes snap up to hers.

"Is your truck out on the street? I'll let security know to let you in. I thought I mentioned you were coming, but it's been so busy with my sister's bakery re-opening that it must have slipped my mind."

"Uh, no, actually. They let me in."

Because I'm the Prince of Argyle and I'm here to see my brother.

"Oh, good," she smiles. "Here's the pool. I think the pump is burned out. It just won't turn on. The electricity went out yesterday, and I think there was a power surge when it came back on. I'm not an electrician, though. You are," she laughs, the sound sending another wave of heat through me. "We're hoping to drain a few inches off it this week to get it ready for winter, but my house manager was saying it would be best to have you take a look at it before we take too much water out."

Her smile is polite. Guarded. She points to a waist-high wooden box, flipping open the lid to reveal the pool pump.

"You think you can fix it?"

"Dante!" My brother Luca throws open the sliding glass door and strides out of the house. His smile stretches from ear to ear.

He looks happier than he did even a couple of weeks ago when I saw him in Argyle. Maybe the cold weather suits him.

Maybe Ivy suits him.

Margot makes a soft noise. "Dante?"

I glance at her, smiling. "Yeah."

Luca bounds around the pool and wraps his arms around me, engulfing me in a hug. "Good to see you, brother."

"Brother?" Margot repeats, her eyes widening. A blush stains her cheeks as horror fills her eyes.

"Margot, this is my brother, Prince Dante of Argyle. Don't be fooled by his size, though. He's a shy little teddy bear."

Luca wraps me in a headlock and rubs his knuckles over my head. I yelp, trying to spin away from him, but my brother won't let go. I shift my weight, trying to push him off me.

His arm stays firmly wrapped around my neck, gently crushing my airway.

Panic starts to lace my blood. I don't like being trapped.

307

I try to get away from his grip again, pushing a little bit harder.

Too hard.

We stumble back, stepping over each other's feet as we both head toward the edge of the pool. Luca laughs, grunting as he struggles with me.

My brother's gotten stronger since we were kids.

Margot takes a step toward us. "Uh, boys…"

With one massive push, I try to get Luca off me. He yelps, letting go of my neck as he falls backward, pitching toward the pool water. His eyes open wide as his heel slips over the edge of the pool.

He's a goner. In a second, he'll be splashing into ice-cold water.

Taking a step back, I suck in a wheezing breath. I put my hand to my throat, finally filling my lungs.

My victory is short-lived, though, because with one last movement, Luca grabs onto my shoulder and drags me down with him.

I yell, falling into the freezing-cold water on top of my brother. The cold takes my breath away. For a second, I can't move. I just sink down, down, down, until my knee hits the bottom of the pool. The feeling of the bottom jars me back to my senses.

I push away from Luca and propel myself off the bottom, breaking the surface to hear Margot shouting. She disappears into the pool house. I swim to the edge of the pool and watch Margot come back out carrying a bundle of towels.

I pull myself out of the water, my clothes soaked and my mood dampened. Luca's head pops up above the water, laughing.

He's in a pretty good mood, considering our half-brother

Beckett just tried to kill him. Does he think I'm here on a social visit?

A black-haired girl appears in the doorway. "What the heck is going on?"

Margot hands me a towel, arching an eyebrow. Her cheeks are still a bright shade of red, and she averts her eyes.

"Babe! This is my brother, Dante," Luca calls out. "You should get in here. The water's nice."

"I'll take your word for it," Ivy answers, laughing.

My whole body is shaking. I don't realize it until Margot drapes a towel over my shoulders and rubs her hands up and down my arms.

"Let's get you inside," she says, glancing at Luca, who's still trying to get Ivy to jump in. "You're obviously more sensible than your older brother."

"It would appear that way," I grin. My teeth chatter, and Margot nods toward the house.

As soon as I step inside, pins and needles erupt over my body. Heat starts seeping into my frozen skin, and Margot leads me up the stairs.

"Bathroom, bedroom." She points to two different doors. "There should be clean towels and toiletries in the bathroom. Warm yourself up. You have a suitcase?"

"On the front porch."

She nods. "I'll get someone to bring it up and leave it in that room."

"Thanks." I swallow, wanting to say something else.

Her eyes linger on mine for a moment, and then she inhales sharply. "And, uh...sorry."

"For what?"

"For thinking you were the electrician, and not the Prince of Argyle."

I chuckle, shrugging. "Easy mistake to make."

Margot's eyes drift over my chest, and I watch her cheeks flush brighter. She smiles shyly, nodding as she turns back toward the stairs.

I watch her for a moment, wondering why my heart is beating so erratically.

~

Keep reading **Wicked Prince** *by copying this URL into your browser:*
https://www.amazon.com/dp/B0843PWYNC

Don't forget to sign up for access to the Lilian Monroe Freebie Central:
https://www.lilianmonroe.com/subscribe

Lilian

ALSO BY LILIAN MONROE

For all books, visit:

www.lilianmonroe.com

Brother's Best Friend Romance

Shouldn't Want You

Can't Have You

Military Romance

His Vow

His Oath

His Word

The Complete Protector Series

Enemies to Lovers Romance

Hate at First Sight

Loathe at First Sight

Despise at First Sight

The Complete Love/Hate Series

Secret Baby/Accidental Pregnancy Romance:

Bad Boss

Bad Single Dad

Bad Boy

Bad Billionaire

The Complete Unexpected Series

Bad Prince

Heartless Prince

Cruel Prince

Broken Prince

Wicked Prince

Wrong Prince

Fake Engagement/ Fake Marriage Romance:

Engaged to Mr. Right

Engaged to Mr. Wrong

Engaged to Mr. Perfect

Mr Right: The Complete Fake Engagement Series

Mountain Man Romance:

Lie to Me

Swear to Me

Run to Me

The Complete Clarke Brothers Series

Extra-Steamy Rock Star Romance:

Garrett

Maddox

Carter

The Complete Rock Hard Series

Sexy Doctors:

Doctor O

Doctor D

Doctor L

The Complete Doctor's Orders Series

Time Travel Romance:

The Cause

A little something different:

Second Chance: A Rockstar Romance in North Korea

Printed in Great Britain
by Amazon